"I did think you were a jerk, Mr. Santini— until I calmed down." Quinn studied the contradictory picture she made—splashed in mud, a florist's bouquet hugged against her ratty sweatshirt, her other hand resting on a shovel. Yet her expression was so open and sincere, Quinn felt a kick of unexpected guilt. Then his resolve returned. He needed to know if April had discovered his grandmother's secrets.

"I'd feel better about the whole misunderstanding if you'd allow me to buy you dinner," he said.

April hesitated.

"You could come in for a glass of wine first and see what I've done to your grandmother's house while I make myself presentable," she finally answered.

"Wine would hit the spot. To tell you the truth, after hearing how much Gram loved this place, I'm curious to see inside."

April hadn't expected him to take her up on her offer, but she could hardly change her mind now.

Dear Reader,

I love clipping articles I find in our local newspaper or in papers I pick up as we travel around to visit friends, family or simply go on vacation. I have a file cabinet in my office *filled* with possibilities for stories.

When my editor announced that Harlequin was going to launch a new line called Everlasting Love, in which the stories would span a longer time period than most of our romance novels, I knew I had two articles in my file that would make for an interesting book.

One had to do with a single love letter found in the wall of a 1918 farmhouse in another state. The other was about love letters that accidentally ended up in an antique store; the woman who bought the chest with the letters was determined to find the owner. The woman the letters had belonged to had lost her husband, who'd written them in the 1970s. But I kept envisioning a man and woman long parted, who each thought the other was dead. Somehow, through the recovery of the letters, they would find each other and rekindle a love that had never died.

That story is this one.

My natural fascination with World War II added the necessary context for that original love story—and I found myself weaving it together with a parallel, present-day romance.

I hope you enjoy it! I love hearing from readers. Contact me via mail or e-mail.

Sincerely,

Roz Denny Fox
P.O. Box 17480-101
Tucson, AZ 85731
e-mail: rdfox@worldnet.att.net

A Secret To Tell You

Roz Denny Fox

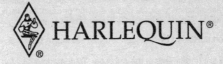

HARLEQUIN®

TORONTO • NEW YORK • LONDON
AMSTERDAM • PARIS • SYDNEY • HAMBURG
STOCKHOLM • ATHENS • TOKYO • MILAN • MADRID
PRAGUE • WARSAW • BUDAPEST • AUCKLAND

ISBN-13: 978-0-373-65415-4
ISBN-10:   0-373-65415-4

A SECRET TO TELL YOU

ABOUT THE AUTHOR

Roz Denny Fox has been published by Harlequin Books since 1989. Her youngest daughter and friends, all voracious readers, were consuming Harlequin/Silhouette books, and the girls badgered Roz to write a romance. In 1986 she took a creative writing class and met other writers, who introduced her to Romance Writers of America.

Soon after, she attended her first national conference and came home to write *Red Hot Pepper,* the book that would be her first Harlequin Romance (writing as Roz Denny). Since then, she's written for Harlequin Superromance, Harlequin American Romance and now Harlequin Everlasting Love (and she wrote a mainstream romance for Harlequin, as well—*Hot Chocolate on a Cold Day.)* We're thrilled to include her in the inaugural year of Everlasting Love.

For Roz, hearing from readers who are in some way touched by her books is like having ice cream with chocolate cake.

Books by Roz Denny Fox

Chapter 1

Dust flew everywhere as April Trent's circular saw bit into the lath and plaster wall of the sixty-year-old Shenandoah Valley farmhouse she was remodeling. Seeing a flash of red and white in what should be empty space, she shut off her saw and set it down on the floor. Then she carefully pulled free a ragged chunk of wall. April shoved her safety glasses into her hair so she could clearly see the item wedged between two-by-four-inch studs.

Since being awarded her contractor's license at twenty-four, this was the sixth Virginia home between Harrisburg and Staunton that she'd purchased and renovated. She always lived in the houses she was renovating; and had managed to accumulate a tidy nest egg. At thirty-one, she was a woman of independent means. Her first project she'd bought with a trust fund left by her paternal grandmother,

Dixie. Early on, she'd struggled to be taken seriously in a largely male-dominated field. Now things were going well. No thanks, though, to her prominent family who, outside of her grandmother, saw her interest as merely an aberrant whim that would pass. Rather than being happy for her and wishing her well, they considered her an embarrassment. Especially her Dad and her brothers....

April plucked out a dusty, rectangular package wrapped in red-and-white checked oilcloth. Bits of fabric, brittle with age, broke off, even though she took care lifting it out. Her pulse beat faster. Generally all she found was crumbling grout, cobwebs or the skeletal remains of long-dead mice.

Coleman Trent, her lawyer daddy, might not be so quick to denigrate her profession if she found a cache of stolen money.

Excited, April carried her treasure around the plastic sheeting that cordoned off the kitchen, one of the rooms she'd completed. A corner nook near the window offered better lighting, and she identified the wrapping as oilcloth of a type used to line kitchen cupboards at the time this home was built. Twine holding the covering in place snapped easily.

Darn! Not money. Letters, bound together with a red satin ribbon. Letters addressed in precise script to a woman named Norma Marsh, at an address in France.

On a self-imposed timetable to complete the house but tempted nevertheless, April couldn't resist tugging open the bow. She eased the top letter out of its envelope. The ink was faded and the handwriting looked like that of a man. Yes, it was signed *Erge ben, Heinz*. April was disappointed when she realized none of the letters were in English. No, they'd been written in German. She'd taken a smattering of college French and high school German, and from the little she could translate, it appeared Heinz was devoted to Norma.

April couldn't help a poignant sigh as she refolded the letter. She'd love to pour a cup of coffee and take a break, try to decipher what—judging by the salutation—were obviously old love letters. But she needed to get that wall down and cleaned up, since she had carpet-layers scheduled the following week. Although she did most of the work alone, a few tasks she subcontracted out on an as-needed basis.

Leaving the letters, she returned to the dirty job at hand. By one o'clock she was exhausted. But the wall was down. Only the promise of coffee and a closer inspection of the letters gave her the final burst of energy she needed to dispose of debris and sweep up.

She was pleased with her morning's work. Ripping out the wall had resulted in a lovely, large open room with a brick fireplace at one end. Homes built in the thirties and forties tended to have small, dark rooms. April liked open and airy.

Filthy, she should head straight for the spanking new shower she'd already added to the refitted bathroom. But coffee enticed, as did those letters.

April filled a mug with the coffee she'd brewed at breakfast and reheated it in the microwave. She'd learned to take her coffee black and strong. She carried it impatiently to the nook and removed the oilcloth around the letters. When she did, a passport fell out and so did a couple of grainy black-and-white snapshots and a pressed flower, a rose. Hesitantly April opened the old passport. A beautiful young woman with long blond hair styled in a manner reminiscent of 1940s movies, stared out. The well-traveled document had been stamped numerous times with dates ranging from the early- to mid-forties. London. Rome. Paris and other cities in France. April sipped the bitter coffee, and let her mind wander. Norma Marsh must have been a debutante. April was familiar with that lavish life-style, since her mother, Bonnie, was from a wealthy local family who still believed the best schools were abroad.

Feeling too much like a voyeur, April tucked the pho-tographs into the passport without examining them and put back the fragile rose. These love letters belonged to a stranger. But she had to wonder how they'd come to be stuck between the walls. Was it accidental, or were they hidden on purpose? Who was Norma Marsh? Born in 1925, she'd be eighty-two now. Was she even alive? And if she was, would she want the letters back? So many pos-sibilities ran through April's mind.

Her doorbell chimed unexpectedly, startling her. She wasn't expecting anyone, and the mysterious letters made her feel oddly vulnerable. Wiping nervous palms down her jeans, she tiptoed quietly to the arch. Through her large front window, she saw Eric Lathrop huddled on her front stoop. His topcoat sparkled silver from a light August rain that had begun to fall in the last half hour.

Eric was an eager-beaver reporter who wrote about politics for the local Turner County newspaper. His long-term sights were set on moving out of Virginia into the big-time D.C. political arena. Her family's law firm, Trent and Trent, dabbled in local politics, which was how Eric had gained the attention of April's parents and brothers.

Apolitical though she tried to be, she sporadically dated

Eric to keep her parents from coming up with worse prospects. In truth, she had zero time for a *real* relationship. And Eric was pleasant enough. He was at least capable of interesting conversation, although at times April found him overbearing.

She gave a passing thought to dashing back to hide her recent discovery, even if it meant leaving Eric standing in the rain. His brashness meant he didn't have much interest in what he called sentimentality—anything to do with emotion, in other words—and April felt oddly protective of these letters. Another part of her, though, longed to share her find with someone—anyone. That impulse won, and she crossed the room and threw open the door.

"What took you so long?" Eric stomped in, shaking raindrops from his buzz-cut sandy red hair. He left muddy footprints behind him.

His surly greeting killed whatever enthusiasm April had mustered for sharing her news. "I'm working," she said, waving a hand toward the enlarged living space.

"So I see." He grimaced at her dusty work boots and smudged safety goggles pushed back in April's short, dark hair.

"To what do I owe this unscheduled visit?" she asked in an affected Southern drawl. She could count on sweet sarcasm annoying the hell out of Eric.

Today, however, he apparently had other things on his mind. "I ran into your brother Miles in town. Had lunch with him. Don't ask me how, but he cadged two invitations to a black-tie fund-raiser. A ball being held by Quinn Santini a week from next Saturday."

"Santini. The name's familiar."

"Good grief, I should hope so! Quinn's running for the

U.S. Senate. My paper opposes him, and his picture's been splashed all over the front page for months. You've probably heard your family talking about him, as well. They're against his election, too."

Eric pulled two gilt-edged tickets from his inner pocket and fanned them under April's nose. "I came here straight-away. If you don't own a suitable dress, something long and slinky, you'll need to buy one. This is a big, big deal, and could be important for me."

"Why would I spend a fortune on a dress I'd wear once, Eric? You know I hate getting even semi-dressed up for the parties my folks throw."

"Yes, but think of the connections you could make at an event like this. You said that in your trade you need social contacts to get your name out through word of mouth."

"It helps," she agreed grudgingly, shutting the door as Eric returned the tickets to his pocket.

"Is that coffee I smell? I could do with a warm-up." Skirting April, he shrugged out of his topcoat and headed for her kitchen. "Hey, what's this?" he asked, weaving around the plastic to drop his coat over a chair next to the stack of letters.

"Something I found in the wall I removed today. Letters, but they're written in German." She hastily poured a mug of coffee and heated it in the microwave.

Before she could place the mug in Eric's hands, he was pawing through the letters. A couple of papers tucked between the last two envelopes floated to the floor. Setting his mug down with a thump, April bent and re-trieved the pages. "Well, these make no sense. They're lists of words that aren't really words in English *or*

German, as far as I can tell. More like scrambled groups of letters."

Eric tasted the coffee, made a face, then leaned over her shoulder. "Huh? Two words are spelled out—they're bird names. See, it says Oriole at the top and Kestrel at the bottom."

"Yes. The second page has Kestrel at the top and Oriole at the bottom." Refolding them, April shoved those sheets into the top envelope. "Maybe they're anagrams."

"Or coded messages." Squinting at the envelopes, Eric grew more animated. "April, who had this farmhouse built?"

"I bought it from the heirs of Dr. David Shuman."

"Yes," he snapped. "But after you researched the deed, I distinctly remember you saying this house originally belonged to Anthony Santini. No wonder the name's familiar! Tony's grandson is Quinn, who's the senatorial candidate. April, what rock have you been under?" Eric demanded when she casually retied the ribbon around the letters and tucked the flattened rose underneath it. He tried to take the bundle, but she yanked it away and walked out of the kitchen.

"Where are you going? April, let me read them." His voice rose. "Have you asked yourself why a bunch of old letters would be hidden in a wall? What if old man Santini was carrying on some tawdry affair? With some German, yet—during the war?" Eric set down his mug and followed April. "Listen, if I don't find anything juicy, I'll give the damned letters back to you. But if I link Grandpa Santini to something sordid, this could be my lucky break. My ticket to the beltway."

She continued down the hall, but called over her shoulder, "Eric, honestly, you're always seeing the next big story in everything you do. These *are* private letters. I didn't see the name Santini anywhere. And if they were my love letters, I wouldn't want them made public. I'm putting them in my bedroom. Then I'm going in to shower. Please let yourself out."

Eric's forward momentum was stopped when April shut her bedroom door. He rattled the knob, found the door locked and pounded with a fist. Then he resorted to cajoling. "You could be holding dynamite, sweetheart. Tony Santini built this farm, but he spent a lot of time in Europe before and after World War Two. I've even read stories that hint he could've been a spy. April? Dammit, are you listening?"

She didn't respond, and thankfully, after a few minutes of shouting, Eric gave up. She heard him say, "I'm leaving, but I'll be back when you've had time to think this through."

What did he mean? She *had* thought it through. But Eric was blind to everything except his career. And he had a temper. She was glad he'd gone with so little fuss.

She didn't dally over cleaning up. She'd observed Eric on the trail of a story. He was like a bulldog. He'd try to get his hands on the letters.

After toweling her hair dry, April grabbed the letters and dashed through the drizzle to her pickup. Someone as astute about the political scene as Eric, but who April trusted more, was her old college roommate, decorator Robyn Parker. Unlike April, Robyn enjoyed the local social scene. She traveled in prominent circles from Virginia to Maryland to D.C. And had the lowdown on everyone of importance. She also could keep a secret.

Twenty minutes later, April burst into Robyn's fabric-cluttered shop, relieved to find her friend alone in her office.

"Did we have an appointment? If so, I doubled up," Robyn said. "I'm on my way to see Mrs. Mason Hightower." The pretty redhead fumbled for her Blackberry and punched up her date calendar.

"I only need a minute, Robyn. I made this discovery out at the farm." Talking as fast as she could, April filled her in on what Eric said.

"Wow! Much as I hate to agree with that know-it-all Eric Lathrop on *anything,* the Norma Marsh in those letters must be Quinn Santini's grandmother. She's pretty much a recluse and has been for years. Her hubby, Anthony, was some kind of government diplomat who put them on the social register. He died quite a while ago. I sure wasn't aware he'd once owned your farmhouse. That'll be a boon when it comes to selling it. Especially if Quinn wins the election."

"I'd forgotten Santini was the original owner until Eric reminded me. He remembered the name from when I researched the deed. It's true that the history of a house in this area does add to its salability," she added slowly.

"You've also got the family tragedy," Robyn said as she tossed fabric in a briefcase.

"Tragedy?" April glanced up.

"Yes. Anthony's son, Brett, Brett's wife and Quinn's wife all died in a small plane accident four years ago. Brett was the pilot. It was headline news, and it's surfaced again with Quinn's campaign. If you ever got your head out of the sawdust bin, you'd know these things, April. I've heard that his grandmother babysits Quinn's daughter. They live on adjoining estates." Robyn rattled off the name of the most exclusive development in their county. "Now, *he's* a man to drool over, my friend. But you probably don't realize that Quinn's considered Turner County's most eligible bachelor. A host of women we know would *love* to become the second Mrs. Quinn Santini."

April shrugged. "Let them. I'm not interested in his type, Robyn."

"Well, I am. Quinn Santini's so ho…ot," she drawled, fanning herself with one hand. "He creates tons of talk around the watering holes. Mostly because he's *not* photographed with models and bimbos. Ask your dad or brothers about Quinn. He's a lawyer-turned-politician. If I recall, last year he beat your dad's firm on some big case. River pollution or something."

"Eric said Dad's firm is backing Santini's opponent, and that would explain why. Dad hates to lose. Anyway, I doubt that these letters are political. They look like love letters to me. If Mrs. Santini loved some guy before she married Anthony, that shouldn't be exploited." April's brow furrowed. "It's—the letters aren't in English. I wish I had time to translate a few of them properly. Then I could decide if I should go see the woman and ask if she wants them back, or would she rather I tossed them in the trash?"

Robyn checked her watch. "Yikes, gotta run, sweetie. You're welcome to stay and pore over them here. I'll leave my safe open so you can lock them up until you decide. I'm pretty sure Mrs. Santini's name is Norma. And if her husband built the house, well…it does suggest they could belong to Quinn's grandmother."

April rose on tiptoes to hug her taller friend. "Thanks. I'll call you tomorrow and let you know what I'm going to do with the letters. I can't waste a lot of time on them, though. I want to finish the farmhouse and get it on the market before Thanksgiving. I've had good luck selling houses over various holidays, thanks to your terrific decorating ideas."

"Yeah, well, all this hoopla over the senate race will blow over."

"Hmm. I may just cast my vote for Santini just to spite my family and Eric. But, honestly, isn't one politician as corrupt as the next?"

"Quinn gets my vote because he's yummy. Matter of fact, if you get cozy with his grandmother, I wouldn't turn down a face-to-face introduction to him." April laughed as Robyn grinned, hefting her case of samples, and sprinted for the door.

But her laughter died when she opened a letter and tried to read it. Her German was rusty. The words she was able to translate left gaping holes and sentences that made no sense.

Her frustration mounted once she determined all the letters were in German. She finally resorted to studying the photos stuck in the back of the passport. There was no doubt that the young woman cuddled up to the handsome man in the first snapshot was the Norma who owned the passport. Oooh—but the uniform her friend wore wasn't that of an American soldier. German. An officer, no less.

Biting her lip, April flipped to the second picture. Norma Marsh appeared distressed. Possibly crying. A set of blunt-tipped fingers seemed to hold her back from the man—the German officer—in the previous picture. This time he was in civilian garb. All but the second man's hand had been cropped. The handsome man who faced Norma looked…stunned, perhaps?

Her curiosity more than aroused, April flipped the snapshots over. The photo of the couple in happier circumstances said *Heinz, my love. Colmar, France, 1944.* The other
said nothing.

Restoring the letters to the order in which she'd found
them, April tucked them, plus the passport and flower, in
a plastic bag and placed it in Robyn's safe. She twirled the
lock, feeling inexplicably unsettled and sad.

On the spur of the moment, she decided to dig into this
now. Using her friend's computer, April went through the
archives of the social register and came up with a current
address for Mrs. Anthony Santini. If the letters *were* hers,
April reasoned she'd get this over and done with, and could
stop worrying about *what ifs.*

In spite of rain and the late-afternoon snarl of traffic,
April never tired of driving though the green hillsides in
this part of Virginia. The Santinis lived in a community of
older estates called Rolling Hills, all twenty or more acres
apiece. Horse properties. Most were fenced and hooked up
to surveillance systems.

She'd never had occasion to visit anyone here but she
wasn't surprised by the ornate wrought iron fencing that
seemed to go on for miles. What did surprise her was
finding the Santinis' gate wide open. To give herself a
chance to organize what she'd say, or maybe to insure that
she could leave on her own terms, April parked outside the
gate and walked up the winding drive. The house was spectacular, with columns, mullioned windows, dormers, all architectural features that attracted her. Stables off to the right
were predictable. So was the four-car garage on the left,
with a garret above, probably for staff. One bay of the

garage was open and empty. Someone was gone, or else it housed the silver Lexus parked in the circular drive.

April glimpsed a second, slightly smaller residence set back behind the main house. She recalled Robyn's saying Quinn and his grandmother shared the premises. She hesitated, wondering if she ought to veer off to the smaller abode. Wouldn't a man of Quinn's stature—a single father, at that—need the larger of the two quarters? Still, *someone* was home in the main dwelling; she might as well find out who.

Bringing up very private love letters with the woman to whom they might belong would be difficult enough, but April couldn't picture herself explaining them to a man. A grandson, and a lawyer no less. She knew how lawyers' minds worked. After all, she had two in her family. In the Trent household everything got hashed over, rehashed and talked to death.

She heard voices, so she mounted the steps. And since the Lexus sat in front, probably awaiting someone about to leave, she pressed the doorbell before she could change her mind.

April expected a butler or housekeeper. She was unprepared when a man in his midthirties—tall, blond, handsome and wearing, of all things, a designer tuxedo—yanked open the door.

For a moment they did nothing but stare at each other. In her old jeans, work boots and jean jacket, clean though they were, April knew she fell way short in the eyes of this man. Those blue eyes were so clear, so sharp, she imagined he not only found her wanting, but as she stammered out her name and asked for Norma Marsh, April sensed that he disapproved of everything about her.

"Trent?" The clipped question came with a scowl.

"How did you get inside the gate? What's your reason for barging in on us? This is private property."

A woman materialized behind the man in the doorway. Her carriage was upright and her figure slender in spite of the fact that her hair was pure white and her face lined. Just as quickly, a sweet-faced child, a girl of five or six, slipped between the two adults. She gaped at April, as if seeing strangers at her door was an unusual occurrence. Which, considering April's dubious welcome, it probably was. She threw back her shoulders and raised her chin. "I'm a contractor who bought an old farmhouse across town—in Heritage Acres. The original owner of record was Anthony Santini. I'm renovating and upgrading the home's interior. Today I tore out a wall and discovered a packet of letters, uh, and a passport. They all bear the name Norma Marsh. A friend of mine said Norma's the first name of the Mrs. Santini who lives here. So I came to find out if the letters— love letters, I believe—belong to her."

The man let go of the door and walked outside. His presence forced April to take a step down toward the car. Rain spattered in her eyes, making her blink.

"Save your breath," he said icily. "Tell Daniel Mattingly it's a good try, but I won't be bribed, nor will I cave in to any attempts at blackmail."

"Who's Daniel Mattingly?" April held up a hand to the rain. "All the letters are signed by a man named Heinz von Weisenbach."

"Come on, *Ms.* Trent. It won't fly, so give it a rest." His beautiful lips curled and he advanced, forcing April down two more steps before the white-haired woman moved into the doorway and said in a low voice, "Quinn, stop.

Invite her in. I need, ah, would like to hear more of what she has to say."

The man came to a halt. "Gram?" He glanced from the woman below him to the one behind him.

The older woman's fingers clutched the shoulders of the little girl. But her hazel eyes reflected a mix of shock and concern. As Mrs. Santini released one hand, her fingers shook noticeably as she crushed the throat of her wool dress. "Hayley," she said, obviously speaking to the child, "would you go upstairs and play? Your father and I need a private word with…Ms. Trent, is it?"

April nodded. The too-handsome man she now knew was Quinn Santini glared at her, then pushed back his sleeve and transferred his glare to a gold watch. "I'm already late for an important gathering, Gram. Can't this wait?"

Mrs. Santini bit her lower lip and shook her head.

Seeing an advantage, April took it. She swept past Quinn and approached the stiff-backed yet elegant woman. "So the letters *are* yours? Yes, now that I see you in the light, there's a resemblance to the woman in the passport photograph."

April felt Quinn Santini's breath on the back of her neck, above the rain-wet collar. It was all she could do not to shudder and spin to face him. Instead, she kept her eyes on his grandmother.

The little girl danced around on her toes. "Daddy, do I *have* to go upstairs? You said Gram and I could watch a DVD."

"Please, Quinn, come in out of the rain. You're both getting soaked." Norma Santini beckoned her grandson and April into the house. "Ms. Trent may hold the key to a mystery that's haunted me for years. And I…would… really like a glass of sherry while we speak."

The man muttered, half to himself, "I don't want dealings of any kind with anyone named Trent. If Coleman or Miles Trent sent her, she's as likely as not to be a sneaky reporter, if not worse."

April tossed her head. "I'm not! A reporter, that is. Cole *is* my father, and Miles and Roger are my brothers. I promise none of them have any inkling I found letters at my farmhouse. Well, n-not unless Eric blabbed." It was April's turn to stutter breathlessly as the possibility of Eric doing just that occurred to her. "Uh, that w-would be Eric Lathrop."

"Lathrop?" Quinn hustled April none too gently inside and slammed the door. "I'm tired of being hounded by reporters. If you're mixed up with Lathrop, I believe I'll call the cops and have you charged with harassment."

"Quinn! Enough!" His grandmother stood in front of a crackling blaze behind a fireplace screen. In the flickering light, she appeared pale and quite fragile. So much so, April wished she hadn't come here at all.

"Mrs. Santini, I swear," April said, "if the letters are yours, I want nothing—"

"Be quiet," Quinn bellowed. "It doesn't matter what *you* want. Hayley, please do as Gram asked," he said, softening his tone as he addressed his daughter. "Go up and play with your dolls for a little bit, okay, hon? I'll come and get you when we're finished here and you can spend the rest of the evening with Gram."

As the pretty blond child flounced across the room and stomped petulantly up the curved white staircase, April almost smiled. Quinn's impatience was very evident in his daughter.

However, it was a noticeably less aggressive man who led his grandmother to a chair flanking the fireplace. He left her and crossed to a bar, pulling out a bottle of Harveys Bristol Cream and pouring a glass, which he carried over to his grandmother. He neither offered April a seat, nor a glass of the sherry.

After a bracing sip, Norma recovered sufficiently to display a steelier persona. "Quinn, perhaps you ought to cancel your meeting. Young woman," she said, leveling April with a haughty stare, "I'm prepared to negotiate a fair price. Why don't you start by stating how much you want? Whatever I pay *will* include return of the letters, and I'll expect your complete silence regarding their contents."

"Grandmother, we're not paying one red cent! Will you please tell me what the hell's going on?" Quinn stepped between the two women, his stance fully protective of his grandmother and combative toward April.

That's it! She'd had it with this family. Regardless of how much she'd like to hear the ice queen's answer to her grandson's question, April resented the implication that she'd come here to shake anyone down. She felt she had every right to the indignation that propelled her out the hand-carved door. And it was definitely satisfying to slam that door hard enough to hear the leaded-glass window rattle.

It was now dark, and the trees around her were deeply shadowed. She ran down the wet, winding drive, holding her breath until she made it through the open gate and climbed into the safety of her battered pickup. She wrenched the key in the ignition, her fingers unsteady. The whole ordeal had shaken her.

Let the letters rot in Robyn's safe for all she cared. Likewise, her friend was more than welcome to Turner County's most eligible bachelor—the jerk.

April forgot to turn on her windshield wipers until she reached the end of Santini's street and realized the world outside her window was one big blur.

All she could think of at the moment was that no way in hell would Quinn Santini get her vote in the November election.

Chapter 2

"Quinn, don't let her leave. Please catch her." His grandmother half rose from her chair. Her glass wobbled, and some of the sherry splashed over the edge, onto the long sleeve of her dress.

"Let her go, and good riddance. If I leave now, I can probably still get to Representative Hoerner's cocktail party. I'll bring Hayley downstairs first. We did shuffle her off without much explanation." Quinn headed for the staircase, but his grandmother called him back.

"I really need you to go after that young woman, Quinn." When he scrutinized her intensely, Norma averted her gaze. Her lips trembled. "The letters she mentioned... It's important...well, suffice it to say I'd like to have them in my possession."

"Securing the letters is more important than meeting

Sam Hoerner's handpicked supporters? I've got a narrow lead in today's poll."

"Politics." She pursed her lips. "I begged you not to get involved, Quinn."

"I've also heard your views on Dan Mattingly." A smile altered Quinn Santini's narrow face and stern features, displaying instead the charm gossip columnists loved to write about.

"This is personal, Quinn." His grandmother gestured with the glass, but her clearly worried gaze focused on the dark, rain-flecked window, as if by staring she could bring April Trent back.

"I know you were never at the farm, Quinn. I loved it so much, and I hated to leave it. But your grandfather decided he needed better freeway access. Tony bought this place and moved us here, right before Brett started elementary school." She sighed. "I'm sure by now Ms. Trent is well on her way home. Quinn, dear, you shouldn't have any trouble finding the farm. It's the only house at the end of Oak Grove Road. The tracts of land adjoin federally reserved forest, which is why there are so few homes on that road."

He expelled a breath. "I might be more inclined to rush out after that woman if you'd explain why a few old letters are so vital. And a passport? It can't be yours. I've seen your passport, Gram. It might be decades out of date, but it's locked in a drawer at the office."

Norma drained her dainty glass and carried it to the sideboard near the compact bar. "Your grandfather filed to replace my lost passport probably a year after we moved to this house. I saw no need. I never planned to travel out of the country. But he insisted and even filled out the paperwork to request a new one in my married name. The

passport in Ms. Trent's possession is in my maiden name—
Marsh. It should be destroyed, Quinn."

"I shouldn't think that it's urgent. Unless you're worried
about some unsavory person getting hold of it and using it
to try and steal your identity. Someone even more unsavory
than April Trent."

"Quinn, it's unlike you to be this unpleasant to anyone.
Especially to an attractive young woman."

"Attractive? It must be time for your yearly eye exam."

"Are you talking about the lady who was just here?"
Hayley Santini sat cross-legged on the upper landing and
took that moment to enter the conversation. Her little face
peered down at the adults through ornate banister spindles.
"I wish I had curly hair like hers. If *my* hair curled, I
wouldn't have to sit for hours ev'ry time Ethel or Gram say
I need my hair to look nice for pictures and stuff." Ethel
was Quinn and Norma's shared housekeeper. Ethel
Langford had been a middle daughter in a family of eight
children, but she'd never had kids of her own. Hence the
housekeeper tended to dote on six-year-old Hayley.

"Exactly how many times a year would that be, Hayley?
Easter and Christmas?" Quinn asked jokingly.

"Attractive means I consider Ms. Trent very pretty,
Hayley," Norma Santini said. "Your father disagrees."

"She *is* pretty, Daddy."

"Aren't you supposed to be playing with your dolls?"

"It's boring up here, and 'sides, Daddy, you guys were
yelling."

Instantly contrite, Quinn hurried up the stairs and
hoisted his daughter into his arms for a hug. Hayley had
been barely a year old when Brett Santini's small plane had

been struck by lightning and crashed in a rugged part of the Allegheny Mountains, killing Quinn's father, mother and wife. At the time, Hayley's pediatrician said he thought Hayley was young enough not to be affected by the accident that had nearly devastated Quinn. Actually, neither one had been quick to recover.

Two women Quinn had tried dating three years after the accident, accused him of overcompensating for his losses by spoiling Hayley. His daughter was bright and sensitive and his *spoiling* just meant he wanted her with him when he had free time. So his response to both women had simply been to stop dating them—or anyone. Dating simply cut into his role as dad.

Since Hayley had entered kindergarten, though, she'd started to notice and exclaim over women she thought were pretty or nice. Last week she'd picked out a clerk in a store, and later during that same outing, a waitress. In a voice the women had to have heard, Hayley declared them very pretty and asked if her dad thought either one was married.

But April Trent? She wore boots like a lumberjack.

Quinn tickled Hayley's ribs as he carried her down to the main floor, and deposited her in a chair by the fire. "Listen, hon, Gram thinks your dad was too hard on Ms. Trent. I guess I'd better go see what I can do to smooth her ruffled feathers. I'll change my clothes and make a few phone calls before I head out. You can pop in one of the DVDs we brought over."

"Is 'smooth ruffled feathers' like saying you're sorry for yelling at her?"

Adjusting the knife creases in his tux pants, Quinn straightened fully and began to rub the back of his neck. His troubled eyes sought his grandmother's.

"Apology might be a bit much, since she showed up here uninvited. But Gram wants me to, uh, discuss something with Ms. Trent." Crossing to where Norma sat, he crouched to speak softly. "I know you said you'd pay her for the return of the letters," Quinn said, "but I won't…can't do that. Gram, think how that could be misconstrued?"

Norma lowered her voice. "Maybe you should listen to Hayley's suggestion. You were rude to Ms. Trent. A simple apology might achieve our goal."

"If *I knew* the goal," he muttered, and left her with a look that said plainly it was against his inclinations to go after April Trent.

On the way to his house out back, Quinn spent more time mulling over what excuse he'd give Hoerner for skipping out on his generous cocktail party. After changing clothes, Quinn called the kindly state representative and explained that his grandmother urgently required his help.

Not until Quinn drove out the gate did he realize it stood wide open. Only then did he feel less hostile toward the woman who'd disrupted his evening. Yesterday, Joseph Langford, Gram's driver, had reported to Quinn that he'd had trouble closing the electronic gate. So April Trent hadn't scaled the fence as Quinn had all but accused her of doing. She'd strolled right through.

Now he'd probably have to apologize. And tomorrow get onto the perimeter-fence firm to fix the system. The company should have phoned him when they detected a breach. Quinn paid dearly for a firm to monitor the gate's daily operation—one more nuisance to add to a growing list, at a time when election meet-and-greets, donor balls, et cetera, were exploding into high gear.

And now this…this letter debacle of his grandmother's. The Trent person had referred to them as love letters. What kind of nonsense was that? Although his grandmother hadn't rushed to deny that claim, or anything else April Trent had said.

Quinn's head pounded as he considered even the hint of a skeleton popping out of his family closet this close to the end of a bitter campaign. His opponent was the king of muckrakers.

Or was he dodging shadows where none existed? After all, they were talking about Grandmother Santini. As far back as Quinn could remember, she'. epitomized grace and dignity. As well, she'd been happily married to the grandfather he'd never met for—what—more than two decades? He'd heard his dad brag that Anthony had rubbed elbows with Presidents Roosevelt, Truman and Eisenhower. Quinn was probably worrying about nothing. Besides, trying to throw dirt on an eighty-two-year-old woman was bound to backfire.

God, those letters must be ancient. Quinn's grandfather had died before Quinn was even born. 1968, he thought. Gram had always lived alone in the big house, but her only son had lived close by. Quinn grew up running in and out of both places. Until he went off to college. Right out of law school, he'd married Amy, and they'd moved to Richmond, where he took a job as a state prosecuting attorney. He'd been twenty-four. No, twenty-five. Lordy, where had those ten years gone? He was thirty-five now, and tonight he felt every minute of it.

Jeez, it was dark in this neck of the woods. The lack of street lights didn't help; neither did the squall that had sprung up.

Straining to see through the hypnotic swish of wiper blades, Quinn suddenly slammed his foot on the brake and felt the rear of the car fishtail before he managed to stop— there was a doe elk standing in the center of the road. Seconds later, a big bull elk bounded out of the darkness. The two magnificent animals cantered across the asphalt and melted into a thicket of underbrush to Quinn's left. Rain hammered on the sunroof of the Lexus, reminding him to get underway. He turned on the radio to a favorite classical station before starting off at a much slower pace. Who knew what kind of wildlife might live out here?

Even though he drove slowly, he passed Oak Grove Road and was forced to make a U-turn. Quinn wondered what had possessed a young woman to buy a home so remote from any neighbors. How old was April Trent, anyway? Her brother Miles, was roughly Quinn's age. Roger had to be a few years Miles's junior, as he'd only recently finished an orthopedic residency in Bethesda. Quinn had also heard that Roger had just bought a practice, located near the Trents' law firm, from a newly retired surgeon. Which didn't tell Quinn a thing about April's age. He considered himself a reasonable judge of age, since he'd spent several years representing men and women from their teens to their midnineties in court. One learned to gauge people quickly and accurately.

Quinn would be willing to bet April Trent was staring down the barrel of thirty. He couldn't imagine why he'd even noticed, but she hadn't worn a wedding ring. Of course, that didn't mean she wasn't living out here in the sticks with a significant other. He decided she probably was. Otherwise, he would've run across her in the parade of twenty-to-thirtyish singles who stalked the favorite cocktail bars of the area's upwardly mobile.

He grimaced, recalling how many of the town's unattached women had gone out of their way to meet him. It had become embarrassing, if not annoying. When he griped to friends, they pointed out that was a normal part of being in the public eye. Married pals were quick to add that if Quinn would pick one of the many available women and settle down, it'd be broadcast far and wide and he'd be out of the market. He would—if he ever found someone who shared his commitment to the environment and to family— someone who wasn't just interested in his money and so-called good looks.

The road narrowed and branches draped low over what had become a series of potholes. There! Lights straight ahead. Hadn't Gram said the farmhouse sat at the road's end?

He could only picture how muddy his car must be as he eased down a drive that resembled one giant mud puddle. Quinn sat surveying the house for a moment after he shut off the car's motor. The building was long, low-slung, with a new shake roof, but with walls solidly built of red brick. Quinn saw the potential in the whole package. People paid well for privacy, and this place certainly offered that.

He opened the door and climbed out slowly. He vaguely wondered if April Trent had a dog she'd trained to take an intruder's leg off.

Except for the patter of rain and the sizzle when raindrops struck the hot hood of his car, he was engulfed in silence. Quinn liked solitude. So did his grandmother. He was beginning to see why she'd hated to leave this farmhouse.

★ ★ ★

April, who'd taken a break from sanding original cove molding she wanted to reuse for its authenticity, heard a car enter her drive. Was it Eric coming back again—to see if he could wheedle the letters out of her?

She jammed the cork into the bottle of white wine from which she'd just poured herself a glass. She glanced at the rows of crystal stemware hanging upside down under a cupboard wine rack she'd added in her full kitchen remodel. If she poured Eric a glass of wine, it might encourage him to think he held a special place in her life, which wasn't true. She opened her fridge and set the bottle and her full glass on a shelf.

She closed the fridge and waited for the chime of her doorbell. *Nothing.* An icy feeling slithered up her spine. Reaching for her portable phone, she turned off the kitchen lights, then slipped between the thick plastic sheeting and around the corner.

It was odd, but until she'd found those letters, and Eric and then the Santinis had gotten so snippy with her, April had never experienced a moment of unease about living in unfinished homes in desolate places. Now she wished she had curtains on the two huge picture windows that flanked her front door. Only one dim outdoor light shed any glimmer through the darkness.

Dropping to her knees, she crawled under the window and crept to the door. The sudden shrill ringing of the doorbell made her yelp and fall backward. "Who's there?" she called shakily, not liking the fright she could hear in her own voice.

"It's Quinn Santini."

Bolting upright, April peaked around the window frame,

and sure enough, there he stood on her porch, broad shoulders hunched forward to ward off the slanting rain.

"What do you want?" A fast examination of the man on her porch told April he no longer wore his made-to-order tuxedo. But, damn, in the feeble, diffused light shining from the single porch bulb, Santini looked even more gorgeous in faded blue jeans and well-worn sweatshirt than he had in that tux. His sun-streaked blond hair, appealingly tousled, curled around his ears from the rain.

In the silence, he announced loudly, "My grandmother wants the letters you found."

"Is she with you?"

"No. Listen, let me in so we can talk terms. I know I said I wouldn't pay...but I brought my checkbook."

April sucked in a narrow stream of air. "Please go. You're wasting your time and mine."

"I didn't drive all the way to hell and gone just to leave again without those damned letters, Ms. Trent."

"Well, you're not getting them," she shouted.

"I want them." Clearly frustrated, he slapped a flat palm against the door.

"I'm holding my phone, Mr. Santini. If you don't leave this instant, I'm going to call the police and tell them *you're* harassing *me*." She didn't add "turn about is fair play," but she wanted to throw his own threat back in his face.

"Don't do that!" Quinn paced over to the window and cupped his hands around his eyes, attempting to see inside.

When she saw what he was doing, April stepped right in front of his face, misshapen by the rain on glass. She snapped on an interior light and shook the phone in a menacing manner, making sure he got her message. Then she punched out the 9 and the first 1 in 911. Where he could see.

"Stop," he bellowed, and raised hands in a placating gestures. "I'll go," he mouthed. "I am going." He backed up. "But we aren't finished," he yelled again. "You haven't heard the last about this." With that final word he stomped down the remaining steps and moved out of sight.

With her finger still hovering over the last number, April stood there until she knew he'd crawled into his expensive vehicle, started the motor and backed up her long muddy drive. When his lights had disappeared and all was dark again, she collapsed against the door. More than ever she needed that glass of wine.

It wasn't until she'd calmed down enough to retrieve her wine that she paused to reflect on the recent scene and wished she'd let Santini know she didn't even have the letters here.

Her phone rang. April snatched it up, somehow expecting it to be Santini. Instead, Eric Lathrop's voice floated across the line. After saying hello, he gave April the same song and dance Quinn Santini had about wanting the letters. "April, my editor authorized me to pay you a thousand dollars cash for the bundle you pulled out of the wall today."

"Why would he do that?" she gasped. "That's a lot of money."

"Because old man Santini, Anthony, did major traveling in Europe for the government before and after the Second World War. The fact that letters written in German were apparently preserved and hidden in a sealed wall in a home he built may implicate Tony in something more unsavory than an affair. What was that guy's name, the guy who signed the letters? Maybe he was trying to blackmail Santini—or his wife. Let me do some digging on the Internet. If I don't find anything, you'll still be a thousand bucks richer."

"I'm hanging up, Eric. I'm not giving you the letters, so forget it. I have them in a safe place." She slammed down the phone and didn't pick up again although it continued to ring. After it finally went silent, she called Robyn, but got her friend's answering machine.

"Hey, Robyn, it's April. I left those old letters in your safe. I'll come by in the next day or so to get them, okay? Meanwhile, I'd appreciate it if you didn't mention them to anyone. Not even friends. Above all, don't let Eric, or anyone from his paper, know you've got them. If you have questions, I'm here working on the house."

Quinn had to get out in the rain and fiddle with the gate to make it lock. That only added to his frustration over having his mission thwarted. He hated coming home empty-handed. Especially since he was no closer to knowing what was going on with his grandmother and those letters than when he'd first learned of their existence.

It was after eight-thirty when he took off his muddy shoes and used his key to enter the big house. His grandmother had wanted to move into the smaller of the two homes after her son's plane crashed. She'd begged Quinn to sell his and Amy's modest house in the suburb and move into the mansion. The so-called cottage out back was where his folks had lived. His mom babysat Hayley while Quinn's wife, Amy, worked for the family firm. Even at Hayley's young age, Quinn had decided she'd feel less traumatized in more familiar quarters, so he'd moved them into the smaller house.

Two things had saved all six of them from going down on that plane. Hayley had come down with chicken pox, and the court had moved up a murder trial Quinn had been handling.

He rarely let himself think about the events that had led up to the accident. It had rained that night, too. He hadn't wanted to go on the trip, and felt guilty ever since, which might be why he felt driven to go after the senate seat his dad had dreamed of one day winning.

Norma rose from the flowered couch where she sat next to Quinn's sleeping daughter. That, too, reminded him of that long-ago evening. Did his grandmother share his twinges of guilt? After all, she'd volunteered to stay behind with the itchy, irritable toddler so Amy wouldn't have to give up relaxing at the condo on Hilton Head.

Tonight, unlike the night her mother and grandparents were killed, Hayley had fallen into an easy sleep watching TV. Norma had thrown one of the many afghans she'd knit over Hayley.

If Quinn had planned for a late night, Norma would've tucked Hayley into the bedroom upstairs that he'd furnished with a canopy bed exactly like the one in her room at home. With his job as attorney and now as a serious U.S. Senate candidate, it seemed that she slept here more than at home. Quinn suffered plenty of guilt over that.

"Mercy, Quinn, you're soaked. And where are your shoes?"

"I left them on the porch. It was muddy out at the farm. Also, when I got home, the front gate acted up. I had to climb around the ditch and jiggle the electronic eye. I'm not sure if it's the same problem Joseph mentioned. I'll call the company tomorrow, and have them check the entire security system. It's because the gate was open that April Trent was able to march right up to the house."

"That irritating system was something your grandfather insisted on before we moved to this house. It was the beginning of his paranoia."

"Paranoia? Aren't you exaggerating a bit?"

"No, Quinn. I thought you knew he started drinking heavily when your dad was Hayley's age. That's when he hired Joseph to drive me to town, and Brett to school, among other eccentric whims."

"Dad mentioned that Granddad had an alcohol problem. On the other hand, he worked for the government. Maybe he couldn't be too careful. Since I've become a candidate for the senate, I worry about crazies. The world is full of them. Come to think of it, we don't know whether April Trent's one or not."

"I hate to be impatient, Quinn, but…where are the letters?"

"I didn't get them."

She looked panicked. "Why not?"

"Because April Trent is cagier than I gave her credit for."

"Goodness, is she holding out for more than you're willing to pay? I'll pay anything within reason."

He shrugged. "She wouldn't discuss how much she wants. When I asked to sit down and talk, she threatened to phone the cops. She wasn't bluffing, either. I was afraid her reporter pal, Eric Lathrop, was waiting to pop out of the bushes with a camera. Wouldn't *that* have been a great photo to see on the front page tomorrow? Along with headlines accusing Quinn Santini, U.S. Senate candidate, of harassing the daughter of a rival lawyer."

"Quinn, I really don't think this has anything to do with you being a candidate."

"Really? Then what reason would she have for flatly refusing to name her top figure—or even a bottom line? And she had me at a disadvantage, after all. I have no idea what the letters are worth. Which brings me back to the question I asked you right after she flew out of here in the first place. What the hell are we dickering over anyway, Gram? Suppose I get a cup of coffee and dry off by the fire while you fill me in."

"I apologize for sending you out in a storm tonight, and for making you miss an opportunity to meet possible contributors to your campaign," she said formally. "Thank you for putting yourself out. It was wrong of me to foist this matter off on you, busy as you are. I'm sorry if my desire to take a trip down memory lane caused you added anxiety. You have enough on your plate. Take Hayley home, and fix yourself a hot toddy. Try and relax."

He rubbed his forefinger and thumb down each side of his nose and over his lips, before sending his grandmother a long, contemplative look. "Earlier, when April Trent barged in with her ridiculous story, I had the feeling you believed it."

Norma twirled a well-kept hand that didn't reflect her advanced years. "It's just an old woman's silliness. Off you go, Quinn. We won't talk about this again."

More relieved than he was willing to admit, Quinn shook his head and bent to pick up his sleeping child, blanket and all. "I have to say it's been one of my more interesting evenings. Probably more interesting than if I'd gone to Sam Hoerner's bash." He smiled wryly. "If you've been to one political cocktail party…"

Norma aimed an equally wry smile in her grandson's direction while preceding him to the door. "You wouldn't listen to me. It's the life you've let yourself in for."

Biting his tongue until she opened the door, Quinn ducked out, pulling on his mud-spattered shoes. "I certainly hope a senator's job offers more excitement than sipping watered-down martinis and pretending to be interested in the cocktail chatter of bored suburban housewives who happen to have rich husbands."

"You'd better hope times have changed, Quinn. In my day, debutantes and wives of the wealthiest entrepreneurs were privy to high-level state secrets and they brought down many a powerful skeptic."

Quinn glanced back and flashed her a broad grin. "Spies, you mean? Like the rumors that floated around about Marlene Dietrich and Julia Child? Gram, if you believe that nonsense, you're spending too much time watching late-night TV."

She rubbed her arms to ward off the chill and listened to his laughter fade as he disappeared into the rain. Going inside, she locked the door, then picked up the phone that connected her to the loft rooms above the garage. "Joseph, it's Norma. I'd like to ride along tomorrow when you take Hayley to day camp. There's a little side trip I want to make…." When he asked where, she said, "I learned that a young woman's renovating the farmhouse where Tony and I lived when we were first married. I'm interested in seeing what kind of changes she's made to the old place. Nine? I'll be ready. But I see no reason to mention our plans to Quinn. He'll think I'm a nostalgic old fool." She paused as Joseph commented on Quinn's schedule. "That's right. One day he'll slow down. Still, I can't fathom my grandson getting misty-eyed over relics from his past, let alone mine." Norma chatted a bit longer before saying goodbye to her driver.

She felt she'd put her dilemma in perspective, but Joseph had underscored another issue. Young men weren't sentimental. She should never have sent Quinn after her old love letters.

Shutting off the lights around the house, Norma went upstairs to get ready for bed. She'd thought the letters were long gone—thought Tony had found them and thrown them away She wondered why he *hadn't* done that, then decided he must have wanted to make sure noone could dig them out of the trash. He'd become more and more paranoid, she recalled sadly, more fearful and suspicious.

Still, her heart felt lighter than it had in…oh, years.

As she washed her face and gazed at her image in the bathroom mirror, Norma Santini imagined herself the pretty girl of nineteen, the girl she'd been when Heinz had written her those letters. Her heart beat a little faster. Heinz—her first love. It was true what the romantics claimed; A woman never forgot her first love.

Chapter 3

Unable to settle down after Quinn Santini left, April spent a good hour mulling over why the man and his grandmother would even consider paying for property that belonged to them. Or at least, belonged to Norma.

As April had been the one to approach them about the letters, she would've thought Quinn was more likely to threaten to sue her for their return than pay her.

Eric's boss—April understood his willingness to shell out the bucks. Knowing Eric as well as she did, she figured he'd probably built the letters into a promised scandal. The lengths to which Eric's editor was willing to go was further proof that politics was a messy business. She'd checked the newspaper online and read back issues. There were editorials against Quinn's platform and twice as many supporting his opponent.

So much for unbiased reporting.

But it was Quinn and Norma's reaction that April found bizarre. It bothered her so much, she let it disrupt her plan to catch up on paperwork tonight.

Of the two Santinis, Quinn had been the one most visibly upset at the existence of the letters. Thinking back to when she'd blurted out the reason for her visit to their home, April recalled Mrs. Santini's face. Unless her memory was completely off base, Norma had been shocked, but overjoyed, too. Then why had Quinn been so anxious to lay hands on the letters? He'd been willing to scrap what he'd declared to be an important previous engagement. Were the Santinis trying to protect themselves—or the identity of the letter writer?

April went back to her laptop. A college friend had located her birth mother through an Internet search. April didn't know where to start. In France, perhaps. Darn, what was the name of that city?

It eluded her, and she didn't own an atlas. Since she lived in the homes she remodeled, she never kept a lot of extraneous stuff. As a rule she scoured flea markets for a sparse quantity of furniture that would show well when she was ready to sell the house.

Scrolling through possible sites, April found a map of France. She hoped the city jotted on the back of Norma's snapshot would jump out at her. But the print on the map was so small, she couldn't place anything. And she'd forgotten her printer was on the fritz and that she'd dropped it off at the computer store for repair last week.

Giving up, she stored the map until she could remember the town. Instead, she Googled missing-person sites. Two that she checked out charged a hefty fee. And even to start, they wanted more information than a name, although one site said they'd work from a name and last-known location. Although disappointed that she didn't seem to be making any headway, she typed in Heinz von Weisenbach's name and requested a general search. No matches came up. She tried adding *France*. To her astonishment, two H. von Weisenbachs popped up. She bookmarked the site in case she wanted to go back at a later date. The first listing was a dud. It took her to a family-owned landscape-architect business in Mulhouse, France. April was positive that wasn't the right city. The blurb listed a Web address should viewers want virtual examples of the family's work. She scrolled on, muttering, "Sorry, folks. Your company's a bit too far away to handle my landscaping needs."

A double click on the second name took her to a U.S. military site with short paragraphs on medal recipients from various wars. Recipients were listed alphabetically. Her excitement quickly fizzled when she saw that this Heinz von Weisenbach, although in a correct age range, must've been an American. He'd been awarded the Distinguished Service Medal for meritorious service—a medal authorized by President Franklin Delano Roosevelt.

Unwilling to give up, April returned to the professional search site. Muttering, "what the heck," she typed in her credit card information, followed by von Weisenbach's name and last-known location as simply France. Satisfied that she'd done the most she could toward solving the mystery of the man in the photograph, April exited the site, and set the laptop on her nightstand.

She'd wasted enough time for one day on Norma and Quinn Santini. Still too restless to dig into boring paperwork but wide awake, she decided to work on something more immediate than worrying about a stranger's old love letters. She went back to sanding pieces of cove molding that needed to be stained and nailed back up in the dining room. After a light sanding and brushing, she rummaged around until she found a small can of stain mixed to match the built-in cabinets.

Her watch indicated nearly 1:00 a.m. before she finished the chore, cleaned her brush and set the molding on saw-horses to dry.

Her busywork hadn't produced the hoped-for effect. Long after she went to bed, her mind wouldn't shut down. She continued to fret over the letters so many people desired. Quinn and Norma Santini. Eric Lathrop. And Eric's boss. Not for the first time, April wished she had a better command of German.

The last time she looked, her bedside clock read three forty-five.

In spite of an almost-sleepless night, April rose early the next morning. Refusing to ruin another day by dwelling on Santini, his family or the letters, April dressed and brewed a pot of her favorite hazelnut coffee. She prepared cinnamon toast and munched on it while the coffee finished dripping through the French press. The French press reminded her of those blasted letters.

Gazing out the window above the sink, she was glad to see that although the sky was overcast, the rain had apparently blown out to the coast before dawn. That was the usual pattern for fall storms sweeping up from the south. The squalls came and went quickly this time of year.

When she'd poured herself a cup of the rich, dark, nutty-tasting coffee, she strolled in to check the cove molding. The stain had dried and looked terrific. Balancing her cup on a nearby sawhorse, she got busy nailing the moldings around the newly painted and wallpapered, dining room. This was the stage of remodeling April loved most, when rooms she'd visualized for so long came together. In this case, she'd waited six months for Robyn to locate period wallpaper that closely resembled the paper she'd uncovered beneath three layers of newer wall coverings. The wait had been worth it. It was these extra touches that had buyers standing in line for one of her finished houses.

After her last project had been featured in the real estate section of syndicated papers in Virginia, Maryland and D.C., her mom finally began to pay attention to April's enterprise. So much so, that at the last family gathering, Bonnie Trent had even ventured faint praise. Unlike the cutting remarks leveled by April's snobbish sisters-in-law or the outright denigrating comments made by her brothers.

Midway through the painstaking task of fitting corner molding, the growl of a car engine forced April to scramble off her ladder, parting the plastic to peer out the living room window. The sight of a big black Lincoln Town Car idling in her driveway rattled April for a frantic second. Her immediate reaction, foolish though it might be, was that Quinn Santini had sent a hit man after her.

Her panic subsided the minute an elderly stoop-shouldered gentleman wearing a chauffeur's cap climbed from the car and opened the back door. April identified the woman who emerged—and stifled the hysterical giggles as her exaggerated fear gave way to relief.

Still, seeing Norma Santini arriving here at all—let alone in such style—was a shock. Especially, dressed as she was today in square-toed boots, jeans and a rather ordinary car coat. April was caught off guard, and yet curiosity sent her scurrying to her door.

"Oh, good, you're home," Norma said brightly as she glanced up. She'd been taking in her surroundings, paying little heed to the mud puddles along the unfinished drive. "I expected to see this place crawling with workmen. Except for the new shake roof, the old place looks much the same as I remember it."

"I generally work alone, except for a few specialized projects and for those I hire craftsmen," April said, talking too quickly. "I stay true to the period of the home, but I do make some changes. For instance, I open up small, dark rooms and create larger ones with more light. Homes built back then didn't have the open spaces we prefer now."

Norma paused on the lowest step and made a second slow circuit to look around. "I see you also opened up the front and made the house more visible from the road than it used to be. I cleared the area near the house to plant a big garden. I liked the privacy provided by the trees between the house and the road." She made a sweep with her right hand. "That's where I hung at least a dozen bird feeders. A useless attempt to keep the pests from eating my corn and tomatoes. This land is on a flyway, so we were inundated with migrating flocks."

"Oh, that explains the birds' names on those papers stuck between the letters."

Norma spun back around and gave April a quizzical look. "Ah…I believe one bird was the oriole," April quickly mumbled. "I forget the other."

"Hmm. As you might guess, the letters are why I'm here."

"I'm sorry you made the trip across town for nothing. I don't have them. I left them in town, Mrs. Santini. But don't worry. They're locked in a friend's office safe."

Wind ruffled strands of white hair around a narrow face that fell noticeably at April's news.

That prompted her to add, "I plan to run into town this afternoon to visit a brick mason—I want him to enclose carriage lamps I bought to flank each side of the drive." April's gesture encompassed a muddy circle cordoned off for the drive. "If you think you'll be home around...say, three," she said, "I'll bring you the letters."

"So...I assume you've decided on a price?"

"What? No. Mrs. Santini, I tried to tell you yesterday, I don't want anything. I realize I lost my temper. Twice—once with your grandson—and I apologize. But please understand...no one has *ever* accused me of attempted blackmail before. He also insinuated that I was a gold digger," April said with a sigh. "I'm sure he repeated every word of our shouting match."

Apparently tuning April out, Norma ran a hand over the brick-and-mortar siding. "I was wrong to send Quinn out here," she murmured. "This farm has no place in his memories. Not the way it does for me. Perhaps you're one of the few people who can appreciate how difficult it was for Anthony to scrounge the materials to build this house before the war ended. He did the majority of the work, since most builders were off fighting. This house was little more than a shell when we got married and he brought me here." She shook her head. "We moved only five years later. I hated to leave."

"Mrs. Santini, since you're here would you like to have a look inside?" April jerked a thumb over her shoulder toward the partially finished interior.

"I'd like that very much. But please, call me Norma."

"Norma, then. The carpeting hasn't been installed, and I have no window coverings yet. I uncovered the most marvelous wood floors in the bedrooms when I pulled out the old carpet. The smallest of the three bedrooms has different wood from the other two. It's lovely—quite unique. Perhaps you'll know if it's a local hardwood."

Following April inside, Norma took care to scrape the mud off her boots, even though April assured her she'd have to clean many times before having new carpet laid.

Once inside, Norma stood completely still, saying over and over, "Oh my, oh my."

"The wall I removed separated a tiny room from the living area. These days a lot of people need a home office, and I thought it'd be perfect as a work-space alcove. I'll install beveled-glass French doors here." April traced out an area. "This was the wall where I found the letters. Without it, I imagine the room looks very different from what you remember."

April retrieved her coffee mug from the sawhorse. Lifting it, she spoke into the lengthening silence. "Could I get you some coffee, Norma?"

"What? Oh, I'd love some. I feel…light-headed. I'm afraid I simply wasn't prepared for all these memories."

"Do you need to sit? I'll help you into the kitchen. That and my bedroom are the only rooms I've furnished in order to live and work here." She led the older woman to the breakfast nook and pulled out a chair. Hurrying over to the carafe, April poured a mug full of coffee and returned to put it in Norma's cold hands.

"You asked about the flooring in the smallest bedroom," Norma said, after taking a bracing sip of coffee. "Yellow poplar. The only stand that's left, I believe, is in Ramsey's Draft Wilderness area." She pointed out the window. "That room ended up being Brett's nursery." Norma set down her mug, crossed her arms and rubbed her sleeves as if warding off a chill.

But she'd never removed her quilted coat and she wore a turtleneck sweater underneath. Seeing the home had obviously been overwhelming. April urged her to drink more of her coffee.

That did seem to help Norma's color. Rather than remain seated, however, she rose and went to examine the kitchen. "You've done a wonderful job with the cabinets. What I wouldn't have given back then to have this kitchen."

"You didn't have a cook?" That surprised April.

"Heavens, no. Tony owned this land, but not much else. As I said, construction materials came at a premium. He had some savings when he retired as an army major and that's what he used. We'd both left the OSS by then, so for a time we had no income."

"OSS?" Slipping in behind Norma as she left the kitchen, April wondered what that was. She'd never heard of it before.

"Yes, dear. The Office of Strategic Services. But you're probably too young to be familiar with it. The OSS was the forerunner to our current CIA. It's how I met Tony. Of course, then I didn't know his name, nor he mine. He was one of several officers picked to train agents. And I was one of a few select women who ended up wearing many faces, my dear."

April gulped, afraid that Norma might be delusional. And as the old woman moved slowly from room to room, murmuring to herself, it was as if she'd forgotten she wasn't alone. She let old memories unfold in almost a whisper. "In 1943 I was a blissfully naive eighteen. I'd completed a year at Barnard, then attended finishing school abroad. I loved Europe. My father was an international banker, and throughout my teen years we spent a month here or there in France, Germany, Italy. All before the war broke out. When it did, my parents called me home. I was eager to do something to help the war effort—anything except fill cocktail glasses at the parties my parents held to raise money for the troops. I guess that made me the perfect OSS candidate."

Pausing at the door to one of the empty bedrooms, Norma turned and walked back to the living room, April not far behind.

Nervous, April bit her lip, but said nothing to interrupt Norma's soft flow of words. She was intrigued, but also wasn't sure any of this was true. But…maybe it was.

"A general who often attended Father's evening fund-raisers was interested to learn that I'd traveled extensively abroad. And that I was fluent in several languages. At one party he pulled me aside and asked questions in French, Italian and German. I have an aptitude for languages. And before he left that night, he slipped me a business card. He said he had a job for me in Washington."

Norma stopped in front of the massive fireplace and ran her fingers over the oak mantel, but continued to ramble. "The war changed everyone. Under normal circumstances my parents would never have approved of me working, other than at home for Father. But my older brother and his friends had shipped out to England. Mother's women's group helped by rolling bandages, which I found too tame."

She crossed to stare out the side window. "At the time I put the general's card in my pocket and agreed to an interview. I told my parents that at most I'd be answering phones, filing or typing in some moldy back office on Capitol Hill. It turned out the general was recruiting me to be a specialized support person in Europe. To be extra eyes and ears for a newly formed counterintelligence unit, he said. I wasn't allowed to tell a soul, my parents included. Real names weren't spoken aloud." She turned toward April and sighed. "A dashing and very attractive officer, whose name I learned much later was Anthony Santini, assigned us code names. Mine was Oriole. He and our other trainers were older and far more experienced than I was. They were so impressive and very serious. I spent weeks in awe of them."

April remembered the page tucked among the letters addressed to Oriole from Kestrel. April guessed Tony Santini might be Kestrel. So, if Norma's story *wasn't* a figment of her imagination, the scrambled letters on the pages she'd seen could be secret, encrypted messages.

April injected her first comment in a while. "When I was in college, I read a biography of the Countess Romanones, who supposedly worked as a clerk in a U.S. company with offices abroad. Part of her job was actually to decode intercepted enemy messages."

Norma's head shot up. "I did that for a few months. I was used to helping my father with his banking, and I discovered I was good at unscrambling codes. Things moved fast, though, and I was transferred to Morale Operations, later called psychological warfare. We disseminated propaganda, so I began delivering messages to field agents, as well. I was taught to kill swiftly and silently when necessary—but fortunately it *wasn't* necessary, not for me. Still, a difficult lesson for a refined former debutante. It was far easier to act like a silly young woman out for a good time. In those situations I was expected only to store the conversations taking place around me in a number of languages. Although sometimes that had serious consequences, too," she said, her eyes blanking momentarily.

Such a sad expression came over Norma that April's imagination ran wild. So wild, she stopped her guest right there. "Mrs. Santini, uh, Norma. I can't bear to think I've contributed to these painful memories." Gently, April tugged the mug from the woman's tense fingers and began escorting Norma back to the entrance. "Those letters and any information they contain should be kept private."

At the door, April squeezed Norma's arm. "I swear I'll return them this afternoon. I'll try for three o'clock, four at the latest. I ought to be able to manage that, but I really should get back to the work I was doing before you arrived."

Her promise seemed to relieve Norma. Still, April had grown more curious than ever about those letters—and why they were hidden in a wall. Obviously, someone had intended they'd never see the light of day. If the letters contained damning secrets, why hadn't Norma simply burned them in the old stone fireplace that flanked the very wall where they'd been discovered?

Teary-eyed, Norma held tight to April's arm as they maneuvered down the outside steps. "April, you can't even begin to know how happy you've made me. I thought those letters and photographs were gone forever. I thought Anthony had destroyed them." Awkwardly, Norma turned back and hugged April.

As they stood there, April glanced out at the road—and recognized Eric Lathrop's battered red compact some distance away but moving inexorably closer.

"Norma, you have to leave now! The reporter I mentioned yesterday…he's on his way here. Eric's not so bad, but he's persistent when he's after a story. I'm sorry to say he saw your letters, and he's sure there's a scandal contained in them. What's more, his boss is biased against your son. So, you need to go." April couldn't have hustled Norma to her car any faster, practically lifting the slight woman off her feet. When the chauffeur opened his door and struggled to get out, April motioned him back inside. She opened the back door and stuffed Norma in, all while babbling that the chauffeur should get moving *now.*

The two vehicles passed as Eric swung into April's lane and the old six-passenger Lincoln shot out onto the two-lane county road.

Eric vaulted from his car, leaving his door hanging and his engine running. He dashed up to April, and grabbed her arm. "Dammit all, did you just give Santini's mother those letters? You lied last night when you said you didn't have them here. You know I want them, and I was willing to pay."

From her seat in the back of the Lincoln, Norma Santini craned her neck to see the reporter. She saw him grabbing April. Tapping Joseph's shoulder, she said, "Slow down please, Joseph. I think that man's up to mischief." The words had barely left her lips when Norma saw April plant her thick-soled work boot squarely on the reporter's instep. He let go of her and hopped around rubbing his foot. April went into the house and slammed the door.

"Never mind, Joseph. Ms. Trent has taken care of the problem. I'm so glad I came to see her." Settling into her seat again, Norma indulged in a satisfied smile. "April puts me in mind of myself at her age. Oh, I wish she hadn't gotten off on the wrong foot with Quinn. Wouldn't they make a grand pair? Did I mention she's dropping by the house this afternoon, Joseph? I wonder if I could persuade her to stay for dinner," she murmured.

The chauffeur, who'd been with Norma since well before her husband's death, threw her a glance in the rearview mirror—a glance that warned her she should proceed with caution in that particular matter.

True to her word, April collected the letters from Robyn, who said, "I got your frantic message. What's the big mystery, April? Why are Eric Lathrop and his boss so interested in those letters? By the way, did I tell you I'm re-decorating his boss's home? Even his witless wife brought up the letters. She pumped me about how well I knew you and asked whether I thought you'd give Eric or her husband the information they want. *What* information?"

April opened her briefcase and dropped the letters on top of the brick mason's bid. "Robyn, in about half an hour, it's going to be a moot point. I'm on my way to Mrs. Santini's place now to give her back her letters." She groaned. "Considering how much trouble they've been, I wish I'd never found them." Briefly, April filled her friend in on Eric's latest attempt to get the letters.

"So I take it you're not going to Quinn Santini's fund-raising ball with Eric? He apparently told his boss you were."

"My brother gave him some tickets. But no, I won't be attending anything with Eric. He's toast as far as I'm concerned."

"Good. You can do better. But I hoped we could go shopping for dresses. I feel a shopping attack hovering," Robyn said with a wink as April prepared to leave her shop.

"I'll tag along. I love watching you shell out money, Robyn." They arranged an afternoon to meet for lunch and shopping.

There were two men working on the Santini front gate when April tried to turn into the drive. "Norma Santini's expecting me," she said after rolling down her window.

The workmen weren't very trusting. One phoned the house and received an okay before letting April pass.

Norma met her at the door. "You came! All day I've worried that you'd change your mind."

April extracted the bundle and placed it in Norma's outstretched hands. "You're welcome to these. My advice— burn them."

The older woman clasped the letters as if they were precious jewels. "Won't you come in?" she said. "I'd love to have you stay for dinner, my dear."

"Thank you, but I can't. I have just about enough daylight left to dig holes for my light poles. The mason said if I get them set, he'll work in bricking around them next week." She tripped lightly down the steps and waved as she got into her pickup.

Driving out the gate where the men were still working, she passed Quinn Santini's Lexus. "Phew, that was a close call." In the rearview mirror, she watched him turn through the gate. April felt a surge of relief at declining Norma's dinner invitation.

Back at the house, Norma settled in her favorite chair to begin reading her precious letters for the first time in almost sixty years. She'd reached the end of the first letter when her front door flew open and her grandson burst inside. Sniffling, Norma fumbled for a tissue and attempted to hide the letters in the folds of her skirt.

"Gram, tell me what that Trent woman said to upset you. I passed her headed out. My gut said I should stop her— that she was up to no good." Quinn jerked up the white phone that matched the room's decor. "This time I *will* press charges. It was those damned letters, wasn't it? Did she come to shake you down for more money? I won't allow her to barge in here and make you cry."

"Quinn, hush. She brought me the letters and wouldn't take a cent. Please, calm down and sit with me. Joseph and Ethel have taken Hayley to her gymnastics class, so you and I have time to talk."

"About what? Those letters?" He saw them now and eyed her with a scowl.

"In a way." Her fingers plucked idly at the faded red ribbon. "I have a secret to tell you, Quinn. One that's burdened my heart for much too long."

Chapter 4

"A secret? That sounds ominous, Gram." Quinn slumped down on the chintz love seat and draped one arm over the padded armrest, his eyes still on his grand-mother.

"I wouldn't say ominous, exactly." All the same Norma shuffled the letters nervously. "Your grandfather extracted a promise from me that we'd carry this secret to our graves. He did. But since these letters went missing, a lot has changed. There are things you don't know that you should."

Quinn sat forward and clasped his hands between his knees. "You'd better tell me, then. Especially if there's stuff that could turn up in the campaign…"

Her eyes shifted to the envelopes fluttering in her hands. Without fanfare, Norma dove into her story at the same point where she'd begun reminiscing at April's. Reaching the spot she'd halted before, Norma hesitated only a few seconds before plunging on. "I never viewed anything I did overseas as a lark, Quinn, even though a significant part of our jobs involved mingling with the patrons at popular night spots. We were expected to keep our ears open and pick up what we could in the way of usable information. By *usable* I mean anything with the potential to help our fighting forces. Whatever we gathered was coded the next morning and sent via teletype or by hand delivery to male agents in the field. Messages came back the same way. Often we were asked to see a particular man again, usually an officer. Or we were dispatched to dig up more information somewhere else."

"I can't believe it—yesterday I was joking you'd been a spy, like Dietrich and Child," Quinn stammered. "And now I find out you were."

"I'm sure it sounds preposterous." Norma paused when he got up suddenly and poured them each a bracing shot of brandy. He swirled it in the two snifters, then handed her one. She took a sip, letting him return to his seat before she went on.

"One day there was a change in my routine that disrupted the entire focus of my mission. Tony, your grandfather, whom I knew only as Kestrel, a man I hadn't laid eyes on since my training days, awakened me in my apartment late one night. With him was a four-star general whose name I recognized and actually recalled seeing at one of my father's weekend gatherings. Kestrel and the general gave me official orders to travel by train from Marseilles to the town of Colmar, near the German border. My task—cozy up to a German officer who'd flirted with me twice at a local café. I had, of course, reported those encounters and our conversations. My first reaction was that I must be dreaming, but no, I wasn't, and those two were quite serious. They wanted me to…seduce military secrets out of an enemy."

Norma heard Quinn choke on his brandy. Her head shot up and she backtracked a bit. "Understand, Quinn, that I was young and reasonably attractive. And the officer they'd singled out was very handsome and charming. So I didn't consider this a hardship. Nor was their request out of the ordinary. I knew female agents who'd been asked to do more."

"But…you must've known how dangerous it was to openly spy on an enemy."

She brushed his comment aside. "At the time, Quinn, every third person in France was spying for one country or another. My cover was that of a clerk working for an American-owned shipping company in Marseilles. Our business was legitimate, but like so many others, it served as a front for gathering intelligence, which we passed to field agents, who in turn got the information into Allied hands. We were told daily that what we did saved lives. So, except for being handed back my passport which I needed to travel to and from Colmar, my new orders weren't much different from what I'd been doing in Marseilles. And Heinz von Weisenbach, the young officer I was to shadow, had never frightened me like many of his comrades did."

Norma wasn't aware that the tenor of her voice changed and her features softened as she spoke about Heinz. "He was witty, cultured and soft-spoken." But Quinn noticed. He glanced sharply at this woman he no longer knew, and felt himself tense at what was to come.

"I had no trouble establishing contact with Heinz in Colmar. He was delighted to see me. I shouldn't have been surprised that there were more men in German uniforms, since we were near the border, but I was nervous and he could tell. I've never doubted that we both entered the relationship for the purpose of obtaining secrets from each other. What I didn't expect was that Heinz would denounce the war so sincerely. But he did. Around me, he revealed himself as a man who enjoyed sitting quietly, listening to Bach, Beethoven and other classical composers. I soon learned he'd attended way more concerts than I ever had. We fell into the habit of taking long walks together. Once he asked a total stranger on the street to take a picture of us. Every day, he brought me a rose from some bushes that grew in pots along the balcony where he lived. I'd never seen his quarters. Couples were more circumspect in my day—at least at the beginning of a courtship."

"You had a courtship with a *German* when we were at war with them?" Quinn appeared thunderstruck.

Sitting up straight, Norma said sternly, "Love doesn't differentiate between uniforms."

"*Love?* You fell in love? With an *enemy?*"

She bit her lip hard for a minute, then her voice dropped, sounding slightly ragged. "Yes, or so I thought." She blinked back tears. "I was a willing participant the night Heinz seduced me with roses, wine and music. It was a momentous experience for me, Quinn. Other female agents had been ordered to submit for the purpose of gathering information through pillow talk, but that wasn't what I'd been charged to do. In fact, Kestrel, er, Anthony, had been quite adamant at the outset of my mission that it did *not* include me going to bed with the colonel."

"Colonel. Oh, great. Now I suppose you'll tell me he was Hitler's fair-haired boy." Vaulting off the love seat, Quinn strode to the fireplace. The fire had burned down and he threw on two logs, stabbing at them with the poker. When flames shot up, he jammed the poker back in place, with the rest of the tools on the hearth. He stood, keeping his back to his grandmother, hands braced on the mantel. "I think I've heard enough," he said. "If those so-called love letters are from *him,* burn them all." Quinn clenched his back teeth.

Norma didn't move, but her voice grew steely. "Hiding them won't alter the facts, Quinn. Nor will turning them into ashes."

He glanced at her over his shoulder, his eyes a cold blue and his face a harsh mask. "Finish your story, then. We'll put your guilt to rest and then forget this ever came up."

"I can't forget," Norma said simply. "That night with Heinz was my first. It was terrifying, but also beautiful. Heinz swore he'd grown to love me with all his heart. He promised he'd find a way for us to be together openly. I believed him. I had no reason not to. Especially since he sent the first of these letters the very next day." Norma picked up the top one.

"Could you cut to the chase? I don't want to hear the details."

"All right. You want it straight, Quinn, here it is. Within days, things on the front heated up and I received notice to return to Marseilles. I sent Heinz a note requesting what I feared would be our last clandestine meeting. To my astonishment and extreme joy, he begged me to help him defect."

"What?"

She smiled at Quinn's yelp. "Yes. I knew it was so we could be together always. But it was more than that. Many times he'd confided to me that he was worried about the decisions Hitler was making. Not surprising, as there were whispers about the atrocities taking place. Defecting wasn't as uncommon as you might think," she said.

Quinn continued to gape. "Well, that puts a more positive spin on this tale than I expected. So what happened? Did you help him? You obviously weren't together always."

"Are you always so impatient? I'm reconstructing what happened long ago. You'll have to bear with me and let me explain at my own pace."

"Okay. More brandy? If you don't mind, I'm going to freshen my drink."

Norma shook her head. "There's still a lot left to tell, Quinn." He heard her take a deep breath. "I mistakenly assumed it would be merely a matter of notifying my contact. Kestrel, uh, Tony. I thought safe passage to America would be arranged for Heinz overnight."

Quinn tipped three fingers of brandy into his snifter and recapped the bottle. "I can't believe you worked for the government and had such unrealistic expectations," he said wryly. "Nothing happens in government overnight."

Her shoulders relaxed a bit. "Did I mention that I was naive? Well, I was. I sent my report, but heard nothing. Days passed, and I had two messages requesting I return to Marseilles. I started to panic, thinking my note had gone astray. Despite the danger that it might fall into the wrong hands, I sent another. Like you, Heinz understood such requests took time. He was fully prepared to continue a long-distance relationship." She held up the packet of letters.

"For a month we corresponded secretly and I hid his letters in the lining of my travel satchel, even though they were just the silly things lovers would write—not one sentence of political import. But all at once, again in the middle of the night, two agents I'd never seen in my life— one American, one French—appeared by my bed. I was ordered to pack everything, and I had no idea why. We left by car. For hours I was grilled. I was expected to divulge every intimate detail of my relationship with Heinz."

"You must've been terrified," Quinn said, just a bit grudgingly.

"Frightened, but not stupid. In those days no one trusted casually. I never breathed a word about our falling in love. I certainly didn't mention his letters to a soul. I prayed fervently that the men wouldn't search my suitcase. I made it seem as if Heinz and I had forged a loose friendship, which was the only reason he'd contacted me about his defection. I also pointed out that I knew the risk to everyone."

"What happened to Colonel von Weisenbach?" Quinn asked intently.

Tears rimmed Norma's reddened eyelids. Her lips trembled and her words were shaky. "My driver finally stopped. Where, I didn't dare ask. To this day, I have no idea. At a farmhouse in the middle of nowhere. Tony was there, although I still didn't know him by name. The other men left. Kestrel said he'd arrange, or maybe he said he *had* arranged for Heinz to come over to our side. He said it was a delicate operation and he needed me to play a part. I never questioned his decision, although I sensed his urgency, and his uneasiness. Kestrel told me I should get word to Heinz to meet us in three weeks on Saturday two hours before dawn. He wrote down some coordinates for me to pass on to Heinz."

She tried several times to say something else. Her lips moved, but no words emerged.

"Here, you need more brandy." Quinn carried her almost empty glass to the bar and added one generous splash, then a second. Returning, he stood over her, urging her to swallow. Quinn knelt and covered the cold fingers that still clutched the old letters. "It doesn't take an Einstein to figure out something bad happened, Gram. I have no desire to hear details that are so painful for you. Let's leave the story here."

"No," she insisted, thrusting her brandy snifter back at Quinn. "Let me muddle on…. I *have* to get this all out."

"As you wish." Nodding, he got to his feet and placed her glass on the square coffee table within easy reach, then went to sit across from her again.

"That Friday before the transfer was a bleak, rainy day. At two the next morning, Kestrel collected me and we drove off. He didn't turn on the car's lights. I suppose I should've been more concerned, especially as the weather got worse. But my spirits were soaring. This was the day Heinz and I had waited for. I admit to being a bit surprised when we drove a mile, stopped and picked up two taciturn Frenchmen whose silence unnerved me. They didn't wear uniforms and they didn't speak, even between themselves. I didn't understand why we needed anyone else along. But I'd learned not to question my superiors."

She reached for the brandy and before she returned the glass to the table, Quinn had slid to the edge of his seat again. His gaze clung to his grandmother's face.

"We arrived at the site of the transfer. The fog was dense, and it'd begun to rain, as well, but as far as I could tell, we were at some sort of abandoned railyard. I remember stumbling over slick railroad ties, and my nervousness increased when lightning struck a rusty rail. It danced along the steel for about fifty yards and lit up the area. I saw a man emerge from a black caboose and my heart nearly stopped until I recognized Heinz. He was dressed in a black watch-cap, bulky black sweater and black slacks. Seeing him, I was distracted for a moment as we closed the distance between us."

She grew agitated, almost dropping the letters. As Quinn lunged for them, she waved him off. "I can't tell you how many times I've relived what happened next. Two rattletrap cars bore down on us from opposite directions. I was blinded by one set of lights. I saw Heinz throw up an arm to cover his eyes. A man jumped from each car. There were shouts. I heard running. Then…shots. I tried to run toward Heinz but someone held me back. I struggled. Heinz's knees buckled slowly, and as he fell I saw blood spurt from his chest. When he brought his hand up, I saw it gush through his fingers. A bullet zinged past my ear. I screamed, but I was blinded by another bright light." She shuddered, and paused to take a drink of brandy.

"Kestrel said later it was a camera flash. I was so numbed by panic and shock, I lost all track of what was going on around me. Kestrel said he grabbed the camera, smashed it, tore out the film. He forced me to run, saying the men who'd ridden with us would bury Heinz and take care of the men in the two cars. For what seemed like a lifetime, Kestrel hauled me in and out among empty rail cars. Every so often, he cautioned me to quit crying or we'd be caught and killed. I have no idea how far we ran—until we reached a cave. Or maybe an old mine shaft. We hid there all day. I was cold, wet and muddy. And when I tried asking what'd gone wrong, I was ordered to sleep. The most he ever told me was that someone had gotten wind of our plans. I assumed it was the Germans."

Falling silent, Norma sorted through the letters. She took out a green passport folder, opened it and two snapshots fell into her lap. As she stared at first one, then the second, her eyes glossed with tears and she touched the dried rose to her lips.

"Gram, now I'm even more curious. There must be more story. How did you get away? You obviously made it home to the States and—hey, are you crying? I don't understand why you or Grandpa felt compelled to hide the fact that you both served as intelligence agents. It's not a criminal occupation."

"Because the story doesn't end there."

Quinn glanced at his watch. "Hayley's due home from gymnastics in about twenty minutes and shortly after that I have to leave for a meeting with my steering committee."

"I'll try to hurry. On the other hand, some things are too important to be rushed," she said, blotting her eyes. "I assumed we'd go back to Marseilles, and that life would go on as before. Kestrel said that wasn't wise. It was the first time he indicated that I was in jeopardy—through my job. He said senior officers thought I'd leaked classified information to Heinz. I didn't! I felt physically sick with fear. We took refuge with a French family, someone in the underground. They got the film developed. There was only one picture on the roll—the one at the transfer site.

It showed me reaching out to Heinz. I didn't see how it could be considered damaging, which is why I stole it from our hosts. I wanted that last memory of Heinz. But Kestrel said if it landed in a senior officer's hands, the photo might make it look as if I'd become a traitor." She gave a resigned sigh. "According to him, my feelings for Heinz were so clear, that photo practically sealed my fate."

"Hardly seems fair," Quinn muttered.

Norma shrugged. "That's how espionage works. The system can turn on an agent in the blink of an eye."

"I'm positive you aren't going to say you two went AWOL, Gram. Otherwise, Grandpa never would've became a diplomat after the war. Dad used to tell me stories about him."

"I eventually went through the proper channels to leave the OSS. A sadder, wiser woman. At the time, Kestrel left me with the French family while he traveled to Marseilles to nose around. What he learned almost undid me. The agency had it on good authority, they said, that Heinz intended to infiltrate the OSS through me. That he was a double agent, in other words. Now you might think my colleagues would feel sorry for me. But no, I was persona non grata to many people who'd been my friends. If that wasn't horrible enough, my life was in danger. I'd become disposable. I was brokenhearted, and I felt totally betrayed."

"Ah, I'm beginning to see. Grandpa, uh, Kestrel, believed in you."

"So he claimed. He also claimed he loved me. Fell head over heels, he said, even before our training days. Apparently he'd attended a few of my parents' parties, although I didn't remember him. I wasn't ready to hear any of it, certainly not his declaration of love. I'd given my heart fully to Heinz. But I wasn't impractical. I knew I could stay in France. After Heinz's death, I slipped into a depression. I couldn't muster up the energy to act, which meant my fate was in Tony's hands. We escaped the country on foot, as it wasn't safe to show my passport. We hiked over the mountains to Spain. A miserable trek. It rained. It snowed. I've managed to block out my worst memories of those days. We rode part of the way in a stock truck, afraid to make a noise. In those days there were spies everywhere. American, German, French, Bulgarian—and even some Japanese. It was truly a miracle we got out alive."

"Gram, don't cry anymore. You did get out. Isn't it time to talk about the good stuff? The part where you realized a good man loved you, and you ended up marrying him?"

"Oh, Quinn. I was ready to run home to my parents. Tony revealed his identity and told me to shape up. I'd taken an oath not to tell a soul about my time with the OSS. He ordered me to destroy any communication I'd had with Heinz, as well as my passport verifying travel to and from Colmar. He didn't know I'd kept these photographs. They were all I had left of Heinz."

She wiped away another tear. "Tony promised to fix my record when he returned to Washington to train a new group of agents. He said I could continue working in Washington at an agency desk job. By then, I'd had enough of the OSS. I wanted to quit and saw no reason to shred my passport or the letters. I hadn't passed any vital information to Heinz. While I admired Kestrel's skill and expertise, and appreciated his help, I didn't love him and I told him so. We had a huge fight. He left my D.C. apartment in a huff, with me insisting I'd dissolve my association with the agency as soon as I could. Honorably. Which wasn't easy, I learned. Rumors about me had already made their way to the Joint Chiefs. I was interrogated up one side and down the other by no-name operatives and assorted military officers. I was glad I'd saved my correspondence with Heinz, should it come to proving that I, at least, wasn't a double agent. Not that I ever believed Heinz was… Thank goodness it didn't go that far. Instead, I was put on paid leave. One day I received a letter signed by the agency chief, giving me a release date three days out, plus the amount of my last paycheck."

"But since you sent Grandpa packing and you quit the OSS while he finished his assignments, how did you two get back together?"

Norma bit her lip, while she held Quinn's gaze. "A few days before I officially left the agency, I found out that the persistent nausea I'd battled for several weeks was really the result of being pregnant." Lowering her gaze to the photograph, Norma added in a whisper, "Pregnant with Heinz's child."

Bounding off the love seat, Quinn paced the room and thrust a hand through his hair. "I know what you're going to say next. You were so overwrought by the whole ordeal, you lost the baby. It was probably for the best. You must've been a wreck at the time."

She seemed to be talking to herself. "I was barely out of my teens and scared to death. My parents were prominent in Boston. My father an international banker. They and everyone in their circle were ultra-conservative. I had no job, no savings and everyone said my baby's father had duped me in order to betray my country. I've always steadfastly refused to believe it. At that point, however, I was so depressed I seriously contemplated ending my life."

That declaration had Quinn flopping heavily onto his seat. He pinched the bridge of his nose. "God, could things have been any worse for you?" He sprang back up the instant Norma set the two photographs on the coffee table and pushed them toward Quinn.

He fought against looking down, but his gaze was drawn to the young German officer—a man who bore an uncanny resemblance to Quinn's dad, Brett. At first Quinn's stomach went into free fall. Then denial propelled him across the room. "Gram, tell me it's not true. All these years… Have you let the whole family live a lie? Brett *Santini* is the name carved on Dad's headstone. Mom's, too. It's the name on their marriage license and death certificates. On my birth records." Quinn threw up his hands, then set them on his hips as he stared at the woman wilting in her chair.

"I'm sorry, Quinn. It's a mess that got compounded—out of compassion."

"Wait! At the start you said Grandpa shared your secret. That doesn't fit with everything I've heard about how hard-nosed he was. I know you were in a bad spot, but…did you lie to him, too?"

If possible Norma's shoulders grew stiffer. "No, Quinn, every word I've spoken is the truth. And I resent your condemnation. You've lived your entire life in comfort and utter complacency, while *I've* lived with this colossal falsehood on my conscience. Your grandfather insisted we distance ourselves from reality, as if Heinz never existed. Did Tony succeed? Hardly. I saw that in his face each time he returned from a trip abroad, even after his military duty ended and later, with his diplomatic assignments. And when he drank... In spite of watching his increasingly erratic behavior and suspecting why, I remained silent to save his reputation. I'd probably have gone on denying all of this had April Trent not found the letters."

Quinn buried both hands in his hair. "Damn! I let myself forget that part of the equation. How much does the Trent woman know?"

"Not much, I should think. Heinz wrote to me in German. She saw the pictures, of course, and I told her how Tony and I were in the OSS."

"Great! But that's what I still don't get. Why would a proud man who served his country the way Grandpa did give his name to the child of a sworn enemy?"

"Is it so difficult to believe that a man could love a woman enough to go to any lengths to protect her?"

"No, of course not. I didn't mean... But you said you two argued and he left."

"Tony visited me the day I contemplated suicide." Norma was so steeped in old angst, she didn't see Quinn flinch.

"Tony saw that something was very wrong. He badgered me until I blurted out the whole unbelievable mess. If he was shocked, he rallied, and he swore again and again that he loved me. He proposed we get married as soon as legally possible. He's the one who repeatedly insisted that no one needed to know my child wasn't his."

"I see. Naturally you'd jump at the chance to solve your problem."

"No," she snapped. "I objected vehemently, mostly because of Tony's exemplary military record. I wasn't convinced the situation with Heinz wouldn't somehow reflect on him. That was early 1945, when Tony said the war was winding down. He said he planned to retire to a plot of land he owned in Virginia. He promised to build us a house, saying he wanted to farm, and frankly, it sounded like heaven. I finally agreed to do things his way. I couldn't have realized at the time that in a few years, around 1949, Russia would attempt to steal the plans for our atomic bomb and that would entice Tony out of retirement. The day he went back to spying for our government was a day I rued."

"What? You mean he was never a diplomat like Dad always bragged? No…no," Quinn said faintly. "Are you about to say he drank himself to death because he sold out his country?"

"Quinn! Shame on you! You may not share Tony's DNA, but until he fell into drinking, he was a wonderful man who instilled excellent values in your father. Values that flowed from Brett to you. For many reasons I'll always owe Anthony my loyalty. And…I was the best wife I knew how to be."

"I take it you never loved him."

"I came to care for him deeply. I truly regretted not being able to give him a child of his own. It's hard to admit," she said sadly, "but I was never able to feel the dizzying passion for Tony that I found with Heinz. And no matter what he and others thought, I'll always believe Heinz truly intended to defect. I think they killed a good man for nothing, Quinn."

"Is that why you sealed his letters in the wall instead of burning them? Gram, what if they *were* right and the man used you? Or tried to."

"No. It doesn't make sense. It didn't then and it doesn't now. The more I rerun those fateful weeks, the less they add up. But Quinn, I wasn't the one who sealed the letters in the wall. I meant to destroy them. I wanted to, but kept putting it off. One day as I lined some kitchen cupboards, I had a strip of oilcloth left over, and I wrapped the letters so they weren't so recognizable. I tucked the bundle underneath my lingerie and never discovered it was gone until Tony bought this house, sold the farm and I went to pack my personal belongings. This was in 1950. Among other things, Tony said our government was actively hunting down Nazi war criminals. I figure after the formation of the new Central Intelligence Agency, Tony must've remembered he hadn't seen me destroy the letters. It wouldn't have taken much digging to find them. I could never bring myself to ask him."

Norma hugged the old envelopes and dabbed her eyes with a tattered tissue. "Brett thought of entering politics, and this is why I convinced him to delay. Now you know why I begged you not to run for office. I didn't draw an easy breath during Tony's entire time in service. When he drank, he tended to wallow in the past. Once he admitted that helping me escape from France hadn't been sanctioned. It's why he was distrustful of reporters. Hardly a day passed that he didn't order me never to speak of our time with the OSS. 'Even these walls could have ears,' he used to warn me. He meant the letters, I suppose. Back then I merely thought he'd gotten more paranoid."

"Paranoid? Mud-slinging is even more prevalent now. Some people will go to any lengths. They even make up dirt."

"I believe Tony lived in fear that reporters would discover

Brett wasn't his child, or worse, that he had German roots. Several times I caught him crying as he held Brett's school picture. Tony died in 1968—acute cirrhosis of the liver. For a short period after that, there were rumors about his real job with the government. Several articles hinted at his involvement in covert operations after the war. To be honest, I never knew exactly where he went or what he did. Not even agents' spouses are aware of what they do. I'm reasonably sure Tony did some work for the CIA right up until his death. I couldn't have verified it to the press, though— even if I'd been so inclined. Yet they hounded me until I became a virtual recluse. I was terrified some enterprising reporter would accidentally stumble on my name in old OSS records. Thankfully, bigger stories made the headlines and the media lost interest in us. Now with you in the limelight, Quinn, it's obvious the rumors have sprung up again. And they're digging into your background."

Quinn arched an eyebrow. "How do you know?"

Norma described what she'd seen at April's. How Eric Lathrop had pounced on April, and how Norma saw April stomp on his instep. "She told me that reporter caught a glimpse of my letters and he smelled a scoop."

"Crap!" Quinn exploded. "The paper Lathrop works for is solidly in my opponent's camp." Although he hadn't digested everything he'd learned about his family in the past few minutes, Quinn was conscious of being the sole protector of his grandmother and his daughter. And he knew he faced some very unscrupulous people.

"Is it too late for you to withdraw from the race, Quinn?"

"I happen to believe I'm the best man for the job. But I can't win if even a hint of this story leaks. You've spent a little time with April Trent. What do you think would convince her to keep quiet about finding those letters?"

"She's a spunky one. I admire that about her. Don't forget, she handed over the letters and refused to take a dime. I offered her dinner, which she turned down, too."

There was commotion in the hall and Quinn smothered what he'd been about to say. His rambunctious daughter skipped in from gymnastics, followed by their puffing housekeeper, Ethel.

His grandmother was already on her feet. "I'm going to put these letters away for now," she said quickly. "Quinn, you've misjudged April. I wish you'd apologize. She's far sweeter than any of those scheming women who fall all over you."

"Gram!" Quinn wasn't willing to attach a label like *sweet* to any offspring of his nemesis, Coleman Trent. The rival lawyer had disliked losing a major case to Quinn last year, and Trent could easily carry a grudge. His idea of payback was to defeat Quinn's bid for the senate by contributing the maximum allowed to Daniel Mattingly's campaign. April Trent's showing up with his grandmother's letters seemed too coincidental to Quinn. At the very least, he wouldn't put it past her to have photocopied them.

Dashing across the room, Hayley threw her arms around her dad's waist. "I think April's nice. I know saying *sorry* is hard, Daddy." She crossed her eyes, and mimicked Quinn in lecture mode. "Santinis are never too proud to 'pologize when they're wrong."

Quinn glanced away and fought a churning stomach. He used to make that statement—before he'd learned he had no right to flaunt the Santini name or code of honor. *A fictional code of honor?* Perhaps his grandparents thought they'd handled a bad situation the best way they could. At the moment it didn't seem like such a good idea. He wasn't Quinn Santini. So who the hell *was* he?

He needed time to sort things through. Above all, he didn't want his grandmother hurt. Damage control definitely had to start with another visit to April Trent.

Chapter 5

Trenching through mud with a hand shovel and then laying wire to power two carriage lamps at the edge of the property was almost easy compared to setting the heavy posts themselves. The job had to be done prior to asphalting the drive, so the mason could work around the posts.

One post was set and wired—it looked good. Wiping sweat from her face, April realized she'd transferred mud from her gloves to her cheek. "Just finish this by four o'clock, then a hot shower," she muttered, and threw all her strength into sliding the heavy post off the wheelbarrow and into the hole. Success on the first try! April danced a few happy steps, even though more mud flew up from her oversize rubber boots and stuck to her gray sweats. She connected and wrapped the wires, and felt joyous again when she threw the main switch for the second time and there was light to both lampposts. April wasn't a licensed electrician, but for a couple of summers during college, she'd apprenticed for Robyn's dad, who was. Handling much of the labor herself was how she made her renovations profitable.

She filled in the holes around the posts, but had to leave the trenches open for the county building inspectors. Just as she was in the middle of tamping down the last shovel full of dirt, she noticed a car rounding the bend. The headlights illuminated her work site. Leaning on her shovel handle, April narrowed her eyes and tried to figure out who'd come calling this time.

The rural road that led to her farm had seen more traffic in the last three days than in the whole ten months since she'd purchased the place.

Darn it, she recognized the silver Lexus as it swung out in a wide turn onto her land, stopping short of the house. By then the driver had seen her, too.

What now? Somewhat perturbed but mostly flustered, April quickly pulled off her gloves and streaked a hand through hair that had become a sweaty, windblown mess.

Quinn Santini stepped out of his spotless car, and April instantly compared her dirty, grungy state to his spit-and-polish appearance. Not only was he flawlessly dressed in black slacks with a razor crease, a tan suede sport coat and a black shirt that was obviously silk, he carried a bouquet of cut flowers. She didn't know whether to cry or laugh hysterically.

He stopped about two feet away. "Those took some work." He gestured to the newly installed lampposts.

April tried to find something condescending in his

remark. "Refurbishing old homes from top to bottom is what I do," she said stiffly. She shifted back a few steps and stabbed the shovel into the ground, as if to set a firm line of demarcation between them.

"My grandmother thinks you've done great things with this place." He gestured toward the house. "Remodeling old houses seems a very labor-intensive way to earn a living."

"I like doing it. If you're out drumming up votes, Mr. Santini, I should tell you that I have neither the time nor the inclination to keep up with local politics."

Quinn raised his eyebrows. "Interesting, since the bills proposed and passed by your legislators quite frequently have an impact on your livelihood. There are several zoning bills stalled in the Virginia state legislature right now."

Those forthright delft-blue eyes of Quinn Santini's spiked a rise in April's blood pressure and sent heat waves galloping through her. Considering that she looked like she'd rolled in a pigsty—while he exuded a masculine perfection guaranteed to rock the good sense of any sensible woman—April found it impossible to act relaxed.

"While you're giving that some thought," he said, "you might want to put these daisies in water before they die." Quinn frowned at the flowers and shoved the bouquet at April as if getting rid of them would revive them.

"You brought me gerbera daisies?" The wrapping had hidden the riot of color—at least a dozen blooms of red, pink, yellow and orange.

"You don't like daisies?" Even in the lengthening shadows, his uncertainty showed.

"They're gorgeous." April moved the shovel and carefully cradled the bouquet. "It's just...why?"

He threw back his head and laughed. "Sorry, I shouldn't laugh. I came to apologize for jumping to conclusions the day you told my grandmother you'd found her letters. It's been a while since I've had to tell a woman I'm sorry. Flowers or candy used to be acceptable. Candy fell into disfavor because of the calories," he said wryly. "So tell me, how can I persuade you to accept my apology? Dinner? I'm guessing you haven't eaten yet. I can usually secure a table at Benny Cinalli's since he and I are old school friends. Would you be interested in joining me?"

The very mention of Cinalli's Ristorante left April's mouth watering. It was her favorite place in town to eat. Thinking about their ravioli made her even hungrier, especially since she'd been too busy to stop for lunch. "Really, the flowers are more than enough. I'll, uh, go put them in water."

"Please, I want to do more. Even my daughter, at six, pointed out that I was rude to you." Quinn knew he was laying it on a bit thick, but he needed to engineer an opening to find out how much she knew about the content of those letters.

"I did think you were a jerk, until I calmed down and realized that the unusual circumstance of finding old letters in a wall might warrant suspicion on anyone's part. And, after all, you have a position to protect. Also, you don't know me."

Quinn studied the contradictory picture she made standing there, splashed with mud, a florist's bouquet hugged against her ratty sweatshirt, her other hand resting on a shovel. Yet her expression was so open and sincere, Quinn felt a kick of unexpected guilt. Then his resolve returned. He wasn't his grandmother, who was willing to buy into every word April uttered. He needed to know if she'd discovered Norma's secrets.

Earlier today he'd researched April with some well-placed calls to his campaign people. Their discreet digging had yielded the fact that Cinalli's was her favorite restaurant. He came prepared to do whatever it took to get answers. "You look plumb tuckered," he said, his southern drawl oozing sympathy. "I'd feel better about the whole misunderstanding if you'd allow me to buy you dinner."

April opened her mouth to decline his offer again. But she couldn't very well blurt out what was on the tip of her tongue—that the flowers made her feel...sentimental. She'd received flowers twice in her life. From her parents on her sixteenth birthday, and from the son of a close family friend who'd escorted her to the senior prom. Neither she nor Graham Merrill had wanted to go out with the other; their mothers had arranged the date. That evening still rankled. For starters, April had been head and shoulders taller than Graham. The gardenia he'd brought her made them both sneeze. Graham admitted his mom had picked out the corsage, and he also revealed that he'd wanted to take Diane Thornton to the prom.

April hadn't thought about that mortifying experience in ages. The memory reminded her that her parents were still pulling strings to fix her up—Eric Lathrop being the most recent example. And here she was holding flowers from a man her folks didn't like.... That more than anything made her accept Quinn's invitation to dinner. "On second thought, eating out after an afternoon spent digging in the dirt sounds fabulous. I'll need time to clean up. If you'd rather, we can meet at the restaurant in, say, half an hour? Or," she added hesitantly, her attention on the bouquet, "you can come in for a glass of wine and see what I've done to the house while I make myself presentable."

Relief flooded Quinn at the out she'd offered—meeting her at Cinelli's. He didn't really want to be cooped up in the car with her, where she'd expect him to make small talk. Coming up with conversation over dinner would be difficult enough. To his own surprise, Quinn found himself saying, "Wine would hit the spot. To tell you the truth, after hearing how much Gram loved this farm, I'm curious to see inside."

April hadn't expected him to take her up on her offer of a predinner drink. But she could hardly say she'd changed her mind without looking like an idiot. "It's far more rustic than the home she currently lives in. If I have the history of this farm correct, after your grandfather sold it in 1950, it served as a country home for the parents of Dr. Shuman. I acquired it from his estate." April propped the shovel against the house and led the way up the steps, where she took off her muddy boots. He wiped the bottoms of his loafers on the bristle mat and checked the soles. April threw open the door. "Don't worry about your shoes. I tiled the kitchen and the bathrooms, so they're easy to clean. Laying carpet will be almost the last thing I do."

"You lay carpet?" Quinn stopped inspecting his shoes.

She laughed. "That's one of the jobs I contract out. I lay tile and I don't even mind roofing. But stretching in carpet takes a professional."

"It's bigger than it seems from the outside." Quinn shut the door, then looked around the room, which was separated from the rest of the house by sheets of plastic. He took in the fireplace and a bank of tall windows that flanked French doors, adding to the spacious feel.

"Those French doors lead to a sunroom. I'm going to tear out the vinyl flooring and put in terra-cotta tile. I have white or red wine. That's it. As you might've guessed, I don't socialize much. Sometimes I serve subcontractors coffee. That's pretty well the extent of my entertaining since I started my business."

"Oh? My grandmother seemed to think you had a boyfriend."

"No, uh, not really. My parents throw dinner parties, and they like me to show up with a partner so it doesn't screw up Mom's place settings. They paired me with this guy Eric, the one your grandmother's probably talking about." She shrugged her shoulders. "We got along okay. We've gone to a couple of my folks' parties together. And Eric needed a date for a yearly July 4th picnic hosted by his boss at the paper, so I was it." She broke off, wondering why she felt compelled to share what was none of his business. Furthermore it was embarrassing, and judging by his look, he obviously thought so, too.

"Um. I'll have red wine." Quinn touched the edge of the fireplace, where it was clear that a wall had been removed. "I take it you uncovered the letters in a section of wall that used to be here?"

"Yes, and they're the most exciting thing that's happened during a renovation. Well, except for early in my career when I mistakenly removed what turned out to be a load-bearing wall and part of the ceiling caved in on my head." She turned the kitchen light on and walked over to the small built-in wine rack before he could laugh or make a smart come-back, the way her brothers and most of her friends did when they heard that story.

"This place is great," Quinn said, gazing around the kitchen as she washed her hands at the sink. "It's a room I wouldn't mind spending time in."

She dried her hands and uncorked the bottle of merlot, then filled a plain goblet. "Thanks." Quinn took the glass she extended, raising it in a brief toast.

"The guest house where Hayley and I live could stand an overhaul. We moved there after my parents and Amy, uh, my wife…died. My mom had planned for some time to enlarge the cottage, but everyone was so busy at the firm. Amy was a lawyer, too. Mom babysat Hayley. These days, Hayley and I are home mostly to sleep and eat breakfast. Otherwise, I'm at the office and she stays at my grand-mother's except during the school year."

"A friend told me about the plane crash. She didn't mention that you all worked together. That must've been even more devastating. I'm sorry for your losses, Quinn. And Norma and Hayley's."

"Thanks." He sipped from the glass and gave the wine his approval. "People say it's a blessing Hayley was so young." He sighed. "I guess I feel guilty about leaving her so often."

"Lawyers put in killer hours—I know that from my own family. Now, with you running for office, I'd be surprised if you're not absent twice as much. But of course I have no firsthand knowledge of that, and I didn't mean it as a criti-cism. I, ah, hope you don't mind if I rush off to shower away three layers of dirt." She brushed self-consciously at her cheek as she backed from the room.

"I wasn't going to say you reminded me of that Pig Pen character in the old 'Peanuts' comic strips," he said with a flash of humor.

"You're so kind," she called back over one shoulder.

After she left, Quinn wandered around on his own. His earlier comment hadn't been mere politeness; he genuinely admired her work. This country-style kitchen had a down-home feel his lacked. April had invested in new, family-size appliances. The stove sported a double oven. Opening it, he inspected the interior. The side-by-side fridge was huge. He wondered if April cooked or if, like him, she relied mainly on prepackaged meals she could heat in the microwave.

The built-in nook had seating for six. A stack of magazines that had been shoved to one side of the table caught his eye. They were all architectural or home-decorating related. Tools of April's trade. Again, like him, it appeared she spent what little free time she had on her career. If she *had* copied the letters, he wondered where she'd keep the photocopies. It didn't sound as if she was all that tight with Eric.

He heard water running at the back of the house, which indicated April had begun her shower. Restless, Quinn swirled the dark-red wine around the bowl of his glass. The color reminded him of blood—the tainted blood that ran through his veins. Up to now, he hadn't allowed himself to think about the German. His true grandfather, he thought disdainfully. A man who'd died, pretending to defect.

Did any of it matter? Would his life have played out differently if his dad had learned about the lies built on lies? At least there would've been an ally with whom he could commiserate.

Expecting a long wait, Quinn decided to take a peek at that sunroom April had mentioned. He crossed the living area, then opened the French doors and found the light switch. The room ran half the length of the house and looked out over a sloping lawn. Removable windows set inside the screens rendered the space usable year-round. Quinn imagined the room as it might have been when his grandmother lived here. She'd probably filled it with potted plants. Would wicker furniture have been beyond her means or even available right after the war? If Quinn owned this house, he'd definitely prefer the red tile floor April planned to install and he'd furnish the room in good solid rattan with thick, comfortable cushions.

"Oh, here you are. When I didn't find you in the kitchen, it occurred to me you'd changed your mind about taking me to dinner."

Quinn spun around, surprised not only by April Trent's fast and unexpected appearance, but also at her total transformation. Gone were all signs of the carpenter. Muddy rubber boots had been replaced by black leather ones with spiky heels.

Quinn's gaze started at the boots and traveled upward to the crown of dark curls. Damp tendrils of hair clung to a rosy cheek as April finished inserting a pair of silver hoop earrings. They matched half a dozen silver bangles dancing up and down the narrow sleeve of a pearl-gray, body-hugging sweater dress.

And what a body. Compact and sexy. The dress that buttoned up the front from hem to midcleavage was a show-stopper in itself. The material looked as soft as kitten fur and twice as touchable. Invitingly touchable. So much so, Quinn's grip tightened on his wineglass.

He tried unsuccessfully to respond to her comment. What astonished him most was the fact that he hadn't been bowled over like this in more years than he could recall. Granted, in the old days before he'd met his wife, a petite blonde, Quinn had gravitated toward leggy brunettes. But he hadn't been moved to take a second look at any woman in such a long time, he thought the urge had forsaken him.

Remembering why he'd invited April Trent to dinner, Quinn marshaled his emotions and downed the remainder of his wine. "All set?" he said inanely, pausing to shove the empty glass into April's hands as he headed for the front door. The thing was, he couldn't leave the sunroom through the French doors without brushing against April. The knuckles of his right hand came in contact with her thigh. Damn. The fabric of her dress was even softer than it looked.

He charged past her in such haste, April frowned at the glass and then at his retreating back. "You must really be starved. I just need a minute to take this glass to the kitchen and grab my purse and a wrap."

Quinn stopped, his hand already grasping the doorknob. "Yes. Get a coat." *A long coat.* "I'll bring the car down from the road so those ice-pick heels don't sink in the mud."

After he sailed out the door, April glanced down at her boots. The heels weren't *that* bad, were they? This was the first time she'd worn the boots. In a weak moment during their last shopping expedition, April had let Robyn drag her to a shoe clearance sale. Her friend had sworn these were the latest style. April let herself be swayed because they were fifty percent off the regular price and they were comfortable. She hated the strappy bits of leather her sisters-in-law called dress shoes. Maybe that was what Quinn Santini expected the women he took to dinner to wear. Traveling in his circles, he likely dated models. Except that Robyn had indicated he was never photographed with them. Maybe he avoided that kind of publicity for the sake of his campaign.

"Well, too bad if he doesn't approve of my boots," April muttered, as she threw on a black knit shawl and made sure her house keys rattled reassuringly in the depths of the worn, black shoulder bag she carried everywhere. She imagined his usual dinner companions toddling around with little sequined or satin purses that weren't substantial enough to hold a tube of lipstick, let alone cabfare home. April made sure her porch light was on and the door locked before she started for the car, which had by then purred to a stop in front of the house.

As her hand closed over the car door handle, it was suddenly covered by Quinn's warm palm. As if irritated, he brushed her fingers aside and opened her door, gesturing curtly that she should climb in.

April's dad opened doors for her mother and other women. But her parents were products of the old Southern chivalry. April didn't fit that mold. She was independent. Which was why she didn't jump to comply.

"Look, we should probably forget this dinner thing. You really don't owe me anything. It's obvious we don't have a lot in common."

His fingers opened and closed reflexively over the upper edge of the car door. "What caused *that* outburst?"

"I believe in equal rights for women. I'm perfectly capable of walking out to a car, and I can open a door without help. Men like you expect women to be helpless— or pretend to be so you can play the big, strong male."

The hell he preferred helpless females. Quinn had married Amy for her independence, hadn't he? And he was attempting to raise their daughter to stand up and speak out for herself. He felt it was an odd comment for April to make, since she'd spent time with his grandmother, who at eighty-two was every inch her own woman.

As Quinn and April faced off with a car door between them, he experienced another jolt. That irritated him. That sense of physical desire had been absent for so long, it was almost unfamiliar. He was, however, intrigued enough to see if it was an aberrant reaction. He shoved the door with sufficient pressure to slam it shut. "There. If you're as hungry as I am, get in however it suits you. I phoned ahead. Benny's holding a table but he'll let go if we don't show up in thirty minutes." Quinn rounded the hood of his car and slipped into the driver's seat. His door closed with a decided bang.

His response was the last thing April had expected. Now she was left with two options, and a grudging respect for the way Quinn Santini had handled her little fit of temper. She opened the passenger door and slid in. "Okay, we're even, Santini. The assumption I made about your behavior is as bad as *your* assumption that I was capable of blackmail. We'll each pay for our own dinner, okay?" Without waiting for a response, she said, "I'm starved. So step on it, unless this fancy car is all show and no go."

Oh, how Quinn wanted to laugh. But he pulled out all the stops to hide even the hint of a smile. "Sounds good to me, Trent." Speeding up the muddy drive, he turned when his front wheels touched the gravel road, and again punched the gas, sending April scrambling to fasten her seat belt. With a half-mocking smirk, he said, "We should get along fine, providing your idea of *starved* doesn't mean picking at a salad no self-respecting rabbit would find satisfying, and after three or four bites tell me you're stuffed."

April snorted. "You do hang out with wimpy women. Don't worry, Santini. I'll match you appetite for appetite."

Quinn took his eyes off the road and cruised leisurely what he could see of her slender figure. Even with the knit shawl flung carelessly over her breasts, his thoughts involved a whole different kind of appetite.

"You don't believe me," April said, mistaking his extensive perusal. "How long has it been since you've done anything physically challenging?"

"Too long, regrettably," he murmured. Quinn turned back to the road, and shifted in his seat. What the hell was he doing, lusting after April Trent? He was taking her to dinner for one reason and one reason only. To learn how much damaging information about his family she'd gleaned from his grandmother's letters.

He left the county road at the first on-ramp and joined the steady flow of traffic heading out of Turner County. Uncomfortable with the silence that had fallen between them, Quinn decided to cut to the chase. "What was your first thought when you came across those old letters in your wall?"

Smiling, April snuggled deeper into the creamy leather. "I thought I'd found something that would make me rich enough so my family would quit bitching about what I do for a living."

When her comment about money sank in, Quinn's stomach rebelled. He felt sick. "Then I was right all along. Giving my grandmother the letters is part of a scheme to shake us down for bigger bucks. I suppose you copied each and every one." Quinn swerved onto the shoulder and his foot hit the brake. His hands flexed on the steering wheel as he scowled at April.

She bolted forward to see what had made him stop. "What? Turn this car around and take me home."

"Quit trying to act so indignant. You just admitted thinking the letters were worth a lot. So why didn't you negotiate with me right from the start? It's because you figure you can get more money by holding onto copies, isn't it?"

"Oh, for Pete's sake! You were wrong then, and you still are. When I noticed the bundle after I cut into the wall, I had no clue they were old love letters. I glimpsed a wrapped package, about this big." She indicated the size with her hands. "What would *you* have thought? I imagined I'd stumbled on a hidden cache of money from a bank robbery or something." April buried her chin in her shawl, looking unhappy. "Now you do owe me an apology. Or better yet, before you take me home, tell me why you'd go out of your way to have dinner with someone you thought had the morals of…of an alley cat?"

Quinn didn't turn around. He returned to the highway and exited soon after. When he pulled into Cinalli's parking lot, he shut off the motor, unbuckled his seat belt and pocketed his keys. Only then did he turn in his seat to face April. "Dan Mattingly's guys paid a hooker to show up at my office one night when I was working late. A reporter claimed he'd just happened along and snapped the picture. She, of course, was plastered to me at that very moment." He shook his head. "That incident required a ton of damage control and we barely managed to keep it out of the papers. I have no doubt he was also behind a couple of inmates claiming my dad took kickbacks in exchange for plea bargains. And there've been other attempts to smear me and my family."

"That's awful. I'd never run for public office for that exact reason. Dirty tactics like that put you and everyone you love at risk." April hauled in a deep breath and unhooked her seat belt. "Mmm. Garlic. I'm fine with letting bygones be bygones so we can go and sample whatever smells so good."

"No argument from me." Quinn walked around the car to assist her out, then in the nick of time stepped back and had to be content with hitting the remote to lock the car. "One more thing before we go inside," he said. "At least let me get the check."

April flung the dragging end of her shawl over her left shoulder. "I could say I'd arm-wrestle you for it, but you'd lose. Okay, Santini, you've got a deal. But I'm warning you, I'm not a cheap date."

Quinn found that funny. He was still laughing when his friend Benny Cinelli saw them. A big man who obviously loved to eat the food his establishment served, Benny beamed and motioned them to follow. "After I show you to your favorite table and pour some of my special *vino,* Quinn, introduce me to this beautiful lady who made you smile. Just promise me you're Italian." Benny kissed April's hand.

She shook her head, blushing at being called beautiful even in a joking way. Grateful for the large menus, she hid behind one while the two obvious old friends bantered back and forth.

"Don't mind Benny," Quinn murmured after the restaurant owner left to bring them wine. "We go way back. To first grade at parochial school."

"You two make me wish I was Italian. I think it's great you have that in common. I *should* be Italian, the way I love their food." She gave a light shrug. "I guess Benny didn't recognize me on my own. I'm usually here with a crowd of women." Smiling, April ordered an antipasto, followed by spinach ravioli and chicken parmigiana. She couldn't realize how her casual comment affected Quinn. She hadn't uncovered *all* his grandmother's secrets.

He relaxed his guard somewhat. Over the course of the evening, he discovered he enjoyed her company. "Who'd have thought you and I would agree on zoning laws and other restrictions that will protect our country's environment?"

Replete and happy, April pushed back her empty plate and offered a lazy grin. "Don't plan on me going door to door, handing out your pamphlets. We might see eye to eye on some issues, but I'm not getting politically involved."

Quinn signaled for cappuccino. They drank two cups each and talked about the area's growth, a subject that affected both their jobs. "You just asked why I wasn't content to remain an attorney and prosecute corporations accused of dumping waste in our rivers or polluting our air," he said pensively. "I jumped into politics because I want to leave a better world for Hayley. Rather than risk losing cases to someone like your dad, who may represent clients who've already done the deed, I want to make our laws tougher."

"I wondered when you'd get around to Dad." Folding her napkin, she set it aside. "It's been a pleasant couple of hours, but we should probably end it now."

"You're right. Let's not rock that boat, because I'd like us to do this again." To Quinn's surprise, he meant it. Signing the credit slip with a flourish, he returned his card to his billfold. He stood and picked up April's shawl, smiling into her eyes as he placed the wrap around her shoulders.

"Tempting. But neither of us have many free evenings." In spite of her doubts, April walked out feeling strangely content. When they reached the entry, she stopped to tell Benny how marvelous her meal was.

He thanked her, then opened the outer door, all the while chatting with Quinn, who without conscious thought rested a hand on April's waist. As they emerged into the night, flashes from a camera momentarily blinded them.

"April, what in God's name are *you* doing with Santini?" Eric Lathrop elbowed his cameraman aside. The reporter grabbed April's wrist and pulled her into the parking lot.

Once he got past being startled, Quinn shoved aside the jerk with the camera and went in search of April. He caught up with her and saw that she'd wrenched herself loose from Eric.

The two men squared off, trading barbs.

"Isn't this great?" Eric shouted, brandishing a pen and notebook. "I get a call from a source at Cinalli's who says Santini showed up here with a woman. My source neglected to say it's *my* woman."

"I beg your pardon? I'm no one's woman!" Planting a hand on each man's chest, April shoved them apart.

"Just get in my car," Eric snapped. "If I don't kill that photo, come morning your dad's gonna have a stroke when he sees his paper."

A mutinous expression settled over April. "According to my mom, a nice southern girl goes home with the person who brought her. Quinn? Shall we?"

"Don't make any sacrifices on my account. Go with

Lathrop if you prefer his company." Quinn stabbed the button on his car keys to unlock the Lexus. Headlights flashed, illuminating a last glare he aimed at Eric before yanking open his door.

"Bro...ther!" April stomped around the Lexus and climbed into the passenger seat. "Quinn, let me apologize for Eric's behavior."

"Maybe we should clear up exactly what Lathrop means to you."

"Maybe that's my business."

"Look, the guy's in Dan Mattingly's pocket. Or at least his boss is. They could twist this evening into something neither of us would care to read about. I wouldn't put anything past them."

"Eric can be overbearing. I know he'd go to great lengths for a story, but I don't believe he'd manufacture one. He has his sights set on a Pulitzer." She frowned. "He said he'd kill the photo. That's decent of him, don't you agree?"

"True—let's hope he succeeds. But he should think about the company he keeps," Quinn added. "Eric's boss and Mattingly are in dirty politics up to their asses. Have been for years."

"Enough, Quinn! Earlier you said we have a lot in common. We don't. You live in the spotlight. I'd rather be a mouse in the corner. Those gutsy things your grandmother did during the war—that wouldn't be me."

"Her war escapades were news to me. As for the spotlight, that's a consequence of speaking out for what I believe. Otherwise, I'm an ordinary working stiff—a single dad."

"Your daughter's adorable."

"Thanks. Have I mentioned that Hayley likes your hair? She thinks you're very pretty." Quinn smiled at April as he left the freeway and turned onto the county road.

Speechless, April was at a loss for any kind of response. Silence prevailed until Quinn stopped in front of her house.

As if he'd forgotten their tug of war over assisting her, he raced around to hand her out. And then walked her to the door. "Except for the scene outside Cinalli's, I thought tonight went pretty well."

"Yes, but like I said, it's…probably wisest if we…" She didn't finish her comment. Quinn slipped his right hand under her black shawl. Bending ever so slightly, he kissed her good-night. The kiss started out simple, but as April's lips parted in surprise, Quinn's fingers stroked her back, then bunched in the angora fabric of her dress. When he felt her sway, he lifted his head. Staring into her lustrous eyes, he murmured, "I want to see you again, April. This weekend?"

She grasped the lapels of his suede jacket, then released them. "You didn't let me finish. I was saying we're too different. And…see how we've gotten carried away?"

"What about Sunday afternoon?" he went on, as though she hadn't spoken. "I'll bring Hayley to chaperon our date. Tell you what, why don't we take in the International Spy Museum in downtown D.C.?"

Prepared to say no again, April hesitated. She loved kids, saw little of her brothers' children. She'd heard about the spy museum, but had never made time to visit it. "Okay, I'll go. After hearing about your grandmother's exploits, I'd be interested in learning more. But don't call it a date. After Sunday, you'll go back to politics, and I'll turn into a carpenter and we won't see each other again."

Quinn narrowed his eyes as he inclined his head in agreement—although he wasn't so sure about her final remark. He'd been right about her dress, though. It was soft and touchable—and so was she.

In the car he still reeled with his ambivalent feelings. Was April as innocent as she seemed, or was she the latest troublemaker in Dan Mattingly's arsenal?

Quinn intended to find out and find out fast.

Chapter 6

She'd kissed and been kissed by Quinn Santini, candidate for the US senate. And, according to Robyn, one of the town's most sought-after bachelors. Inside the house, April slumped against the door and let her shawl slip to the ground. She rubbed her still-tingling lips as Quinn backed up the muddy drive. His headlights cast ghostly shadows across her fireplace.

April bent to retrieve her fallen shawl. Her thoughts remained on Quinn as she made her way to the bedroom, reflecting on the series of events that had led up to that kiss. Receiving gerbera daisies, a dinner invitation and plans for a second outing with Mr. Eligible.

Always cautious when it came to her love life, April mused over how little resistance she seemed to have to this man. Tugging off her sweater dress she returned it to a padded hanger. Little about the last few days made sense. For starters, it was unlike her to let anyone bulldoze her. Yet in hindsight, that was how she felt.

After tonight she'd begun to understand how her father, a force to be reckoned with in his own right, had lost to Quinn in court. Quinn Santini was focused, persuasive, charismatic.

In the middle of pulling on sweats, April stopped dead. Okay, she could buy the apology angle that had prompted the flowers and even dinner. Why the all-out good-night kiss? And what about Quinn's unwillingness to accept *no* when April had twice made clear that there was no future in seeing each other again?

He wanted *something*. What?

Idly she sat on the bed to tie her sneakers.

She'd achieved her primary goal of returning the letters to their rightful owner. Now she wondered if the letters contained more than declarations of love. Maybe she should have let Norma Santini ramble on. At the time, her story had sounded more like fiction than truth. Perhaps therein lay the real crux of the matter. If Quinn's grandmother was slipping mentally—to the point of spewing fantasies about her and her husband's involvement in espionage—that would surely worry a man running for the Senate.

No, the letters weren't fake. They were definitely real— which suggested her story might be, too.

April dived across the bed and grabbed her laptop. What if, by some remote chance, her computer search turned up the man who'd signed those letters? April opened her notebook and flipped the power switch. As she waited impatiently, her cell phone rang. She remembered she'd dropped her purse near the door—while kissing Quinn Santini. Her face heating even now, she ran out, grabbed the bag, then returned and dumped its contents on the bed. "Hello," she said breathlessly, not bothering to see who was listed on her caller ID.

"April, what's this I hear about you showing up at Cinalli's tonight with that Santini bastard?" Her brother Miles's scornful denouncement of her evening grated on April's already raw nerves.

"Gee, Miles, Robyn told me Quinn comes from as old and eminent a Virginia family as ours. *Bastard* is hardly an appropriate term, do you think?"

"Don't be smart. You know what I mean."

"Do I?"

"April, we have a score to settle with Santini."

"We, the *firm?* Or you and Dad personally? I'm not nor have I ever been connected to Trent and Sons. As a matter of fact, Roger isn't, either. You really should change your sign to read *and son,* singular."

"As if the Trent name hasn't benefitted your business! Oh, why do I even try to reason with you? I know you're perfectly aware that Dad and I oppose Santini. Eric said he told you when he invited you to Quinn's fund-raiser."

"Now that you mention it, Miles, why would you ante up four hundred bucks for tickets if you're so dead set against Quinn? The tickets did say the money was tax-deductible, and a hundred percent went to his campaign."

"I traded with a client—my Redskins' football seats for next Saturday night in exchange for the Santini tickets. The object was for Eric to go and keep his eyes and ears open for anything useful to Dan Mattingly. I thought he'd take a fellow reporter. To be fair, Eric said he had no idea you were playing footsie with the enemy."

"Enemy? Bro…ther! That's pretty strong language to apply to such a silly game. While we're on the subject of politics, Miles, let's be clear. I don't care who wins. I'm not convinced it make any difference. Most assuredly, though, I'm not playing footsie with anyone. Quinn's grandparents built the home I'm currently renovating. I found and returned something that belonged to his grandmother. He took me to dinner at Cinalli's by way of thanking me." She said nothing about their next excursion.

"Eric said you uncovered Norma's old letters in a wall you took down. That's another thing, April. I wish you'd let Eric have a closer look at your find. He should've said straight out that there are some old news stories that raise questions about Anthony Santini's war record."

"What about it?"

"Nothing I plan to tell you unless you swear on Mama's Bible that you're standing with us against Quinn. Dan Mattingly's the incumbent and we want him to stay in office."

"Don't tell me, then. I didn't vote last time, but after seeing the way Eric acted tonight, I'm giving more and more thought to voting for Quinn." April had the satisfaction of hanging up on her older brother. Ever since Miles passed the bar on his first try, he thought he knew everything worth knowing. Actions, not titles, impressed April.

She fumed over his call for so long, she forgot why she'd turned on her laptop. Maybe because it was time to pay her bills. With a few taps on the keys, she called up her online bank account and dispensed payments to all her suppliers. When she signed off, April again felt in control of her life but no less irritated with her family for attempting to manipulate her.

Eric's strong-arm tactics at Cinalli's—followed by Miles's phone call, which made it blatantly evident that he'd been in touch with Eric—only confirmed April's decision to say yes to Quinn's second request.

Over the next few days, in spite of drizzling rain that delayed work on her asphalt drive, April found herself looking forward to Sunday's trip. The rain let her attend a lunch-and-shopping trip with Robyn on Saturday. April bought a beautiful velvet dress on sale. It shocked Robyn, who was sure April had changed her mind about going to the black-tie benefit with Eric. She said she hadn't; she'd just purchased the dress because Robyn had urged her to try it on and she liked how she looked in it.

Sunday, any remaining clouds drifted off into the Appalachians, leaving pleasant weather in the latest storm's wake. Preferring comfort over fashion today, yet aware that she should be prepared for an ever-changing climate, April dressed in layers. She paired a cotton turtleneck with stonewashed blue jeans and a pair of knee-high boots with walking heels. She filled an old leather tote with bottled water, wet wipes and cheese-and-cracker snacks. Her brother Roger's wife never took her kids anywhere without a supply of all three.

Or would Quinn think she was another of the many women apparently lining up to mother his motherless child? Twice April took out the bottles and packages, then put them back before his knock sounded at her door. Faced with the final decision, she hastily scooped everything into her tote.

A bit harried, she swept the hair out of her eyes and swung open the door. Quinn Santini stood on her porch, taking her in at a glance. A slow light of appreciation warmed his blue eyes, sending heat throughout April's body. They both let the moment pass as his daughter scrambled out of the Lexus and ran up to April, waving madly.

"Miss April! Are you happy that Daddy's taking us to see the spies?"

"Hayley, it's a museum," Quinn gently corrected her. "We won't be seeing any spies."

"Oh, I thought that's why I wasn't s'posed to tell Gram, 'cause she'd worry about us going to see spooky guys and stuff."

April noticed that Quinn looked partly flustered and partly exasperated when he made a second attempt to explain. "Honey, I…just didn't want her to worry because we're driving into D.C. when traffic will be exceptionally heavy."

"I wondered if you'd bring Norma." April slipped on her leather jacket and slung the bulky tote over her shoulder.

Quinn tensed. "I'm not so sure that's a good idea."

"Quinn, are you concerned that Norma may…well…be imagining she, uh, you know, lived a glamorous, exciting life?" April finished lamely because Hayley zeroed her attention in on April, then her dad.

"I'll admit it crossed my mind that she…padded her story," he muttered, lowering his voice.

"Except that I saw the postmark on the letters. Why else would she have been in Europe during the war?" April gave him a serious look. "Frankly, Norma strikes me as being a woman in possession of all her faculties." The more she considered it, the clearer that seemed.

"Yeah, probably." He nodded, although he didn't appear overjoyed by April's assessment, which further confused her.

"Daddy, can we go see the spy place now? Or are you and Miss April gonna talk all day?"

April locked her door and dropped a ring of keys into her voluminous tote. "No, Hayley. Let's get this show on the road. I'm ready to learn about phone bugs, invisible ink and secret codes." She winked as she fell in beside Quinn.

At the car, she realized she hadn't expected him to lift Hayley into the back. She should have, though. Her sisters-in-law both insisted their children ride in the safer back seats. Hayley Santini had a booster seat belted directly behind her dad, which left April to join him in front. She slid into the passenger side, while Quinn made sure his daughter was buckled up tight.

April loosened her seat belt and turned slightly sideways in order to include Hayley in any conversation. "This is my first visit to the International Spy Museum."

"Mine, too," Hayley chimed in.

April rummaged in her tote. "I printed off some information about the museum from the Internet." While shopping with Robyn, April had picked up her repaired printer. Now she unfolded several sheets of paper as Quinn started the car. He backed up April's as-yet-unpaved drive.

"It says there are children's events that change from week to week. Gosh, right here it says visitors will meet *real* spies who'll teach us spy skills." She glanced up. "I guess your dad was wrong." She ignored his wry chuckle. "They have fifty years worth of information and technology on display, including gadgets and disguises a spy might use."

Hayley, who'd listened raptly, asked, "What's a disguise?"

"Hayley," Quinn said, "you remember the trunk Gram gave you filled with dress-up clothes, and hats and grown-up shoes? You wear those things and pretend you're a movie star. That's a kind of disguise. Although I suspect a real spy has to alter more than his clothes. Or hers," he added hastily. "I wonder if Gram…uh, never mind," he finished, swallowing whatever he was about to say.

April guessed from the twitch of his jaw that Quinn disliked the fact his grandmother had almost certainly been involved in spying. Why would it bother him?

"Daddy, I'm thirsty."

Quinn had just made the transition from highway 81 to 66, the busy thoroughfare that led into the heart of the District of Columbia. He sighed in resignation and switched to an outside lane where he could find an exit. "Hayley, I warned you this would happen if you didn't finish half your milk."

"I wasn't thirsty then. 'Sides, I was afraid if we were late, Miss April wouldn't go with us. I *wanted* her to come. I only ever get to go places with Grams, Mr. Joseph or Miss Ethel."

Quinn aimed a shrug at April. "Damn, why are there never any convenience stores when you need one?

Not altogether sure he'd appreciate her interfering, April pulled out a bottle of water. She displayed it for Quinn's eyes only and motioned with her head to ask permission.

"You're a life-saver. Next thing, though, we'll be looking for a bathroom."

Quinn met his daughter's eyes in the mirror. "Hayley, you're a lucky kid. April has a bottle of water and is willing to share with you. What do you say?"

"Thank you, Miss April," she murmured, then added,

"My best friend, Tammy Sikes, her mother always has water for Tammy on field trips. She said it's what moms do." The implication hung in the air, forcing April to clear her throat.

"I brought us each a bottle, Hayley." Uncapping it, April handed it back. "If it's okay with your dad, call me April and skip the Miss."

Hayley took the water. "Daddy, may I?"

"Sure, I guess." He eyed April. "Were you offended by her calling you *Miss?* As you can tell, Gram and our house-keeper, Ethel, drill old-fashioned manners into Hayley."

"Heavens, I wasn't offended. My mom insisted on those same southern courtesies. It's your call, Quinn. I can live with being called Miss. After all, it's a fact."

"At the risk of being told to mind my own business, why? Are you against marriage?"

"Daddy, I didn't finish my lunch, either, and now I'm hungry."

The interruption gave April a moment to collect her thoughts. Because she didn't quite know how to answer, she foraged in her tote again and came up with the cheese snacks. This time she passed one back to Hayley without running it by Quinn.

He noticed, and an expression of cautious reserve appeared. "It's obvious," he said, drowning out Hayley's *thank you,* "that I've crossed a line. Sorry, it was presump-tuous of me. I asked because the majority of women I meet who are anywhere near my age are married—or have been, at least once."

"It's okay, Quinn. I'm not going to accuse you of prying." Reaching back, April automatically ripped open the package that was giving Hayley trouble. "I'm not anti-marriage. But I'm building a business, which takes all my energy. Most men I've met assume they'll be a woman's priority. I haven't figured out how to give a hundred-and-twenty percent to my business *and* a relationship."

"Men are expected to do it."

"Touché!" April's lips curved. "I have a good friend who seems to manage. Although she's not married... Robyn Parker is a top interior decorator. She rarely goes a weekend without a date and says I'm just lousy at organizing my time. Maybe she's right."

"Or maybe you haven't found anyone about whom you feel strongly enough to rearrange your life."

April gave an uncomfortable laugh. "Are you sure you chose the right field, Mr. Santini? Maybe you'd do better writing an advice column."

Quinn guffawed. "Right. You go ahead and propose that idea to Lathrop's editor."

"Are we almost there?" Hayley broke in from the back seat.

Sobering, her dad focused on the passing scenery as if he'd lost his train of thought. "As a matter of fact, we're close. The building housing the museum is adjacent to Ford's Theatre and the Smithsonian American Art Museum."

April saw they were on Pennsylvania Avenue. Georgetown University was her alma mater, so she was no stranger to the mixed commercial and residential district in this section of D.C. Judging by the confidence with which Quinn navigated the crowded streets, he felt at home here, too.

"April, April, look out my window." Hayley stabbed a finger against the glass. "See that white building? That's where my daddy'll work if people choose him to...be what, Daddy? I forget the word."

"Senator. If the people's vote sends me to serve in the United States Senate."

"Yeah." Cracker crumbs flew from Hayley's lips. "Daddy told me'n Gram it's 'portant to serve people who live *everywhere*. People need clean air and water, huh, Daddy?"

"You're exactly right, honey."

April sneaked a peek at Quinn. It was a father's pride she saw creeping over his face. Underlying that, she recognized his resolve. "You're serious, aren't you, about passing legislation that'll slap federal fines on businesses that ignore environmental guidelines?"

"I'm dead serious. But I find that an odd thing for someone to know who claims to be totally oblivious to politics."

"Uh, well…after the scene at Cinalli's, my brother let it be known that I'm in the doghouse for consorting with the enemy," she said, rolling her eyes. "So I reviewed some of your rally speeches, and some of Dan Mattingly's."

"What's the verdict? Will I get your vote come November?"

She glanced away. "One vote won't make or break you, Quinn."

"How do you know?" he challenged. "At least I can promise I won't waste the opportunity. It's a travesty to squander a single minute in office. Mattingly's had eleven years of doing nothing."

"There it is, the spy museum. Oh, isn't that the most fabulous wedge-shaped old building?" April rhapsodized. "Holy cow. Is that the waiting line to get in? I never would've expected so many visitors." She effectively changed the subject.

"I heard that's what happens on weekends. I phoned for

reservations. Once we park it's a matter of collecting our tickets and bypassing the crowd."

A car pulled out of a parking spot and Quinn nabbed it. He let April fend for herself while he helped Hayley out on the street side. The second the girl's feet touched the ground she began to fidget.

"Hayley, what's wrong?" Quinn took her hand and crossed to the sidewalk.

"I hafta go potty bad," she told him. She pulled free, then slipped her fingers through April's.

"Concentrate on something else for however long it takes us to walk there. I'm sure the restrooms will be near the museum entrance."

"What should I think about?" Hayley asked. "Can we walk really, really fast?" The girl sped up, tugging April along.

Quinn jogged beside them. "Fine thing. I invite two beautiful ladies out for an afternoon and they both run off and leave me."

Hayley squeezed April's hand and smiled up at her. "I knew Daddy would change his mind. Me'n Grams told him you were pretty. But he said—"

Quinn did a quick-step, swinging Hayley high into his arms. He gave her a scowl. "I hope *he* said it's not nice to eavesdrop and really not nice to repeat anything you hear." Spotting the will-call line, Quinn strode toward it, leaving April stuck behind a meandering family of four.

She shouldn't fret over what Quinn's assessment of her appearance might have been. But was there a woman alive who wouldn't let it bother her? Once more, April felt unsure as to why he'd included her in today's trip.

An innocent comment dropped by a child seemed to

have drained some of the pleasure out of the day for both April and Quinn. He was careful to place Hayley between them, and each looked as if the two hours they'd need to make their way through the museum was an interminable stretch.

Hopping up and down, Hayley reminded them of her need to visit a restroom.

"April, would you mind taking her?" Quinn asked. "It's difficult for a single dad raising a daughter. She's at the age where I can't very well take her into the men's room, but if I let her go into the women's by herself, I get all kinds of dirty looks for hovering outside the door."

She was only too happy to put a bit of distance between her and Quinn. They left him reading one of the information plaques. An introduction to espionage.

One line jumped out at him. *A spy must live a life of lies.* Man, didn't *that* underscore everything he'd learned from his grandmother. A woman he'd never have dreamed capable of leading a double life.

When April and Hayley joined him again, he remained withdrawn.

The exhibit began with a tribute to the original agents of the OSS. April noticed Quinn's tension mounting when they moved to an area that named the agency's first director and listed some of the men and women who'd worked for him.

Sidling up to Quinn, April murmured, "Neither of your grandparents' names are here. Is that a relief, or does it make you worry about Norma's mental state?"

"I don't know. This brochure indicates there were a number of agents not listed here for various reasons."

Continuing, Quinn paused for a long time in front of a

volunteer who was lecturing about famous deceptions and double agents.

April found that curious, and she wondered if Quinn's grandmother had told him things that were revealed in the letters. The picture of the German officer came instantly to mind. The camera had certainly captured Norma's frightened expression in the second photo. Had she been involved in something unsavory? Or illegal? Some kind of betrayal?

It wasn't until they were in the area called *a school for spies,* where observation skills and surveillance ability were tested at interactive stations that April remembered her computer search on Heinz von Weisenbach. If Quinn's mood had been lighter and more carefree, she might've confessed that she'd paid for a probe. But Quinn remained stiff and acted uncomfortable until they entered the contemporary section of the museum, so April allowed the moment to pass.

She'd forgotten about the incident by the time they finished the tour and Hayley begged to have an early dinner at the Spy City Café. It was a casual place. Gradually Quinn relaxed, and because he did, they all had fun.

Ten minutes into the drive back to Virginia, Hayley fell asleep. April smiled at Quinn. "Hayley's a delight. She goes full-tilt and then, splat, she's done. Were you as surprised as I was about all the things she's taken in?"

"The kid has the makings of a good lawyer. Thanks for being so patient when it came to Hayley's endless questions."

"I have to admit she did better than I did in the spy school. She loved it. Good luck convincing her now not to let on to Norma where we spent the afternoon."

He drummed his fingers on the steering wheel, but didn't respond to April's observation.

They were on the gravel road that led to her house when a dark sedan traveling too fast passed them going the other way, flinging so much gravel across the driver's side of the Lexus the noise woke Hayley.

While April reassured the girl that everything was fine, Quinn gazed steadily in his rearview mirror. "I only caught a glimpse, but was that Lathrop?"

"What? No, you must be mistaken. Eric drives a beat-up compact. It's red. Someone probably missed the turnoff to the lake resort. It happens a lot, which is why I've decided to invest the money in fencing this property. I'll hang an ornate gate between the carriage lamps. When your grandmother lived here, there wasn't as much crime. Well, maybe in the District, but here it was relatively safe."

"It's not safe anywhere now. Aren't you nervous living alone this far from town?"

April shook her head as Quinn drove between the partially finished carriage posts.

He pulled up in front of her house. "You really aren't worried about whoever was in that car? Yours is the only house around." Quinn reached for the key to turn off the engine. "I'll go in with you while you have a look around."

Grasping his wrist, April stopped him. "Honestly, there's no need. Like I told you, people going to the resort often get lost. Anyhow, Hayley's fallen back asleep."

"Yeah? I'm still walking you to the door. I've wanted to kiss you all afternoon," he admitted. "This way I won't get the third degree from the peanut gallery."

April slid out, his words causing prickles of anticipation. Even though she could list a hundred reasons why not to foster a relationship with such a complicated man, she moved eagerly and naturally into his arms. April assumed that the last time he kissed her she'd exaggerated how good it felt. But, no, their lips met and it was as if an electric arc passed from Quinn to her. Her chin went slack and he didn't hesitate to deepen the kiss.

It wasn't until he had her pressed against the door and they were slipping to their knees that he came to his senses. Breathing hard, Quinn touched his sweating forehead to hers. He straightened, drawing her up until they were both standing. "Tell me you're thinking this is the beginning, not the end," he murmured.

April opened her eyes ever so slowly. "I'm afraid…I… can't think at all."

"Exactly." He let go of her with one hand and jerked a thumb toward his car. "Next time I'll leave Hayley with Gram. Do you have your house key?"

Fumbling and disoriented, April managed to pull the big ring out of her tote.

Taking it, Quinn tried two different keys in the lock. "Oh, wait, it's open. I must've had the right key after all." Handing her the ring after she'd stepped over the threshold, he leaned in and kissed her one final time. "I'll call you and set something up. Or you call me. I have an obligation next Saturday, though." He broke off suddenly, grasped April's hands and brought them to his lips. "It might cause a stir, but…will you come with me? Saturday's my last big fund-raiser. It's a buffet."

He looked so boyishly endearing April couldn't have refused him anything. "When? I have an asphalt crew coming that day."

"Late. Nine o'clock. Dressy." He stroked her knuckles and gazed into her eyes.

"I…ah…happen to have a dress that'll work. Listen, Quinn, you'd better leave. I see Hayley's awake."

He had a hard time letting her go, and that, too, counted for much in April's book. She stood in the open door and watched him lope back to the car. She grinned when he stopped twice and foolishly blew her kisses.

After he'd driven off and she closed the door, excitement and pleasure remained with her. Until she turned on the light in her bedroom and discovered her things flung everywhere. "What the…?" The room had been ransacked. Rushing around, April picked up blueprints and began rolling them up. Her brain numb, she noticed her laptop sitting on her bed, its lid open. Racing over to it, she hit a few keys and gasped aloud when her e-mail came up—the first on the list was from the search company she'd engaged. On the subject line she read Heinz von Weisenbach, Mulhouse, France.

She scanned the brief report. To her disappointment, the search had only located the landscaper. Still, whoever was responsible for this mess had opened and read that e-mail. It became apparent the minute April saw that four e-mails from Realtor friends had been skipped over. Who would do this? That hadn't been Eric's car, but he could've been riding with his cameraman.

She shut down the power. Furious, April dug out her cell phone and punched in Eric's number. She hadn't given Quinn's suspicion any credence before; now she did. The instant Eric answered, she shrieked, "You creep! If you damaged *anything* while tearing up my bedroom, I'm presenting you with a bill. As for the information you stole from my computer on Heinz von Weisenbach, the joke's on you. That guy in Mulhouse, France, plants trees and flowers for a living. He's a landscaper with the same name as on the letters, you idiot."

"April? I didn't tear up your house. What landscaper in France? Are you drunk? What in hell are you talking about? I'm at a warehouse fire in midtown, and I've been here interviewing people since four this afternoon. You're on my list of people to call, however. I want to say I'm sorry for the way I acted that night at Cinalli's. I'd still like you to be my date for the Santini fund-raiser."

"No, Eric." Calming down once she realized she'd attacked the wrong man, April accepted Eric's apology with as much grace as she could muster.

"Yeah, well we hafta get together soon. I want a rundown on anything and everything you can tell me about Norma Santini's letters. I found this guy, see. An old government agent. He's a drunk, but when I got him sober he said some interesting things about Tony and Norma. I need facts to corroborate his stories. Particularly when he claims they both lived in Europe way past the time most Americans came home to wait out the war."

"So, your apology's just so much hot air? You're just after the letters."

"April, come on. I shouldn't have to tell you what an exclusive on any Santini dirt would mean for my career."

"Well, I wouldn't want a career based on digging up dirt on nice old ladies. I don't believe you didn't break in here. We're finished, Eric. Stay away from me and stay off my property." She jammed the Off button so hard, the phone flew out of her hand and struck her computer keys, making the screen go black.

"Great!" As she attempted to retrieve the lost document, April worried. What if Eric wasn't lying? Who else had an interest in the Santinis or the German soldier?

The e-mail reappeared. With a sigh, she debated again whether or not to call Quinn. And say…what? Admit she'd gone behind his back to run a secret search on a man from his grandmother's past? "Right," she muttered. Do that and it'd spell the end of anything further developing between her and Quinn.

For the first time she could ever recall, April *did* want something to develop between her and a man. Not just any man. Quinn. Senatorial candidate Santini.

Was she out of her mind?

Chapter 7

Monday, Quinn searched his closet for clothes to wear in court. Since the start of his campaign, he'd cut his client load by half. But this week a civil suit had finally landed a spot on the docket. He was prepared for the case, and he'd gotten up in an unusually good mood, which boded well for his presentation.

The phone rang while he whistled and fastened his tie. The ringing stopped abruptly, which told him Hayley had answered the call.

She tapped on his bedroom door. "Daddy, Gram's on the phone. She fixed breakfast this morning and we're 'vited."

Pushing up his cuff, Quinn looked at his watch. "Tell her I'll drop you off. I need Joseph to drive you to day camp. I'll grab something to tide me over at the Starbucks drive-through. I'm meeting a client at eight-fifteen."

Hayley disappeared and Quinn heard her footsteps skipping along the hall. Moments later she was back. "She wants to talk to you before you go to work. And, Daddy," Hayley said in hushed tones, "she knows we went to the spy museum."

"What? How?"

Shrugging, Hayley twisted her lips to one side. "She said she read it in this morning's paper. Why would a paper care?"

"Exactly!" Quinn tried not to swear around his daughter, but something slipped out that left Hayley shaking her finger at him. "Sorry," he said resignedly. "Tell Gram we'll be right over." He slid up the knot of his tie, muttering to himself. So much for his good mood, which was shot to hell. *Who saw them yesterday?*

As calmly as possible, he checked the contents of his briefcase, then with the efficiency that came from single fatherhood, did the same with Hayley's backpack. Today kicked off the last week of her day camp. After that, there'd be a week in which she had nothing going on but dance class. Following that came the Labor Day weekend. Then school. *First grade.* Quinn had a big X on the calendar.

Jeez, he had to make time this week to run Hayley out to the mall to fill the supply list they'd received from school. A flash of guilt shot through him. Granted, he'd been busy, and Gram had offered to purchase school supplies. But Hayley wanted *him* to take her.

Grabbing his briefcase and the backpack, he called to Hayley, "Come on, honey, time's wasting." Sometimes Quinn wished he could be in two places at once. Ha! His secretary, Marvella, said at least twice a day, "Quinn you should find a wife."

As he clattered down the stairs, it occurred to him that for the first time since Amy's death, he didn't dismiss Marvella's advice out of hand. Like a bolt from the blue, he remembered how good it'd felt holding April last night. Kissing her hadn't been enough. He'd left her, only to drive home aching with unfulfilled need.

Hayley met him near the front door, carrying her pink raincoat. "Is Gram mad at us for going to see the spy place without her?"

"No. Actually, I'm not sure."

"I don't want her to be mad, 'cause Daddy, I really, really like April."

"Uh, speaking of April. Did Gram say the article specifically mentioned April?" He raised a large umbrella over both of them.

"Nope!" Hayley skipped to keep abreast of Quinn's longer stride. "But it musta said something, 'cause Gram asked what woman went with us."

He swore—under his breath this time. Judging by April's negative response to politics, he could guess how unhappy she'd be to find her name linked with his in a gossip column. He should've been on the lookout yesterday at the museum. Since he'd decided to run against Dan Mattingly over a year ago, every move Quinn made had been dissected in the local newspaper.

They entered the main house via the side door. Quinn shook out the umbrella and left it under the awning. The cold drizzle this late-August morning contrasted with the warmer air inside, which was permeated with the scents of maple syrup and cinnamon.

Hayley let go of Quinn's hand and skipped into the

kitchen. "Goody, goody! Gram fixed my favorite blueberry French toast."

Quinn lagged behind, trying to assemble his thoughts. His grandmother reserved her signature breakfast for holidays or special celebrations. What was this all about?

He looked at the table set for three with his grandmother's everyday pottery. She poured coffee into two mugs, then assisted Hayley into her usual seat. A tall glass of milk had already been poured.

Quinn extended an arm and tapped his wristwatch. "I'm really pressed for time this morning. Is everything all right?" He propped his briefcase and Hayley's backpack against the island counter, and draped his raincoat over them before brushing a kiss across Norma's cheek. He noticed something different about her. A new outfit? Maybe. Or a haircut? Both, he decided. She'd always been energetic, but he liked this more youthful look. "What's the occasion?" he asked, accepting the steaming mug. "I know I didn't miss your birthday." Quinn gazed blankly at a plate piled high with blueberry French toast she set in front of him. Hayley's plate was slightly smaller.

Tightening her grip on the mug she held, Norma sat sideways in her chair. "Quinn, I'm going to France. This week if I can find a direct flight."

"Fr…rance?" He dropped the silver knife he'd picked up to cut Hayley's toast.

Wilting a bit under Quinn's laser stare, Norma ended up glancing away. "I see you're shocked. But I can assure you I've thought this through."

"Shocked is putting it mildly. I thought this—" his wave encompassed the food "—was your way of grilling us about our trip to the spy museum."

Norma dismissed that idea with a flip of her wrist. Her plate sat empty, while Quinn's food was neglected and cooling. Hayley was the only one interested in eating.

"You went there seeking answers." There was faint accusation in her statement. "Which is exactly why I'm going to France. I should've done this after Anthony died. I did mention the trip in passing, but your dad wouldn't hear of me traveling alone. He insisted I wait until he or Marsha could accompany me, unless I booked a trip with a seniors' group. With the galloping growth of the firm, of course, they never could arrange a time. Anyway, had they tagged along or had I gone with a tour group, I couldn't have done what I needed to. So I kept putting it off."

"Gram, what can you possibly find in France so long after the war?"

She pleated her napkin. "There must be some official record in Colmar or in a neighboring town telling where Heinz was buried. Seeing his grave and making sure there's a proper headstone is too little, too late, I know, but…it's necessary."

"No, it's not necessary at all."

Briskly shaking out her napkin, Norma helped herself to a small portion of French toast. "Quinn, don't think me an old fool, but his image visits me at night. I can almost hear his voice. But that's not the only reason. Going there…is something I have to do—for *me*." Her voice trailed off dreamily.

"Why?" Quinn's jaw tightened perceptibly.

"I'm not sure I can explain it," Norma murmured. "Heinz had such a zest for life. And a passion for roses. I plan to buy several dozen in all colors and blanket his grave."

"Whose grave? My mama's?"

"Mercy no, Hayley." Norma redirected Quinn's attention by gripping his forearm. "I should've waited to talk about this until you and I could be alone. But, you're always running hither and yon. And at my age, I no longer have the leisure of frittering away days, weeks, months. That's what I've done, let months evolve into years. Too many. My mind is made up, Quinn. I have to do this soon."

Quinn didn't like his grandmother's urgency, so he gulped his coffee. "My calendar's really crammed," he said, feigning regret.

"Tonight, Quinn. We'll discuss it this evening. After Hayley's bath and bedtime story."

He removed a thin silver BlackBerry from the breast pocket of his suit coat. "I've got a campaign strategy meeting with our media managers once I leave the courthouse this afternoon. I'll be lucky to make it home by seven."

"Eight then, or nine," she said with finality.

"Please promise you won't do anything rash before we talk. Such as phoning the travel agency."

"A day's delay? I suppose I owe you that. Although," she added as Quinn rose and collected his coat and briefcase, "you didn't intend to inform me of your excursion to the new museum. What did you see there?" Her pupils narrowed ever so slightly.

"Nothing. I mean, we saw a lot. Have Hayley fill you in. But not to worry," he said, finally understanding the worry behind her question. "According to the pamphlet, names of former agents only show up if they or a descendant have authorized their inclusion in an exhibit."

"I'll walk you to your car, Quinn. Hayley, honey, I'll eat

when I return. I hear Ethel coming in. I made too much food, so tell her to help herself and fix a plate for Joseph. I'll be back in a jiffy."

Quinn realized she had something else on her mind. He'd guessed right, because Norma launched her second salvo the minute they were out the door. The rain had stopped, for the moment anyway.

"When I saw in today's paper where you'd gone, I was mystified. Then I recalled receiving a letter from the Central Intelligence Agency about collecting memorabilia for a museum. Goodness, that was several years ago. The very idea scared me half to death. The notice came right when we were dealing with the plane accident and I tucked the letter away in Tony's desk. I tossed it out later, assuming such a museum would never come to fruition. The work of agents is clandestine for a reason. At times they're asked to do things that would not make their families proud."

"People visiting the museum didn't appear to think along those lines. From what I saw, everyone was awed by the courage of agents. Kids, like Hayley, and teens, seem to consider undercover work a very cool job."

"Perhaps times have changed. I worried that my name or Tony's would surface on some foreign agent's hit list. There were rumors about a group called ODESSA tracking and killing former agents years after the war ended. Tony always took precautions to keep us, Brett and me, secure. He thought I didn't notice, but he was always jumpy. Always checking over his shoulder, as if afraid he'd been followed. That's a heavy burden to carry. I suspect it's what caused him to start drinking. A million times I begged him to retire permanently. He said he couldn't."

Quinn lingered, his hand on the car door. "You can't still think there's any danger. The war's been over for sixty years."

She gave a shrug, crossed her arms and vigorously rubbed them.

"Here, you shouldn't have come out without a sweater. The weatherman's forecasting more rain later today. Go inside before you catch a cold." He sighed. "Ever since those damned letters surfaced, it's been wearing on you. I can't help thinking this should all be left buried. Damn, I'm going to be late."

"If you're late, you're late, Quinn. Don't risk an accident on the freeway. I'd like your blessing in this venture, so I will wait. Shall I ask Ethel to prepare something for dinner that can be reheated when you come in?"

"I'd appreciate it. Unless that's inconvenient."

"Of course not. Don't worry about it."

"What worries me is the thought of you going to France by yourself to dig in God knows what mess. You say there must be records and in the next breath you tell me your name may be on some long-ago hit list. Given the violent way *that man,* von Weisenbach, met his end, did you stop to consider that one or more of the people involved in killing him could still be alive? What if they want to silence you? Who ordered his death?"

"That *man* is your real grandfather, Quinn. And I have no idea who ordered him killed. I want people to know he was loved. This trip is a risk I'm willing to take. Now, you'd better go."

He did, but he felt surly over this latest turn of events. He punched the gate release button, realizing his life, the one he'd been comfortable in for thirty-five years, was spinning out of control.

Late or not, he didn't drive away from the property until the gate had fully shut behind him.

During his morning commute, Quinn usually rehearsed whatever case he'd be presenting in court. Today, his mind refused to cooperate. All he could think about was Norma…. The German soldier… Spies… Lies…

Lawyers relied on past cases to help make sense of current problems they needed to solve. Somewhere, someone must have experienced a situation like the one his grandmother had blown the lid off last week.

For the life of him, Quinn couldn't recall a single case he'd read about with similarities 'enough to give him comfort. Nor could he run known facts by colleagues, who were too sharp to buy the vague term *hypothetical* in a case this unorthodox. How many people in the cars around him weren't who they'd grown up believing themselves to be? No one, he'd bet.

Stuck in traffic, he took out his cell phone and notified his client that he was running ten or fifteen minutes late. He started to tuck the phone back in its holder, then stopped. He'd consciously pushed from his mind the one person with whom he could discuss this latest development. *April*.

Quinn hadn't yet programmed her number into his cell, but he had it memorized. The minute her cheery hello wafted through the receiver, his heart tripped erratically, but his stomach settled. At the sound of her voice, his troubles began to recede.

"I hope I'm not calling too early."

"Quinn, is that you? Hang on a sec. I'm juggling a paint roller in one hand and a coffee mug in the other."

He pictured her lithe figure in paint-spattered jeans.

She'd probably covered those springy dark curls with a scarf. He asked if she had.

Her throaty laughter reduced the miles that separated them. "You called me before eight for a fashion update? Don't tell me you've heard a rumor that I'm not capable of looking presentable enough for your fund-raiser?"

"I hope you already know me better than that."

The intensity of his denial changed April's tone, bringing a swift apology, followed by, "Is something wrong? You don't sound like yourself, Quinn."

"My grandmother's just told me about a ridiculous plan of hers. She's got it in her head to fly off to France."

"Why on earth?" April accidentally inhaled coffee and began to choke. "Oh, wait," she sputtered a moment later. "It's because of Heinz, isn't it?"

"You got it," Quinn said grimly. "Some nonsense to do with the bastard who wrote her those letters. He used to bring her roses, apparently. She's obsessed with the idea of finding where he's buried so she can return the favor. Cover his grave with roses, I mean."

"Heinz von Weisenbach is dead?" April's shock vibrated in Quinn's ear.

Traffic began to move, forcing Quinn to shift the phone. "I wasn't sure how much of that old story Gram told you. She saw him being shot."

"Quinn, that's awful. I think she…loved him. I read enough in a couple of her letters to know *he* loved *her*. I had the impression that the feeling was mutual."

"So? Anything they had ended over sixty years ago. She married someone else. Anthony Santini. She's romanticizing this old lover way out of all proportion."

"Quinn, is Norma absolutely positive he died?"

Swerving into a different lane due to a fender-bender, Quinn failed to answer immediately.

"Quinn? Do you think maybe he's still alive? Living in or around the city where she knew him in France."

"What? I just said Gram watched him die. Obviously she didn't give you the whole story." He paused to negotiate the snarled traffic. "Sorry, April. I'm weaving around a wreck on the freeway. I shouldn't be on the phone while I'm driving. I'd better—"

"Don't hang up yet!" He heard her take a deep breath. "I thought about calling you last night, but I didn't want you to get upset. Because…I've got no idea who burgled my home. Technically not burgled, I guess, because nothing's missing. But someone pawed through my stuff and dumped out drawers. My laptop was open and my e-mail's been accessed. Someone read a preliminary report that came in response to a search I activated on Heinz. Norma's Heinz."

"Hold on! You're talking so fast I can't follow. Someone broke into your house? Last night? Are you okay? Did you call the police?"

"I found the mess after you dropped me off, and no, I didn't call the cops. I suspected Eric, because he refuses to believe I don't have the letters and because you thought he was in that car. He's definitely the most logical possibility. But Eric swears he spent all afternoon and evening at a warehouse fire. He can't lie worth a damn, so I believe him. Sort of. Can you think of anyone else who might be interested in Norma's letters?"

"Suppose you back up and tell me why you'd conduct

a search for a guy you know nothing about." Every terse word revealed his anger.

"Listen, Quinn, I'm not a criminal you have on the witness stand. I don't care to be cross-examined in that tone. If you must know, I started the search after you and Norma implied there was something about the letters that made them blackmail material. And maybe you're right, since *somebody* wants them," she said, sounding more congenial. "But I stand by my belief that politics is full of dirty business and politicians are slimeballs. Any woman with half a brain would have to be nuts to get seriously involved with one."

"So you're saying you're serious about me, slimeball or not?" Quinn broke into a foolish grin.

"I was happier before our paths crossed, Quinn Santini. Anyway, I'm hanging up. You're a danger on the road—and the paint is drying on my roller."

"Wait. I'm driving carefully, I promise. I never thought of doing a computer search on Gram's, uh…friend. You haven't found this von Weisenbach, have you?" Quinn was nowhere near letting himself think of the German as his biological grandfather. He was even further from letting any hint of that slip—to anyone.

"Looking around on my own, I came up with two references to that name. Neither man lived in Colmar. I'm pretty convinced neither one is the man who wrote the letters. Anyway, I wasn't aware he'd died or I would've saved my search fee. For all of their supposed expertise, the company only gave me one name. One of two I found on my own. They wanted a lot more money to dig deeper. So, I'm done. Dead or alive, your grandmother's lost love will have to stay lost. What I tried to say, before you so rudely jumped all over me, is that whoever broke into my house read that report. Who knows? Maybe it means nothing. My intruder might've been trying to hack into my online bank account."

"I didn't intend to jump all over you, April. I value your opinions."

"Didn't sound like it."

"I do. And now I'm concerned for your welfare. I'll bet whoever broke into your house drove the car that nearly sideswiped us. Damn, I wish I'd gotten his license number. The driver looked familiar and Lathrop was my first guess. Are you *sure* his alibi holds up?"

"I'm no detective, and I'm not sure of anything except that if I don't get back to work I'll have to toss out this paint roller and open a new one. I can't afford to get tangled up in this, Quinn. My part ended when I brought Norma her letters. Maybe you're used to stuff like this—break-ins and mysterious men in fast cars. I'm not and don't want to be. So, I think it'd be best if you scrounged up a new date for Saturday's fund-raiser."

"I don't want anyone but you. I'd cancel the damned party, except my campaign manager says we need to refill the coffers for another media blitz."

"You can't cancel. That's not even realistic. Tickets were presold. I know that because, in a roundabout way, Eric acquired a pair. He invited me to go before you did, but I turned him down flat. Twice, in fact."

"Please don't turn *me* down flat without giving me a chance to change your mind. In person. Not tonight, though—I really have to squelch Gram's overseas trip. Will you be home tomorrow, around six? And do you feel safe staying out there alone after what happened? If not, Gram has several guest rooms."

"I'm fine, Santini. Whoever broke in must know by now that I don't have the letters—or any real information about them."

"Dammit, I'm just pulling up to the restaurant where I'm meeting my client, and I'm late as it is. I'll handle my grandmother. It's probably best if you forget you ever saw those letters."

"I'd like to, but... I'll talk to Eric again. He *is* the most logical suspect. I mean, who else knows I found the letters? Well, to answer my own question, my brother Miles. And Robyn Parker," she muttered. "Eric blabbed to Miles. But that wasn't Miles's car, either." She sighed. "I'm not making sense. I'm free at six, tomorrow. See you then. Bye, Quinn."

The buzz in his ear told him she'd hung up. Quinn felt as if they'd left things hanging. It was an unsatisfactory feeling.

After that, however, Quinn was so busy that he had no time to focus on anything personal.

In his car, finally headed home, it all came back in a rush. Quinn stripped off his tie and opened the top button on his white shirt. Little by little he swept away the remnants of his exhausting day. Part way home, his mind switched gears and moved onto the next issue facing him. Namely, his grandmother's sudden travel plans.

Should he tell her about April's break-in, which in all likelihood *was* connected to her letters? Say someone was shooting in the dark, hoping to dig up dirt on him or his family—maybe even his hidden ancestry, a fact still too shocking for Quinn to accept. In the wrong hands, it would be effective ammunition against his candidacy.

Could the information contained in the letters bring real harm to the people he loved? Other than cast dishonor on his grandfather's good name, of course. His grandfather Santini, who wasn't really his grandfather. Quinn reached for a roll of antacids he'd been using too liberally during this campaign. He popped two tablets into his mouth and threw the pack in his briefcase.

It was dark when he rolled through the gates. As arranged, he stopped at his grandmother's house.

She left him alone to eat the plate of food he warmed up in the microwave. Hayley ran into the dining room as Quinn sat down to eat. "Hi, honey. Let me get you a bedtime snack, and you can tell me about your day."

"Okay. Ethel made tapioca pudding. I didn't have any with dinner. Can I have some now with a glass of milk?"

"Sure, you bring the pudding and a bowl, and I'll get your milk."

They both ate, neither saying anything for the first little while. Hayley reached the bottom of her bowl before Quinn finished his noodle casserole, green beans and whole wheat muffin.

"Today at camp my teacher talked about how a lie is a lie is a lie. You know, Daddy, how kids cross their fingers behind their back? Well, Mrs. Crosley said it doesn't work. And she said a little white lie isn't any littler or whiter than a whopper. She said every lie ends up hurting someone. Is that true, Daddy?"

The bite Quinn had taken stuck in his throat. He had colleagues who bragged about how easy it was to twist the truth in order to win cases. The bigger instance, by far, of course, was the lie his grandparents had told his father, and by extension, him and now Hayley.

"Honey, your teacher was right. Telling the truth, no matter what the consequences are at the time, means that problems won't crop up later and come back to haunt you."

"Like ghosts?" She polished off the last of her milk.

"Ghosts aren't real. Saying something comes back to haunt you is a figure of speech." Quinn got up and carried his plate and her bowl to the kitchen, and took another stab at explaining. "Honey, people who tell a lie live every day knowing they should've told the truth. How do you think they feel?"

"Bad. I think their tummies hurt." She clasped her hands across hers. "Daddy, I did have tapioca pudding with my dinner."

Quinn turned from rinsing off his plate. "Hayley Santini!" He bit back the lecture on the tip of his tongue. The pain etched on her sweet face said it all. Quinn scooped her up and hugged her tight. "The bigger the lie, the worse the tummyache. Think about it while you take your bath. When I come to tuck you into bed, I want you to tell me if you'd say you didn't have dessert again when you really did."

"I already know," she said, wiping tears from her eyes. "I won't, 'cause with dinner it tasted yummy. This time it tasted yucky, 'cause I lied."

"Lesson learned, Hayley. I'll run your bath. You get your pjs and choose the book you want for your bedtime story."

Dark thoughts swirled inside Quinn's head throughout the bath and bedtime process. Nothing to do with Hayley's transgression, but with the one committed by his grandmother and Anthony Santini. How could they think there wouldn't be consequences someday?

He warily approached the room where his grandmother sat knitting. She never just sat and relaxed. Quinn wondered if her inability to simply sit in repose had to do with all the memories that must weigh her down.

"Is Hayley asleep?"

"Yes. I only made it halfway through her favorite Junie B. book. The one about starting first grade." He crossed to the fireplace, picked up the poker and turned the crackling log.

"How did your day go, Quinn? You seem restless. Did you lose your case?"

"No. It went well. If I'm restless, Gram, it has to do with what we're about to discuss. Today I learned that someone broke into April's home. Quite likely he hoped to find your letters."

"No!" Norma's knitting needles stopped clicking. "What makes you think my letters had anything to do with a break-in at April's?"

Taking a seat across from Norma, Quinn described the details he'd obtained from April, including the condition in which she'd found her laptop.

Norma blanched. "Why would she launch a computer search for a dead man? Did I trust her too readily, Quinn? If so, I'm sorry. I ought to have listened to you and relied on your instincts."

"You misunderstand what I'm saying. I'm not casting blame on April. It's no fault of hers that Eric Lathrop dropped in right after she discovered the letters. Nothing was stolen but her computer was breached and all the intruder appeared to look at was a report of her search efforts, so we're pretty sure the letters were the reason for the break-in. You can put an end to further problems, Gram. Go get them, and I'll help you burn every one."

"Unless whoever's searching for them *knows* they've been destroyed, it won't make any difference." She raised one hand to wipe away a tear that trickled down her face. "Besides, I don't want to burn my letters. They're all I have left of Heinz. Let me assure you, Quinn, anyone who breaks in here won't find them. I placed the packet in the floor safe Tony installed years ago. It's where he stowed government pouches he carried to and from foreign…agents is my guess. Believe me, he would've made sure his hiding place was very secure."

"You have a floor safe? What kind of stuff did he transport? To whom? This is all news to me!"

"I never asked. I assume he carried classified documents to field reps, and brought back foreign intelligence. A lot went on during the Cold War"

"Dad thought Grandpa was a diplomat or a civilian ambassador." He shook his head. "Your marriage sounds pretty unsatisfying—a husband who was either away or emotionally distant."

Norma shrugged but responded only to his earlier remark. "Officially, your grandfather's business credentials said he was a U.S. emissary for the District of Columbia's Department of Tourism. I'm sure he tailed Russians or spied in Japan and North Korea. Back in the late '60s, an enterprising reporter said Tony always took red-eye flights to and from Europe, but never checked into the hotels where he'd preregistered. Wild rumors circulated after Tony died—that he carried a briefcase chained to his wrist when he traveled for…business. Neither your dad nor I could ever verify that with a reliable source. Which didn't stop the press from hounding us, or saying we were uncooperative."

"Can you swear that everything Gramps did was above-board? Or did he operate in gray areas and do things that could be dragged out now and made to appear suspicious?"

"I trusted him. Colleagues trusted him. I learned first-hand that a person can't stop anyone from embellishing the truth. Even patriotic acts can be manipulated. I believe to this day that Heinz intended—was eager, in fact—to defect and join our side. He wouldn't have been the first young man coerced into joining Hitler's army. Something went wrong that night," she said sadly. "Very, very wrong. I just have no idea what."

"You said yourself you were nineteen years old and crazy in love with the guy. I wish there was someone else who could attest to your version of what happened that day. We could sic Eric Lathrop onto the story," he muttered, conscious of the irony. "He claims all he wants is a bona-fide scoop."

"Your tone implies that isn't really his goal."

Quinn folded his hands between his knees and shook his head. "I don't know if Lathrop bears me ill will. His boss is certainly biased in favor of Dan Mattingly. I know for a fact that in the last election, Eric's editor miraculously dug up damning information on Dan's primary opponent—and he did it so close to the end of the race there wasn't time for rebuttal."

"Which is why you think I shouldn't go to France, in case it starts tongues wagging?"

"That's one reason, Gram. Right now, anything con-nected with me is newsworthy. If you book a flight to

France, it'll leak out. If Lathrop is even a mediocre reporter, he's bound to link your sudden journey abroad to April finding those blasted letters."

"Mere conjecture. What does it prove?"

"There's another reason I don't want you flying off to France. Say, for instance, that Eric told his editor, Paul Benson, about the letters. Is Benson determined enough to torpedo my chances that he'd pay an unscrupulous person to break into April's house, just to see what he could find? Said intruder uncovers the report and a name in France. What's to stop Paul from having you followed? And would it stop at following? I don't want you or April hurt on my account, Gram. I'd never forgive myself if something happened to you."

"Heavenly days! You're saying April was harmed?"

"No, no. Luckily, the intruder left before I dropped her off. But if she'd been at home there's no telling what the outcome might have been. Please humor me in this. I promise…when the election's over—" Quinn raised a solemn hand "—win or lose, I'll take you to France. It's possible Heinz has relatives living in that area."

"Impossible. Heinz didn't know his parents. He grew up in an overcrowded boys' home in Dusseldorf, which was why the army was his only option. He liked military life at first and moved up in rank. Oh, I can see you think he fed me a pack of lies. You're wrong, Quinn."

"I didn't mention that April's preliminary search found other von Weisenbachs living, not in Colmar, but in another French town."

Norma's color faded and she clasped her throat. "All the more reason I can't delay my trip. I need to see his grave for my own peace of mind. What…who did April locate?"

"She mentioned two Heinz von Weisenbachs. The firm demanded more money to dig deeper. Since April was only fooling around, and you had the letters, she cancelled her search. Anyway, you never told her your Heinz had been shot or that he died. Otherwise she'd never have instigated any search."

"No, I didn't. Our conversation ended before that. And the memory's painful. It's a difficult time to relive."

It was clear to Quinn as he watched his grandmother collect her knitting that he'd lost her to the past. Especially when she rose and wandered toward the stairs. She grasped the newel post, then turned. "Quinn, I wish I could explain this…odd sense of urgency I feel. I can't so I'll sleep on what we've discussed. Perhaps I'll see everything more clearly in the morning—figure out what steps I need to take. Good night, now. There's no need to interrupt Hayley's sleep to take her home. Bring her fresh clothes in the morning. And plan to stay for breakfast. I'll leave you to lock up and set the perimeter alarms. In case…" She didn't finish.

"Don't worry that someone will break in. I don't think Eric Lathrop would risk his career by setting off our alarms."

"Is he the culprit? He struck me as too young to under-stand how things really were during the war."

"Me, too. I find it hard to believe that anyone, other than historians, can work up much interest in what individuals did that long ago. What can they hope to gain?"

"Don't kid yourself, Quinn. Every war leaves enemies behind, sometimes for generations. People who fancy themselves U.S. political power-brokers even lay claim to grudges reaching back as far as the Revolutionary War. Now, good night. I'll see you in the morning."

She left then. Quinn watched, hating that he was making things harder for her. He banked the fire for the night, locked up and drove back to his house, all the while worrying about his grandmother's vague warning. All it served to do was make him less sure about the safety of his family.

He wished he could talk about these murky feelings with April. But it was late. Quinn pocketed his keys after unlocking his front door. He switched on a light and was suddenly overwhelmed by waves of loneliness. He *would* call, he decided, promising himself he wouldn't keep April long. He merely wanted to hear her voice.

Chapter 8

Quinn found a hanger for his suit jacket, then flopped down on his bed and pried off his shoes without untying them. He dragged the bedside phone within reach.

Leaning against the antique headboard, he punched in her number. She answered on the second ring. "Hi," he mumbled, because now that he had her on the line, he couldn't quite recall what he wanted to say.

"Quinn, is that you?" Her voice conveyed pleasure. "I've been thinking about calling you. Three reasons," she said hastily. "To see if you won your case. To find out if you talked your grandmother out of dashing off to France. And…" she hesitated, "to ask if you saw the article in this morning's paper about our Sunday jaunt to the spy museum. The society pages," she added sarcastically. "As if anyone would expect to see *me* there."

"Gram mentioned the article. I didn't have time to even glance at a paper today. But the answer to your first question is yes. As for dissuading her, I did temporarily. That article…was it really snarky?"

"Not with regard to you. Especially if your standing in the community gets jacked any higher based on the number of clever ways a reporter can say you're a side of sizzling beefcake."

"Jeez, April." Quinn bolted into a sitting position and drew a hand through his hair. "I hope you're pulling my leg."

"Nope. And you've got no idea how thankful I am to have a low profile in our community. The article refers to me as your—and I quote—'fashion clueless gal-pal.'"

"Who the hell wrote that crap?"

"Tori St. Clair. Know her? I've been imagining her office desk, decorated with a voodoo likeness of me stuck full of pins."

As he collapsed on the stack of pillows again, Quinn's laugh rumbled. His mood improved. "If only Ms. St. Clair knew the truth. You kept me so preoccupied, I didn't notice her or anyone else tailing us."

"Santini, you are so full of it. I figured out before we'd passed two exhibits what you were preoccupied with. You were worried we'd see your grandparents' names on a document or plaque."

"I was that obvious?"

"I can't figure out why it concerns you so much. They left you quite a legacy. I should think you'd be proud. Especially of Norma. What she did was more than gutsy. Both of your grandparents were trailblazers during a tough time."

His mood sank fast. Would April change her opinion if she knew the real story? "I'll tell you what worries me.

Besides the fact that I didn't have an inkling about their secret lives until you produced those damned letters. It now appears that someone outside the family is interested in Gram's past. The only reason I can think of, is to turn her stint with the OSS—and the whole von Weisenbach mess—into something they can use to blacken my background. Character assassinations are all too common in campaigns. If old scandals hit the news in the last months before voting, a candidate can be destroyed."

"Oh. Ohhh! The letters, the photographs… I suppose they could be made to look bad. As if she was…a traitor. And it's my fault someone has the colonel's name! Quinn, I know you said he died. Is it possible he didn't and went on to exact revenge against the U.S.? Well, I don't see how, but…" She sighed, the sound futile and a little sad. "Quinn, you can't know how sorry I am for tearing into that wall."

"Yeah, me, too. With one exception. I never would've met you otherwise."

"Do you mean that? You're not just being nice because you still think I'm in cahoots with Eric and you're trying to trick me into admitting it?"

"I believe you. At first I had my doubts, but you're wide open, April. The reason I called is to try and change your mind about going to my fund-raiser."

"Um…after I backed out, I realized it's probably too late for you to invite another woman. I guess I can still pose as your date, Quinn."

"There's no posing involved. I'm not stringing you along, April. Ask anyone on Saturday. This will be my first appearance at a campaign function with a date."

"Really? My friend Robyn said…oh, never mind."

"Robyn said what?"

"If I tell you, it'll make me blush."

"Would you blush if I said I'm sitting on my bed, wishing like hell you were here beside me?"

"Quinn! You have a young daughter to consider."

"She's bunking with Gram tonight. But I don't want you thinking adult sleepovers are the norm for me if Hayley's not here. They're…just…not."

As April said nothing, Quinn let it ride. Frankly, he didn't understand the out-of-kilter emotions she aroused in him. "Okay…let's get back to your friend's comments. If anything Robyn said had to do with the ridiculous things they call me in gossip columns, I'm not to blame. The first time I saw *Virginia's most eligible bachelor,* I phoned the reporter, mad as hell. She claimed she'd done me a favor with younger voters. She said I'd look boring if she'd written the truth about how I spend my days lawyering and my nights being a dad."

"What happened to truth in journalism? Are you saying that when Eric climbs on his soap box and blathers on and on about digging for the truth, he's actually lying?"

"In hard news, they try to get their facts straight so they don't get their pants sued off. Where they can legally stray are gossip columns and the like, which are all about innuendo and supposition."

"I guess if they say how handsome and charming you are, you can't really charge them with character assassination."

"No, but what does physical appearance have to do with my ability to do the job? I instruct my media team to counteract with articles that state where I stand on the issues. Which is what Eric does for Mattingly, by the way.

Speaking of Eric, did you ask him again what he knows about your break-in?"

"I left a message on his cell, but he hasn't called back. Quinn, do you remember seeing me lock my house before we left for the museum? I ask, because I'm usually so careful. There's no sign of forced entry and no broken window. If anything creeps me out, it's that."

"I watched you lock your front door. Who else has keys?"

"Um, my carpet-layer. I dropped one off last week after I okayed his specs. But, that's been true for all my jobs. He's a family friend of long standing. Oh, and Robyn Parker. She does my interiors at a cut rate, so I like her to be able to deliver orders or come and hang drapes or whatever when it's convenient. My mom has duplicate keys for obvious reasons. Like, if I fall off a ladder or lacerate myself with a saw, she'll dash out here and let the paramedics in. Provided I manage to reach my cell phone, of course."

"Didn't you say Robyn Parker knows about the letters?"

"I left them overnight in her office safe. But she's not the culprit. We were college roommates for four years. I'd trust Robyn with my money or my firstborn."

"Okay, don't bite my head off. Look, it's late. We're both tired. How about if we talk about this tomorrow? Are we still on for six o'clock? Can I grab some takeout?"

"Sure. Tomorrow I'm ripping up vinyl and setting tile in the sunroom. Whoa...Quinn, I just flipped on my outside lights. It's pouring rain. Sheets of it."

Quinn sprang off his bed and crossed to the window. "The weather report this morning said to expect a storm. It wasn't raining when I came in a few minutes ago. Holy moly, it's definitely coming down now."

"If it keeps up at this rate, you may have to call off your fund-raiser. The creeks and rivers will flood and no one'll get there."

"Folks who shell out for candidate's buffets like to get their money's worth. Seriously, most of my supporters live in or near town. It'll have to dump more than a foot of rain before there's a problem. What about your job? Doesn't bad weather bring construction to a halt?"

"Most of what's left is inside. Although the carpet-layers prefer a dry day so they can cut carpet on the patio. I'll cross my fingers that it doesn't last. I'd like to list this place soon and have it sold by Thanksgiving."

"Then what?"

Excitement resonated in her voice. "I'm making an offer on an eighteenth-century, three-story brick home on Captain's Row in Alexandria. It's got great potential but needs tons of work. What'll make it really worthwhile financially is if I can turn each of its levels into a condominium. The area's already zoned for multiple dwellings, which is a plus."

"If I'm elected, it sounds like the type of place I might be interested in. The commute from here into D.C. is worse every day. I'll have to move."

"Wow. What about Norma?"

"We, ah, haven't discussed it yet. She's got too much house here, even with Ethel coming in during the days to clean and fix an occasional meal. Besides, Ethel's going to be retiring soon. But I'm getting ahead of myself. First I have to win the election."

"You will, Quinn."

"Says she who doesn't follow politics."

"I'll have you know I've pored over Mattingly's speeches. He rambles a lot. And his voting record stinks, to put it mildly."

Quinn did his best to quell his laughter. He was slowly winning April over, and that made him want to turn handsprings around the room.

"Are you laughing at me, Quinn Santini?"

"Who, me?" Then he broke into a chuckle. "I knew you had the makings of a first-rate activist."

"Not until I met you. It's your fault for inviting me to your fund-raiser. I started thinking how badly it'd reflect on you if I stood around like an airhead, keeping quiet because I didn't know your views on significant issues. Then the reporters would criticize me for more than my lack of fashion sense."

"The hell with 'em. Just be yourself, April. I like you as you are." Quinn's voice dropped, conveying deeper feelings than the word *like* implied.

"Quinn, I'm not... I haven't... Is our relationship heading into new territory? If so, you should be aware that...I, uh, am not very experienced."

Quinn strained to hear her and finally figured out that the faint tapping in the background was April pacing nervously on an uncarpeted floor. "Don't let it bother you. We'll take things easy." He shut his eyes, calling up a vision of how she'd responded to his kisses the other night. He hadn't felt this rush of desire in so long it was almost scary.

Clearing his throat, Quinn muttered, "I've all but drawn you a picture showing you how out of practice I am. I've asked a woman out twice in five years. Both times, you were that woman. Dinner and the spy museum."

"Quinn, I can't believe—"

"Believe," he cut in roughly. "I've had dates, yes, but not of my own choice," he said with a shrug. "Friends fixed me up a few times, or my campaign manager did for photo ops, but…hell, this is hard to admit." He walked to the window where he cooled his forehead against the glass. "I thought I was…finished. You know, the, uh, urge. Gone. Until… Crap, if lawyers and politicians are supposed to be orators, I'd do better asphalting your drive."

"It's done. Today. In fact, it's cordoned off. So, if Tucker Creek floods, you'd have to park a half mile out on the road and walk to my house. I hope the asphalt sets before the storm hit, so the rain doesn't dig furrows in my expensive driveway."

"I'm afraid our evening's looking less likely by the minute. Are you still watching? That lightning is incredible."

"I see it." April couldn't quite conceal her disappointment. "There's no real necessity for us to get together tomorrow. If Eric phones me, or if I come up with another suspect, I can always call you."

Quinn continued to monitor the rainfall, and when his breath fogged the window he wiped off the condensation and saw his frown reflected in the glass. "Judging by this downpour, I'm afraid the creek will overflow its banks."

April had nothing to add.

Quinn had another thought. "If your street's still passable now, why don't you pack a bag, including your dress for Saturday, and stay here in town?"

"With you?" she asked lightly.

"That idea has appeal. But, as you were quick to point out, there's Hayley, who's very impressionable, not to mention nosy."

"Precocious is the term. So where should I go if I pack my bag and slog through this awful rain?"

"Last time I offered Gram's guest room. You refused, but it's still an option. Otherwise, can you stay with your folks?"

"Oh, right, Quinn! They'd love to accommodate me so I'll be handy for you to escort to your fund-raiser. He…llo! My dad isn't exactly in your camp."

"Ouch. I knew that. Your friend Robyn, then? Can you crash with her?"

"No. Well, I could. But…okay, now this is embarrassing. I did date in college. Until the guys got one look at my roommate. Long red hair. Green eyes. Voluptuous. In a word, she's gorgeous. When I put Norma's letters in Robyn's safe, she let me know she's dying for an introduction to you. Needless to say, I'm forestalling that."

"I prefer slim brunettes. Ethical ones, who can't be bribed."

"That's a nice thing to say, Quinn. In addition to ethics, I have a four-wheel drive Dodge Ram truck equipped with all-weather tires. If this rain keeps up, maybe I'll come and chauffeur you on Saturday night."

Quinn formed a mental picture of April in some clingy dress, climbing down and handing her truck keys to the valet at the city's most upscale hotel. His mind lingered on April wearing a form-fitting dress, and he was momentarily lost.

"Are you still there? Or are you plotting how you can meet Robyn, after all?"

"Actually," he lied smoothly, "I'm praying for a flood of Biblical proportions. One that'll ground flights and keep Gram from running off to France in search of heaven knows what."

"Looking outside, I think that scenario's possible. I'd

better sign off and go put a tarp over the tile I'm putting down in the sunroom tomorrow. It was just delivered today."

"Sorry, I didn't mean to tie up your evening. Take care covering that tile. Oh, weather permitting, I'll be in court until about four o'clock. Why don't I give you a holler to see if I should still come over—and what kind of food you want me to pick up."

"That's easy. Ribs from Frank's Barbecue. We'll test a theory I have about how to tell if a couple's compatible. Let them roll up their sleeves and share a rack of ribs."

"Oh, yeah. Plus corn on the cob and ice-cold beer."

"You'd enjoying that?"

"Yep."

"Hmm… Bye, Quinn. We may just be compatible with a capital C."

"I already figured that out."

He could still hear her sweet laugh after she'd hung up. Quinn gripped a sweaty receiver even after the dial tone had returned. He was starting to feel so many things for April. Respect. Liking. *Desire*.

She stoked a fire hotter than any he recalled with Amy. Granted, he could have forgotten details in the ten years since they'd met. That troubled him, as his grandmother still carried a torch for her first love. He and Amy had met in law school. They'd been two people who shared long-range professional goals and fell into dating exclusively. Then they'd ended up at the altar. Joining his dad's practice had, for Amy, taken precedence over their marriage. But Quinn had never let on that his marriage was anything but ideal, as ideal as he thought his parents' relationship was, and his grandparents' before Tony's death. Which he now knew to be utterly false.

Examining those years with Amy as he unbuttoned his shirt, stepped out of his slacks and welcomed the sting of a cool shower, he recalled that sex was often put on hold until he or Amy won a case.

It was rare that he let himself reflect back, especially to the day she'd announced her pregnancy and declared that having this baby would ruin their lives.

What did any of that matter now? Quinn could attest that from Hayley's first squall, he loved that tiny human being enough to be both mother and dad. A vow Amy held him to. Neither of them could've known that all too soon his promise would become an everyday reality.

Bracing his arms against the cold shower tile, Quinn let the slowly warming water beat down on his head and shoulders.

Earlier that evening, he'd chastened his grandmother because she'd stayed in an unsatisfying marriage. And he'd done the same. With nothing to distract him now, he saw he'd felt angry with his grandmother for claiming to still love a…foreigner—an enemy. He'd been angry because it seemed to invalidate her life with Tony. And because it forced him to unravel too many of his own tangled emotions.

Not only that, anything controversial exposed near the end of a hotly contested senate race could take him out of it.

Damn! April had no knowledge the letters were there when she tore out that particular wall. Even Gram didn't know where they'd gone. He wrenched off both faucets and buried his face in a towel.

He'd devoted nearly two years and a lot of money to this neck-and-neck race for a U.S. Senate seat. If he lost now, a lot of good people who'd worked hard and stood behind him would be adversely affected, too.

He could drop out. Say he needed to spend more time with Hayley.

But could he in good conscience hand Mattingly a win?

April had said she hadn't deciphered much of the letters. The best thing for everyone would be if his grandmother got rid of them once and for all. Then anyone engaged in surveillance and spite would have only hypotheses—nothing they could prove.

She didn't want to burn them, though. And was it fair of him to expect her to destroy good memories? After all, she'd buried a husband, a son, daughter-in-law and grand-daughter-in-law. Steeped in his own grief back then, Quinn hadn't considered the toll so many losses would take on a woman almost three times his age.

What did the jerk who'd gotten into April's computer really know, any way? Pondering that, Quinn dived, naked and still damp, under the comforter. He lay awake watching raindrops spatter with ever-increasing regularity against his bedroom window.

Toward morning he slept, no closer to any answers. Including what steps to take if his grandmother couldn't be talked out of going to France.

Luckily, the rain storm helped Quinn's cause. Flooded intersections snarled traffic and virtually shut down cities from Georgia to D. C. Quinn's court dates were postponed. Hayley's day camp was canceled. And all flights out of Dulles and Reagan National airports were delayed for hours, possibly a whole day.

Around eight o'clock, he joined his grandmother and Hayley for breakfast. Norma was arranging bacon on three plates that already had steaming waffles. "Instead of waiting,

I wish I'd packed a suitcase and booked the one seat available yesterday. A nonstop to Paris. How long is this storm going to interfere with air travel?" she fretted, pulling aside the kitchen curtain.

Quinn shrugged.

Hayley couldn't sit still. "I *love* puddles, Gram. I wanna go out and jump in them. Can I, Daddy, after breakfast?"

Quinn shuffled his utensils—made to feel guilty by his grandmother. "Sure, but it looks like I need to clean the gutters first. Eat up, then run to our house and get your boots and slicker. I'll come out after Gram and I have a private word."

"*Another* private talk?" Hayley propped her curly head in one hand, and assumed the injured air six-year-olds pulled off so well. "All you guys do anymore is talk, talk, talk."

Quinn dusted the tip of her nose with his napkin. "You're a lucky kid. You don't have to sit still and listen to all the boring stuff adults need to discuss."

She grinned, flung her arms around his neck and delivered a sticky kiss. "Talk fast, okay? I love you, Daddy 'n Gram."

"We love you, too," Quinn said, returning her hug. She scrambled down and crammed what remained of one waffle into her mouth. Pulling on a sweatshirt, she skipped out. They watched her through the window, happily jumping over rivulets of water in her running shoes.

"She's beautiful, Quinn. Before you lecture me again, dwell on that for a minute. Some of Hayley's heritage is in Germany. Not Italy."

Quinn extended his legs and laced his fingers across his stomach. "That's been on my mind every hour of every day since you gutted the history I thought I knew. Tell me, did Grandpa Tony's parents ever see my dad?"

"Thankfully, no. They married late in life. Tony was a change-of-life child. And quite a bit older than me. His parents died before our marriage. Anthony was an only child, and my brother, my only sibling, lost his life in the invasion of Normandy. We visited my mother and father twice, I think. As grandparents, they weren't very involved. Since they died in the early fifties, when Brett was only about four, there was no further opportunity for a relationship…."

"So there are two people left who are affected by this—Hayley and me. Do you want us to change our last name? Not that I'm saying we will, but—"

"Heavens, no! For all intents and purposes, Tony was Brett's father. Your grandfather."

"But Dad wasn't adopted, was he? He thought he was a Santini by birth. I know people were very bitter toward Germans after the war. Would you agree Dad was fortunate that things worked out the way they did?"

"Tony, more than I, understood that."

"Hmm. Have you considered how your life might have turned out if your plan with von Weisenbach had come to pass?"

"Yes. Often, in fact. Quinn, defectors provided us with much-needed information that helped win the war. Our government treated them with respect. As a colonel, I'm quite sure Heinz was privy to particulars that would've been useful." She waved a hand. "I know Tony said someone in our agency intercepted a message that said—that said his defection was false. In my state of distress, I accepted his reasoning, even though it went against every-thing I knew of Heinz. It still bothers me. Even with all the time that's passed, I can't rationalize why—if he was double-crossing us—our team ordered him shot rather than captured for interrogation."

"And you hope there's someone in France who can answer that question? What if you went to the CIA and asked to examine archived records from that time period?"

"I did that the year after Tony died. I couldn't be truthful about why I wanted to examine reams of formerly classi-fied material. I indicated that I'd witnessed an incident over which Tony and I disagreed. I said we had vastly differing memories and that although it was too late to prove anything to him, I wanted to satisfy myself. They bought it. A person who's worked in intelligence is often left with annoying puzzle pieces that need to fit before the agent or former agent can let it go."

"You didn't find the missing piece, and you haven't let it go."

"I found no communication out of France that even mentioned Heinz. Nor did he appear in a single one of the four microfilms of data shipped from the Marseilles office. Something that important, Quinn?"

Sitting up straighter, he planted his elbows on the table. "Wasn't communication pretty poor? I'd think a lot happened that no one wrote down. Especially if, as you said, spies were everywhere."

"I scrolled through a number of defections. I first learned that they passed through many layers of our agency and were signed off at very high levels, up to the presidency. Then they went back to the field office to handle the transfer. On Heinz, I'm telling you there wasn't a thing."

"Do you have any idea why?"

She shook her head, her eyes damp with tears. "That's what keeps nagging at me. Had I not witnessed every terrifying moment, I'd believe that entire part of my life was a dream. Or a nightmare."

"But Heinz did exist. Your proof is in the letters and photographs."

"Yes. And if they aren't enough, one has only to place Brett's college photo alongside the ones of Heinz. You pretended not to look, Quinn. I know you did, and you saw the similarities."

Unfolding himself from his chair, Quinn walked to the window facing the home he'd moved into after his parents and his wife had died in the plane crash. "I saw," he admitted grudgingly. And he'd spent every day since trying to block out the image. "I apparently inherited more Marsh characteristics. My mom used to say I resembled pictures of the brother you'd lost in the war."

"Sidney. You're pigheaded like him, too."

"Thanks a lot. I have to go, Gram. I see Hayley's got her rubber boots and rain slicker. She's ready to jump in puddles." He shrugged into his jacket and put on a baseball cap. "I'm asking you again to delay going on this quest until after the election in November. You know you can count on my word. I promise, no matter what, I'll make time to travel overseas with you. I owe it to Dad and Hayley to quit hiding my head in the sand."

"I hate waiting. At my age, three months can equal a lifetime. But I will, if you'll promise me one more thing."

"I promise." Quinn brought one hand to his heart.

"If, God forbid, anything should happen to me between now and then, I want your word that you'll still go and make an honest effort to locate Heinz's grave." Norma blinked rapidly, then began gathering up dishes. "I'd like to share something Heinz said to me the night Brett was conceived. He spoke of growing up in an orphanage unloved and unwanted. His greatest fear throughout his military career was that if he died for an evil cause, his punishment would be to lie for all time in an unmarked grave. I made a solemn pledge that as long as a single breath remained in me, I'd never let that happen. But…I did. Now I beg your help in keeping my vow."

Quinn felt his hand slide off the doorknob. "Gram, are you ill? What aren't you telling me?"

"Nothing, for heaven's sake. I'm in fine shape for a woman my age. Unfortunately, no one can predict when old bodies will fail. I'm not planning on leaving this planet between now and November, but every day I get out of bed these days is a gift from God. Is what I'm asking of my only grandson so impossible to grant?"

Quinn shook his head. "If I thought for one minute that you might be hiding some health problem, I'd say to hell with the campaign, I'd hand my upcoming court cases to Morris Greenburg and we'd go to France on the first available plane out. I'd even delay starting Haley in school next month so she could go along."

Tears leaked in earnest now from Norma's eyes. "Thank you." She made shooing motions with her apron, which she then used to wipe away her tears. "Go on, now. Hayley's getting rambunctious. Oh, no—she's trying to set up the ladder to help you clean gutters. Listen, Quinn, my vow to Heinz has waited for over sixty years. It can wait another three months."

"It's more like two. August is almost over. My upcoming fund-raiser is on the Labor Day weekend. The election's in the first week of November."

"Well, see? Time's flying. Go outside and pose with your daughter so I can take a picture. This storm is a windfall for Hayley. You so rarely have time to play with her."

Guilt coursed through Quinn. "I know my schedule's been crazy. Do you think I'm shortchanging Hayley?"

"You shouldn't ask for my advice. I'd probably look at you, think of Anthony and say you're shortchanging yourself. There's only one reason people crank up the speed on the treadmill of life—they're fleeing from... something."

Norma's voice trailed off as she crossed to stand by the window. Still, he couldn't forget what she'd said. Last night in the emptiness of his house, he'd admitted there was one thing missing in his life. A woman to love. Yet he'd tried to convince his grandmother to ignore what was missing in *her* life. All she required of him was his help in placing a few damned roses on some far-off grave.

Only...what if there was no grave? Bingo! That was what bothered him. April's casually dropped query the night before coiled in Quinn's mind like a cobra waiting to strike. Now that it had, Quinn panicked. What if Heinz *had* miraculously survived the shooting? There was every probability he wouldn't want to be found. Especially not by a former lover. An old enemy of Germany. A woman capable of delivering unwanted news. The man couldn't know he had descendants in America.

April had instituted a search and discovered two mentions of men named Heinz von Weisenbach, living in France. What were the odds of *that?* Unless von Weisenbach was like Smith or Jones, which he doubted. However, investigators had verified one match. And now someone else, someone here, possessed that information.

Quinn supposed he could continue April's search. If he could track down the Heinz in her report, and if the name Norma Marsh meant nothing to that man, then Quinn would stop worrying. Satisfied that he at least had a plan, he spent the next two hours sweeping gutters and chasing Hayley in and out of puddles, which she thought was great fun. They both got soaked and laughed like hyenas when Quinn slipped on some wet grass and rolled down the hill to land in a muddy puddle.

"Yuck, I'm completely wet. The rain's stopping now. Let's go in and change. If the streets are dry enough, we can go buy your school supplies."

"I liked the storm, Daddy." She wiped her wet face and pouted as they walked inside. "Because now you'll go back to being busy and forget all about me."

Her words shocked Quinn, but before he could decide how to respond, he noticed the message light on his phone. He took a moment to check and heard April's voice. "I put down the last tile and I'm about to mix grout. Guess who got stuck in my neighborhood and had to hike here to phone a tow truck? Eric. Quinn, he swears he's not my intruder. I wanted to let you know that. Also, my road isn't passable, so I guess tonight's off."

"Daddy, who is it?"

"April."

"Are you going to her place? Can I go, too?"

"Honey, she said there's water all over the road." Quinn deleted the message and hung up. "We'll take advantage of my free afternoon to go buy school supplies."

"Can April meet us at the store? I want *girl* supplies and I want her to help me choose."

"I think you're safe. School supplies are generic. So, you like April, huh?"

"A lot." Hayley bobbed her head. "Don't you?"

"Yeah, as a matter of fact. A lot," he mumbled under his breath as they went their respective ways to change. Quinn wondered if his feelings were returned. He wondered, too, if April was too trusting of Lathrop. Why, for instance, had he even been in her neighborhood?

Eric knew about the letters, and April said he salivated after a juicy story. She'd also brought up in passing that Eric had wangled tickets to Quinn's fund-raiser.

On Saturday, Lathrop just might get more than a plateful of hors d'oeuvres.

Because Quinn was nowhere near as trusting as April.

Chapter 9

Saturday, the flood waters had receded enough that life returned to normal. April wanted to let Quinn know that the county road that led to her house still had pockets of water, but was open to traffic. She had difficulty getting through to him on the numbers he'd given her. His cell and home phones were constantly busy.

After she'd tried numerous times, he answered his home office phone. "Santini," he said. "Okay, Jim, what's the final count?"

"Of birds, bees or sycamore trees?" April chuckled merrily.

"April? Sorry, I'm expecting a call from campaign head-quarters with an exact count of tickets for tonight. Our caterer's been given three different figures. We're talking a discrepancy of fifty people."

"That's quite a few. But this isn't your first event."

"It's the first of this size. The others have been town-hall meetings. We served coffee and cookies from a local bakery. At this stage, every penny's vital. How hard can it be to tally that figure?" he asked in frustration.

"You sound harried," she said. "Would it help if I drove myself to town and we met at the hotel tonight?"

"Is there some reason you'd rather not be seen walking in with me?"

"No! Quinn, how paranoid is *that?* We haven't spoken in three days. I just offered in case—oh, never mind. I'll be ready at eight. Isn't that what we agreed on?"

"Eight, yes," he muttered with a deep sigh. "If I sound paranoid, it's because I figured you'd heard that the press has been calling. They're demanding complimentary tickets. I remember how you felt about the last article."

"No wonder you're stressed. There'll be speculation if you bring a date and haven't done so before. Maybe we shouldn't do this, after all."

"Are you kidding? It's what's held me together all week. Nothing else has gone right. Let me count the ways. This fund-raiser has caused all kinds of problems. Then Hayley's going to be starting first grade on Tuesday and the school phoned to say they somehow missed the fact that she's short a set of immunizations. My trial that got postponed due to the weather was rescheduled for the same time as Hayley's doctor's appointment. Gram would've taken her, but she woke up yesterday with a head cold."

"You should have called me. I would've been happy to ferry Hayley to the doctor. Did you work it out? They won't let her into school if she's missing vaccinations."

"I appreciate the offer, April, but I got Ethel and Joseph

to take her. I bribed Hayley to be good for them by giving her money to buy the new *Kim Possible* DVD she's been wanting."

April laughed again. "I hope your phone isn't tapped. Bribery isn't a good thing to have on a would-be senator's record."

"Ha, ha! Wait until *you* have kids and you're faced with a desperate situation."

"I'd be a wash-out. I've never heard of the DVD Hayley wants. I guess I'll blame it on living in the sticks for nearly a year."

"That reminds me. Dare I ask about the condition of your road?"

"It's the reason I phoned. Your car will get muddy. If the second storm they're predicting hits, the creek will overflow again. I'm thinking of packing a bag and asking you to drop me at my folks' place after the fund-raiser."

"What are the odds of that storm hitting within the next twenty-four hours? I've been counting on us swinging by Frank's Barbecue after tonight's affair. Ever since you suggested ribs, I've practically been able to taste them."

"You just said your event includes catered food."

"If by food, you mean a stuffed olive stuck on a square of cheese or a shrimp speared with a toothpick, yes."

"Ah. Frank's it is. But fair warning. I plan to change out of my new dress first. And if you dig into the ribs without me, I may have to do you bodily harm."

"Rats, there goes my cell. Just as I was about to suggest some other, uh, bodily alternatives."

"Hold that thought," she teased. "Go catch your phone. See you at eight."

The phone went dead in Quinn's ear. Grabbing his cell, he was in decidedly better spirits. His stressful week faded away. He finished the call with his campaign manager and realized when he hung up that this was the first time he'd looked forward to one of the campaign events. Mostly he considered them necessary evils.

At seven, dressed in his best tuxedo, Quinn escorted Hayley to his grandmother's. Ethel had agreed to make chicken stew and a hot toddy for Norma, after which Norma planned to retire upstairs, and Ethel would watch a movie with Hayley until her bedtime.

"I have loads of pretty dresses, Daddy. Why can't I go to the hotel with you and April?"

Quinn noticed her protruding lower lip. "I've attended a dozen of these campaign events without you. Why this sudden desire to go tonight?"

"Gram said tonight's special 'cause you ordered April roses. You always say *I'm* your special girl. You don't buy me roses."

Quinn halted a few feet from his grandmother's back door. He shifted his daughter's favorite blanket and sleep-puppy into the hand that held a bag with her robe, slippers and pjs. He tipped up the quivering little chin so their eyes met. "A few days ago you said how much you liked April."

"Yeah, but I don't want her to be *that* special." The pout grew more pronounced.

Crouching in front of her, Quinn straightened Hayley's jacket and brushed back a strand of hair. "I love you more than anyone, Hayley. You'll always have the biggest piece of my heart. No one I meet will *ever* crowd you out. Which isn't saying it's always going to be just you and me in our family. Do you understand?"

"Gram's in our family. We love her."

He pushed to his feet again, frustrated by the stubborn glint in her eye. Hayley's pediatrician, one of Quinn's political supporters and a personal friend, had warned him a couple of years ago that if he put off dating much longer, he'd be facing his daughter's jealousy. He'd scoffed. And here it was.

Ethel stuck her head out the door. "Norma said she saw you leave your house five minutes ago. Did you lose something?"

"Hayley and I were having a father-daughter chat. The first of many, I suspect."

"Chat in here where it's warmer. Hayley, my girl, I made buttermilk biscuits. Better hurry in and take the ones you want while they're still hot."

"Biscuits. Yum. They're my favorite with chicken stew. Bye, Daddy. Tell April I'm going into first grade. My friend Tammy Sikes? Her mother said school has open house and we get to 'vite people to come and see what we draw and color. I don't know when it is, but I want April to come." The girl batted long eyelashes. "Maybe you can give me roses then, 'cause Tammy's mom said open house is special."

Quick as that, her fit of jealousy was over. It left Quinn thinking that he was going to need a woman's help in understanding his daughter's changing moods.

Relieved, Quinn went inside to drop off Hayley's things and to check on his grandmother's condition. He walked into the living room and found her clutching a tissue as she read a letter from the stack in her lap. *The letters from the wall.*

Norma made no attempt to hide the letters or her watery eyes. "You know what Heinz did that I miss most, Quinn?

Held my hand as we walked. He used to talk about the things he wanted to give me for our wedding. An ivory silk dress with a drop waist. Satin shoes. A three-layer cake with white sugar frosting. All rationed items. We both knew it was a fantasy. But with my hand in his, I believed in the possibilities." She smiled tearfully. "I doubt you think holding hands is such a grand romantic gesture."

Quinn set Hayley's stuff in the rocker. "Gram, why torture yourself like this?"

"It's not torture." She separated a dried rose from the packet of letters. "I'll see Heinz again one day. I feel it here." She closed her fist, still gripping a tissue, over her heart.

"Huh?" Quinn's body jerked. He felt a brief surge of anxiety—was she talking about death? Did she believe she'd die soon?

She smiled softly, as if she saw something Quinn didn't, and then confirmed his fear. "Maybe we won't meet in this life. He and I were aware that we'd fallen in love at a time when death waited around every corner. Love that strong surely crosses normal boundaries, don't you think? Did I mention that he had the most beautifully cultured voice? I loved listening, whether he read poetry to me in German, French or English."

"I have to go, or I'll be late to my fund-raiser," he muttered.

"You think I'm a foolish old woman. I'm not. You have a second chance to find the kind of love I'm talking about, Quinn. Don't squander a single minute on less than the real thing."

"What's that supposed to mean? That I shouldn't get involved with April? Or that I should?"

"It's not up to me. I hope you won't get mad if I say this,

but you let your head rule in your decision to marry Amy. She was a lawyer first and a wife second. I'm confident that you have enough of me in you, Quinn, that you'll recognize the difference a second time around. You'll choose a life partner with your heart, not your head."

He bent and dropped a kiss on her short white hair. "We'll talk later. Eat some of Ethel's stew, then get a good night's sleep. I'm glad Ethel's staying to keep an eye on you and Hayley. I don't know what time I'll get home. I promised April some real food afterward. I expect I'll be quite late, so I'll go directly to the cottage and then collect Hayley in the morning if that's all right."

His grandmother stared at him with an arched eyebrow. Quinn escaped before she could decide it was her duty to lecture him about safe sex. As if someone shouldn't have lectured *her* way back when, he thought sardonically—then chastened himself for reacting that way.

But once the prospect surfaced, Quinn checked his pockets to be sure he'd remembered to bring condoms. Just in case… He started the Lexus. On the drive to the florist, he reflected that preparing in advance stifled the spontaneity of lovemaking—and yet anything else would be irresponsible. Which brought up the question: would he even be here if the German colonel had other options one particular day?

Quinn didn't like thinking about von Weisenbach—the rose man. It irritated him enough that he was short with the clerk. "My name's *Santini*. Quinn Santini. I phoned in an order for a dozen pink roses. Is it too late to change my order? How about those purple flowers, instead?"

"Oh, you're *that* Santini." The flustered clerk studied him for a minute. "I must say you're nicer-looking in person than in your news photos. Er, excuse me." She blushed profusely. "Uh, these Dutch irises are out of season. They just arrived from our Holland grower. I hope they're for a special lady." She cast Quinn a coy glance as she nipped stems and arranged a bouquet with greenery and sprigs of tiny white flowers.

He shoved his hands in his pockets and glowered. She took the hint and went quietly about tying on a ribbon. Quinn checked his watch after he'd paid the bill and carried out the vase. What if April didn't like irises? Should he have stuck with roses? Damn, he hated the way this man, whom he'd never heard of until a few weeks ago, made him question his decisions, to say nothing of treating a defenseless clerk rudely.

He got to April's with five minutes to spare. Planning to park on the road and walk down her new driveway, he noticed that the tape she'd told him about had been removed. So he drove around the circle instead and parked directly in front of the house.

She opened her door before he rang the bell. A smiling vision in a dark purple gown held up by straps so thin they were practically nonexistent. The neckline plunged invitingly, creating an effect so tempting, Quinn could hardly force air into his lungs.

April pulled him inside and snapped her fingers in front of his eyes. He figured they were glazed and might even be crossed.

"For me? Wow, they're even more gorgeous than the gerbera daisies." She continued to admire his gift.

Quinn placed the tipping vase into her thankfully steadier hands. She turned to carry the flowers into the kitchen, and what little sanity he'd cobbled together slipped from his brain and landed—rock-hard—a few inches below his cummerbund. The reason—April's back was naked to slightly above her hips. Her dress was held together by crossed bands of fabric glittering with diamond-like jewels. Surely not real diamonds, Quinn thought inanely. Although, her only other adornment, a single strand necklace that lay close to her throat, and matching studs in each ear, sparkled like the real McCoy.

As soon as he was able to shake himself out of his stupor, he nudged the door shut and trailed after April.

She stepped back to examine the flowers after setting the vase on the table. "Those irises look perfect. I may have to keep a bouquet here once I list the house. What do you think?"

Quinn stretched his neck and tugged at his bow tie. "What's perfect-looking is you. You outshine the flowers."

Still wearing a soft smile, April took her time making a head-to-toe appraisal of him before she moved close, reached up and straightened his tie. "You don't look half bad yourself, Mr. G.Q. If you don't meet the fancy of the media's fashion mavens tonight, the likes of Tori St. Clair should get their eyes examined."

Quinn realized why April Trent was the first woman in years to hold his interest. He was attracted by her looks, but even more so by the way she remained oblivious to compliments. He found it a rare and refreshing trait.

She gave his tie a last pat and headed out of the kitchen. "Let me collect my handbag and wrap, and we can be underway in nothing flat. Can't have the guest of honor waltzing in late. Especially not the first time you take a lady. If we show up late tonight, wouldn't *that* be a field day for the media?"

"I suppose it's not a good thing if someone running for pubic office expresses negative opinions about the media. Given the constitutional right to free speech and all."

Grinning, April passed Quinn her wrap, a long velvet cape. She turned so he could arrange the cape over her bare shoulders. "Why, thank you, Mr. Almost Senator."

"You look like royalty in this outfit. Makes me think that if you wave your dainty little hand and say *off with his head*, yours truly is history."

"Dainty?" She gave a little snort. "These hands are calloused from swinging a hammer. It's a cinch you've never laid tile. My fingers are raw from the grout chemicals."

He tied her cape securely with twin satin cords. Lifting her hands, he inspected them, front and back. Then he pressed a kiss in the center of each palm and closed her poor battered fingers around them.

The pupils of her eyes dilated and flickered darkly. April's lips parted. Had a clock in the kitchen not chimed the quarter hour, they would've been lost in a kiss by then.

Quinn sighed and frowned at his watch.

April worked a hand through the side slit in her cape and hooked his elbow. "Keep that thought, Quinn. We'll save it for when you bring me home."

"Am I bringing you home? You said you might stay with your folks tonight."

"Not if three weather channels are right about the storm skirting the coast instead of blowing inland."

They went out and he locked the door with a key she handed him. They both twisted the knob, to make sure the door had locked.

Conspiratorial smiles on the way to his car said they understood each other. That they both looked forward to sharing kisses—and more—after they'd dispensed with the boring task ahead. And this time if anyone entered April's home, there'd be no question that the intruder possessed a key.

They touched on a variety of subjects on the drive to the hotel. Quinn found it interesting that April had always felt like the odd person out in the Trent family. "If I didn't have so many of my grandmother Dixie's traits," she said, "I'd swear I was stolen off someone's doorstep. And Miles and Roger fed my insecurity when we were kids by telling everyone in the neighborhood I was adopted."

Her admission had a profound effect on Quinn. If it wasn't for the fact that they were half a block from the hotel, he was sure he would've confided the troubling truth about his dad's paternity. But a minute later, they were in a line of cars waiting to unload passengers under the hotel's brightly lit portico. April clasped nervous fingers on the padded dash.

"Relax," he murmured, dredging up the consummate politician's smile for the young man serving as valet. The kid raced around the hood and all but bowed and scraped as he flung open Quinn's door.

"Please attend to my guest first, David." Quinn passed him the key to the Lexus as he slid out. "David's a volunteer with my campaign when he's not working here," he told April.

The young man stumbled over his feet as he dashed back to April's side. He was so obviously bowled over once he got a look at his boss's guest, the poor kid dropped the keys and had to scramble under the car to retrieve them.

April and Quinn were both acutely aware of shock

waves preceding their walk up the marble stairs and over to where wraps were checked prior to entering the ballroom. Talk briefly stopped and then began again in their wake. It rose markedly in volume after Quinn untied April's cape, handed it to a checker and pocketed the ticket stub.

He caused a second stir when he placed a warm, proprietary palm on the bare, triangular spot just below April's natural waistline. Quinn acted nonchalant, but it seemed to take him an hour to guide her out of the lobby and into a room filled mostly with Santini supporters, plus press and a few opponents. Supporters cheered and the mood shifted, growing lighter.

Still, April felt like a biology specimen under a microscope. Had Quinn's hand not anchored her to his side, she could never have made that stroll through the packed room.

Ever the gentleman, Quinn introduced her to huddles of two and three who yakked a mile a minute while juggling drinks and plates. April was grateful she didn't have to shake anyone's hand, hers was so cold and clammy.

Then a man she recognized, Dennis Granger, a onetime client of her dad's, placed his rotund body directly in her path. "April Trent? You're here with Santini?" Granger had a booming voice. "Won't that just make your daddy turn purple. Sorta like the color of your dress, little lady." His guffaw projected as loudly as his voice. Dennis clapped Quinn on the back. "Ever think maybe she's a clever plant, Quinn? I saw Miles Trent leaving a bar last week. When I went in, the first person I saw was Paul Benson of the *News Register*—and the only empty seat was next to him. I took it and asked what he had to smile about. Paul insinuated that he's sitting on an explosive story guaranteed to bring down my choice for senator. That's you, my man."

Quinn and April gaped at Granger, then each other.

Others immediately paused to listen. One of the people who edged forward was Eric Lathrop. Spotting him, April stopped him with a glare. "Eric, you toad. Just what are you planning to do with the information you stole from my computer? Tell me, or I'll call the cops."

Eric turned shades of red. "I didn't touch your computer. I'm not sure who did, but I'll admit Granger's right—Benson thinks he's onto something huge. He knows you're hanging with Santini, so he cut me out of the loop. The bastard keeps saying I blew my chance to write the story after you found those letters and I didn't nab them. Anyway, I'm not here for the *Register*. I was let go yesterday, April. If you want to scoop Paul, give me the story. I'll freelance the article uptown. The odds are always in a candidate's favor if he breaks his own scandal."

April felt Quinn's fingers dig into her arm. The look on his face gave her pause. Yet all he did was crook a finger at two security guards. Both big guys, they flanked Eric on either side. "Lathrop, this event is for supporters. If you bought a ticket, we'll refund your money."

Quinn jerked his thumb and the guards hustled Eric out. All the while, he bounced up on his toes, locking eyes with April. "I can help. Call me."

The low hum of voices in the room rose again after the doors shut behind Eric. He continued to introduce her, acting for all the world as if nothing had happened.

She discovered two things in the next few hours. Quinn's supporters were loyal. And every woman in the room, young, old, married or single, envied her. Eventually she was able to put aside the threat of Benson, relax and absorb an endless list of reasons the people in this room backed Quinn over Dan Mattingly any why they gave him their money and their trust.

"Bye, April," several campaign office workers called as the evening wound to a close and they were filing out. "Drop by headquarters if you have some time to stuff envelopes or knock on doors. The next six weeks is crucial."

April waved. "Maybe I will. Our state needs him to win."

The minute David, closed her into the Lexus, she folded her cape around her pencil-slim dress and kicked off her spike heels. Bending, she massaged her toes. "Who would've thought glad-handing would be so hard on the feet?"

In the dark interior of the car, after they left the brightly lit hotel behind, April thought Quinn had fallen into a bad mood, brooding about something. They hit the outskirts of town, and it was patently obvious that he'd withdrawn from small talk.

She was surprised when he swung into the drive-through at Frank's Barbecue. She surged out of the slump she'd retreated into. "No need to stop here on my account, Quinn, since you're mad at me for some reason." That reason could have to do with Eric. Or worse, her brother Miles...

"At you? No, I'm mad at the circumstances." At the drive-through window, Quinn gave their order after consulting with April. They drove to the next window, where he paid and collected their food. He spoke to the top of her head, because she'd opened the sack and had her nose buried in it, checking their order. The spicy aroma of southern barbecue filled the car.

"I'm contemplating dropping out of the race," Quinn said casually.

Astonished, April flung up her head. Frantically, her fingers rolled the sack shut. *"Pardon?"* She couldn't conceal her shock. "Because of that dumb verbal brawl I had with Eric? Quinn, no. I shouldn't have reacted like I did. But what Dennis Granger said about Benson made me think Eric had lied. Now I'm back to not knowing who broke into my house. I don't want to think Miles did it, even though he's tight with Benson."

"The way you flew to my defense meant a lot to me. M-my reason is…hell, things are a mess." He avoided looking at her, staring at the well-lit freeway.

She waited for him to continue, but he left the highway and turned on the county road without clarifying. "You can't give up, Quinn. You'll disappoint a lot of folks."

"Yeah. Well, the big story Dennis and Eric alluded to stands to hurt my whole family." Propping his left elbow on the window ledge, Quinn raked his fingers through his recently cut blond hair. "I'd let them drag me through the muck, but Gram's old and Hayley is innocent."

"You've lost me, Quinn." April clasped his knee. "Did… you, ah, have an aff…affair while you were married? Is that what this is about?"

"Not me. Gram. With the man from those damned letters." Quinn slowed to make the swing into April's drive. A brief flash of moonlight revealed the extent of his anguish. "Anthony Santini isn't my real grandfather," he said slowly. "Von Weisenbach…is."

Quinn stepped on the brake and brought the Lexus to a shuddering halt. The air between him and April crackled as if this wasn't a placid night, but one charged with lightning.

"I heard you, but—" she shook her head "—I don't understand."

"It's my fault for dumping this. I've tried like hell to deny it's true. After Lathrop's hints…well, I believe Paul Benson knows." Quinn opened his door, slid out and circled the car to assist April. She let him, which showed him how rattled she was. Her hand shook as she searched her handbag for her keys.

"I'm betting Paul's waiting, like the snake he is, to print the story when it'll hurt me most." He took her key, opened her front door and handed back the key. "Give me the ribs before you drop them," he said, noticing her unsteadiness. "Do they need reheating?"

"I've lost my appetite, I'm afraid. The ribs will keep in the fridge. I, ah, need to change, anyway." She fumbled with her cape.

Leaving her for a moment, Quinn snapped on a kitchen light and went to store the food. When he returned, he saw she hadn't yet untied the cords holding her cape. He gathered her hands between his and as he kissed her knuckles, his steady regard remained on her ashen face.

"If my brother Miles is involved," she said, biting her lip, "it would explain why there was no forced entry. I have his old laptop, so accessing my e-mail account wouldn't pose a problem."

"We're not even sure if there were one or two people in the car that tore past us that night. I thought it was Eric, but Benson's hair color is similar to his and they both wear glasses."

April was finally able to fling off her cape. She dropped

it on the only chair in an unfurnished living room. "I brought this down on you." A low cry escaped. "Eric saw the letters. He went to his boss. Paul Benson and Miles are old friends. Fraternity brothers. Oh, Quinn, how can you ever forgive me?"

"Shh. There's enough blame to go around." He ran warm hands up and down her bare arms. They stood inches apart. Neither moved, then suddenly tension arced between them and erupted in the desire they'd banked earlier.

"Quinn?"

He pulled her into a tighter embrace.

"This has been brewing since the night you brought me daisies," she whispered, snuggling into his arms.

"I came prepared tonight." He kept her slender body plastered to his while he dug in his tux pocket and pulled out some sealed packets.

The heated look in April's eyes was all the consent he needed. She tugged open his bow tie, undid the top two buttons of his pleat-front dress shirt and pressed her lips to his drumming pulse.

"Where?" Desperation exploded in a voice grown hoarse. Quinn's body had begun to shake as April popped the studs on his shirt and nuzzled in the opening with teasing lips. She let him feel the weight of her breasts. His smile spread provocatively across his mouth. "No drapes or carpet in here. Bedroom?"

She wriggled out of his seeking hands.

Blindly, he followed the sparkle of her dress straps down the hall, all the while thinking she was right—this *had* been brewing since the night she'd threatened to call the cops on him. She was gutsy, and he liked gutsy women.

In the glow cast by a night-light in the base of her bedside lamp, she dispensed with his troublesome jacket and cummerbund.

"I can't figure out how you got into this dress," he muttered.

She showed him the hidden buttons, which he unfastened in a matter of seconds. He breathed out a satisfied sigh when at last she stood before him in black lace panties and her diamond choker.

"Here, I'll get rid of this." April reached up to remove the necklace.

He stayed her hand. Quinn was through talking. Impatiently he stripped off his underwear and hers, and almost before she'd yanked back the covers exposing cool ivory sheets, he pulled her on top of them. He was grateful to see that he hadn't forgotten how to love a woman. Not just *any* woman. April. Her skin tasted like sweet almond. Her sighs of delight were poetry to his ears.

With gestures, not words, she urged him to rip open a pack and to feel her readiness.

Quinn changed their positions to make a good thing last longer. His hands spanned her hips, and together they moved faster and faster until their control broke simultaneously.

She collapsed across him. "What a wonderful ride," she murmured, raising herself to kiss him.

Quinn stroked her hair, unable to express his feelings. When his body and brain floated back together, he managed to mutter, "Too short."

"Um, so we'll call it a trial run."

"I like the sound of that." He continued to graze her back with the tips of his fingers. "April, my marriage was never like this. Amy…I——we weren't impulsive. When Gram talked about how she and *that man* got carried away, I was angry. I thought she should've shown more self-restraint." Lifting April's chin, Quinn said, "Tonight, the way I wanted you… Let me say I understand Gram a lot better."

"Good. So, have you changed your mind about walking away from the race?"

"I don't know what to do." He slid up so his back was supported by pillows, and brought her against his side. He began haltingly, but his words gained momentum as Norma's story tumbled out. He continued to stroke April's skin, and she did the same to his. She reserved her questions until he was finished.

"What exactly do you think Paul got from my preliminary search? He might be bragging that it's a big story, but he can't know what you just told me. And, if Norma's colonel died in 1944…does he really have anything at all?"

"You asked me a question before. What if he's *not* dead?"

April scrambled up, tucked the sheet around her and grabbed her laptop.

"What are you doing?" Quinn was slower to move.

"Maybe Paul's simply guessing that some impropriety took place. If the Heinz I unearthed, the landscape designer, is the man Norma had her fling with, I doubt he'd blab about it to total strangers. You, though, are connected to someone he used to love. If I can find his phone number, Quinn, call and see how much mischief Eric's editor has done. I swear, if Miles is in on this, I'll never speak to him again."

She tapped into her e-mail. One popped up from an anonymous sender, someone who'd written I Am Watching

You. A background of swastikas intertwined with roses made them both gasp. "Who could've sent this—without a name?"

"Anyone using the public library computers."

Quinn read the message aloud. "*Drop Santini. His family are Nazi lovers.* Well, does that answer part of your question? They've found…something."

In an instinctive act of revulsion, April deleted the offensive page. "Okay, look, I bookmarked a site—for a landscaper by the name of Heinz von Weisenbach."

"Landscaper? Didn't I say Gram's Heinz grew roses in pots on his balcony and always brought her fresh flowers? I think you might have found our man," he said, sounding glum.

Frowning, April turned her laptop toward Quinn and handed him her bedside phone. "That's not proof. Norma's sure her Heinz died. Call this one. Here's home and office numbers. What time is it in France?" They calculated, and after a couple of false starts, Quinn punched in a string of numbers. "What'll I say?"

"Start with your name and where you live."

"Hello. Have I reached Heinz von Weisenbach? My name is Santini. I live in the U.S. I, ah—you know someone in America by that name?" To April, Quinn mouthed, *This guy doesn't sound old enough to have known Gram.*

"Santini?" the voice at the other end snarled. "My father hasn't heard a word from you in years. He thought you were dead. What kind of trouble are you trying to cause now? Last week when that newsman phoned, it sent Papa on a wild goose chase."

Quinn's grip on the phone tightened. "I'm *Quinn*

Santini. Was the man your father knew called Anthony? If so, he's my grandfather, and he is deceased."

The man on the phone spoke English with a French accent. "I don't know what this is about. I only know I'm trying to landscape gardens for a prominent resident, and Papa...my father, Heinz, decided to buy a plane ticket from Paris to Washington, D.C. I can't afford to have him *and* my son gone, but neither could I let him go off alone. So Marc, my son, is also on his way to America."

"They're coming here?" Quinn jumped off the bed, oblivious of his nakedness. "Can you stop them? I'm not sure you understand. My grandmother knew your father, or I think she did. If he shows up unannounced, it'll be a huge shock. And a bigger inconvenience," Quinn muttered.

"If her name is Norma Marsh, Papa thought she died trying to escape France during the war. Alas, it's too late for me to stop them. Papa and Marc were to leave from Orly an hour ago." Heinz rattled off a flight number and the time of their arrival at Reagan National Airport in D.C.

Quinn sank down on the bed, his eyes frantically seeking April's. "Who's supposed to pick him up? Paul Benson or...Miles Trent?" He said the last name with hesitancy.

"Papa spoke with Mr. Benson, who wanted to wire plane fare. Papa said Benson hedged too much to suit him. My father's no fool. He handled tricky situations for your military during the war. So well, may I add, that your government bestowed on him a Distinguished Service Medal." The man spoke so loudly April heard every word.

She'd mistakenly discounted the man who'd received that medal as the wrong Heinz von Weisenbach. Apparently they were one and the same, which was even more confusing.

Quinn transferred the phone to his other ear. "I'm no closer to making sense of this than you are, Mr. von Weisenbach. I damn well intend to get answers, though. Trust me, it's not a good idea for your dad and son to link up with Paul Benson. I'll do my best to meet them first. If I miss them, or you hear from them, please ask them to phone my cell." Quinn gave his number. He repeated it to make sure the man got it right.

Hanging up, Quinn reached for his pants and shirt. "You heard? Heinz is coming here. He and his grandson arrive tomorrow afternoon." He shook his head. "I guess that's *this* afternoon."

"It's surreal, Quinn. How will you break the news to Norma?"

He buttoned his shirt and paced up and down the room. "I don't intend to. At least not yet. I'll meet his plane and find out why—if he was so madly in love with her—he let sixty years go by with no attempt to verify her death."

"It's so sad. They each thought the other had died."

Slinging his jacket over one shoulder, Quinn bent to kiss April. "I'll ask Ethel to stay with Hayley. Will you meet me in town and ride with me to the airport?"

"Are you sure you want me there?"

"I've never been more sure of anything."

"Okay, then. I'll see you out and lock up." Sliding off the bed, she went to the closet and pulled out a quilted robe and slippers.

On the porch, Quinn indulged in a last goodbye kiss that was interrupted by the noise of a gunning car engine.

They jerked around toward the road and saw a car speed off into the night.

"That's Eric's car," April said, brow furrowed. "Quinn, be careful, okay?"

He cupped her face in both hands. "I don't like him keeping tabs on us. I'll wait while you dress and come with me."

"I'll have to shower first."

A slow smile warmed features that had turned harsh. "In that case, I'll join you." He stepped back into the house and shut the door.

Chapter 10

"As long as you're staying, Quinn, why don't we dive into those ribs before heading off to shower? I'm starved, and the ribs are pretty messy."

"I could be talked into breakfast in bed."

They sat naked and cross-legged with a tray between them. April served ice-cold beer from a six-pack she'd bought for the occasion. "I shouldn't ask, but have you ever done anything that feels so decadent?" she asked, giggling as she wiped sauce off her chin and Quinn licked off a blob that fell on her breast.

He nibbled his way up her neck to her earlobe. "Believe it or not, I was a serious kid in high school and college. You're a bad influence," he said, grinning. Which was even funnier to both of them, given that each had sauce spread from ear to ear.

"Time to hit the shower so I can corrupt you further, counselor." Her eyes smoldered with promise as she set the tray aside and slid off the bed.

They emerged from the shower after using up all the hot water. Quinn toweled April's dripping hair. "Where's your hair dryer?" he asked after he paused to kiss her.

She had difficulty focusing on anything as mundane as drying her hair, because Quinn continued to kiss her in ways that left her weak. April wasn't even sure she had strength left to lift a hair dryer.

He gave a brief bow, and she waved off his formal gesture. "I'm offering my services," he said. Holding her at arm's length, Quinn trailed a hand along her shoulder and made shivery spirals down her arm with cool fingertips. "For drying hair," he added with a wicked half grin. "I'm all tapped out, otherwise."

"Me, too," she said, loving the erotic brush of his damp skin against hers. "I vote we grab an hour or so of sack time—for sleep." She passed him a portable dryer she took from a drawer. Stifling a yawn, she smiled as he turned on the dryer and played it over her hair. "I wonder, do your constituents fully appreciate the many talents you could put on your résumé?"

"Believe me, eating in bed and leisurely showers are not my norm. With a kid who wants food the minute she wakes up, I'm lucky to get five minutes under the spray." He laughed, and the towel tied loosely around his hips began to slip. Quinn passed her the hair dryer and tightened the knot before he again aimed the nozzle at April's head.

She almost purred as his fingers followed the flow of air. "I know it's not environmentally responsible to use so much hot water. But let's consider it a special event—something to remember on the days we're taking speedy showers."

Quinn kissed her dry hair. "You make me laugh, and I can't tell you how good that feels. Being with you like this is the best thing that's happened to me in…years. I've been on a constant treadmill since starting this campaign."

She put the dryer away and got out a fresh sheet to replace the one splotched with barbecue sauce. Deftly making the switch, she set the alarm, giving them until 5:00 a.m., then dived under the covers. "I feel I need to apologize again for inadvertently allowing Eric to see your grandmother's letters. I had no idea…."

"How could you possibly know what they meant—or what he'd do?" Quinn turned off the light, slid down and held her in his arms. "I'm just grateful you returned them to Gram. Other people might've sold them to the highest bidder."

"You're okay? You weren't at first."

With one hand he steadied her head and kissed her hard. By the time the kiss ended, they were both breathless. "We'll never get any sleep if you keep *that* up," she murmured.

"I know. But I want to convince you that I don't blame you. Or Gram. Although I can't say I wouldn't be happier if this von Weisenbach character hadn't turned up."

"You don't mean that, Quinn," she said, touching his lips in the dark. "Aren't you a bit curious to meet him? You share his blood, after all."

Quinn sighed and reached for her again. "There are a lot of…unanswered questions."

She yawned against his chest. Several minutes later she said in a sleepy voice, "I refuse to believe that disgusting e-mail and what it implied about Norma. I also refuse to believe that Miles played any part in sending it. We were raised to respect everyone. Oh, I know my dad and Miles didn't like losing a case to you, and I can see them funding your opponent. But I promise that neither Dad nor Miles would *ever* condone these tactics. That e-mail went beyond malicious mischief."

"I agree. But I am worried. Who's to say that the man on his way here—ostensibly to reconnect with my grandmother—isn't a war criminal who managed to slip under the radar?"

"Quinn! Norma wouldn't have fallen in love with a traitor. She loved and trusted Heinz."

"Yeah, well, Dad and I loved and trusted her. But she let us live a lie, didn't she?"

April had no comment, and in no time at all they fell asleep.

A scant few hours later, they woke up and stumbled out of bed when the alarm sounded. In the dark April managed to find jeans and a long-sleeved knit shirt. When she entered the bathroom Quinn turned on the light. He put on his badly wrinkled tuxedo.

Neither made any effort to resume making love. Their interlude was over. April knew that his mind, like hers, was on other things—leaping ahead to the important meeting at the airport later in the day.

Refreshed and wearing clean clothes, she watched Quinn tie his dress shoes. She'd stuffed her jeans into knee-high leather boots. "Wow, anyone who sees us will be able to tell what *we* did after leaving your benefit."

Straightening, he brushed his knuckles over a whisker burn that had reddened her chin. "Maybe I don't care."

"And maybe that's how your grandmother feels about having loved van Weisenbach. Quinn, I know from what you said last night that you're deeply hurt. I can't, in all honesty, identify with how you feel. Betrayed, I imagine. But earlier you said you'd begun to understand how Norma could let things get out of hand. We're all human, and humans aren't perfect by a long shot."

"No, but when they make mistakes, they should take responsibility for their actions." He briefly closed his eyes. "I recently had a version of this conversation with Hayley. Lord," he said as they placed last night's dishes into the dishwasher and prepared to leave the house, "how do you tell a kid your great-grandmother told a major lie, but it's not okay for you to do the same?"

"I don't think you have to worry, Quinn. You've done an excellent job of raising Hayley. She's happy, charming and outgoing."

"Oh, she can be willful and stubborn."

"Then I've only seen her on her best behavior." April collected her jacket from the closet. "Which brings up another point. Considering it's just after 6:00 a.m., how are you going to explain my presence so early in the morning? Will that upset her?"

"If you'd asked me that question a week ago, I'd have shrugged it off. Today I can't be so cavalier. We had a display of jealousy before I left home to pick you up yesterday evening. She senses that you're the first woman since her mom who's special to me. That's how she put it, in fact. She wants to be the special one in my life."

April stepped close to Quinn at the car. "I'm glad you told me. A child's ego is fragile. Maybe we ought to take separate vehicles. Instead of going home with you now, I can meet you at the airport or in town."

"No—let's go together."

"For moral support?"

"I haven't got any idea how I'll identify the right men. Not to mention avoiding Paul Benson. Nor have I figured out how to get answers without starting a brawl."

"Whatever else Heinz might be, Quinn, he's an old man. His son cares enough about him to leave their business shorthanded while the grandson accompanies him. Does that put you in mind of anyone? I mean you," she said when he looked blank. "Who didn't want Norma flying off to France by herself?"

April lifted one eyebrow pointedly.

"Get in," he said, having opened her door. "Oh, you brought your laptop." He chuckled wryly. "A little late— like locking the door after the cow got out. Do you want to carry it around with you, or shall I lock it in the trunk?"

"I don't know. Now I wish I hadn't dumped that awful e-mail. It's hard to confront anyone without evidence. But…you're the lawyer. Why didn't you tell me to hang on to the proof?"

"I was just as shocked as you were. But if it becomes necessary we can have the message recovered from your deleted e-mails." He frowned. "Paul Benson is well aware of the damage he could do to my political career by merely hinting that my grandparents were linked in some way to a man who wore a Nazi uniform."

"No one saw his photograph, except for you, Norma

and me." She climbed into the car and tossed her laptop in the back seat. He followed, and suddenly April grabbed Quinn's arm, alerting him to the hoot of an owl.

He examined their surroundings. A meadowlark warbled off to their right. An answering call nearer the house startled a rabbit, who hopped for cover. "Something I noticed last night," he said in a low voice, shutting his door as carefully as possible, "is how quiet it is out here. No city sirens. No hum of traffic. I can see why Gram balked at moving into town. Do you mind telling me your asking price?" he said unexpectedly. "It occurred to me that Gram might like to live out the rest of her days back here. Not that I don't think she has plenty of years left. It's… I want her to be happy."

"That's sweet, Quinn. But what if Heinz flies in, sweeps her off her feet again and whisks her away to live in France?" She laughed when he cringed.

"She's eighty-two, for God's sake!"

"So? Why else would a man drop everything to come halfway around the world?"

"Don't imagine it's out of love." Quinn snorted and stepped on the gas. "He obviously didn't pine away for her. The guy got married. He has a son and a grandson."

April tugged her jacket collar up around her chin. "I suppose I am romanticizing the long-lost-love idea. I grew up loving fairy tales. Don't you read to Hayley about a handsome prince galloping in on a white charger to claim his true love forever more?"

"I explain that those stories are utter fantasy."

"Spoilsport. Okay, Quinn, I'll give you a price on the house as soon as the market analysis comes in. I've had one inquiry from the newlywed son of a former customer. But

I do rather like the thought of the farm going back to its original owner. If you're serious, I'll see if I can work up a quote in a couple of days. This is strictly business. I can't take a contingency offer and wait for you to sell Norma's home. I need my money out in order to buy that place in Alexandria I told you about."

"Right. I expressed an interest in a unit. But if I drop out of the race, I won't need to move closer to the beltway. I'll find a smaller place in Turner."

She gave him a black look. "I'd hoped you'd rejected that idea. How can you let slime like Paul Benson scare you off?"

Quinn opened his mouth to answer, but April's cell phone rang. She pulled it from her leather handbag, checked the readout and frowned. "It's my mother. I wonder what's wrong. She never phones this early." As if expecting bad news, April breathed out a tentative, "'Lo, Mom?"

"April, dear. I knew you'd be up at the crack of dawn, even though I understand you had a late night last night."

Quinn heard laughter very like April's before she punched a button and turned off the speaker portion of her phone. "Really? And who told you that?"

She rolled her eyes, and it was all Quinn could do not to burst out laughing. If her mother only knew how they'd spent the night....

"Dear, a mother doesn't give away her sources," she said briskly. "It's been months since we had time to sit and chat. I realize this is short notice, but I have a spa appointment with Monique at eight. How about coming into town to meet me for breakfast at that new place off Court Square."

April hesitated, again sharing consternation with Quinn, who merely shrugged. Running a hand through the curls he'd blown dry after their shower, April made her decision. "Fine, Mother. I'll meet you in, say, half an hour? And will you bring me the spare key to the farmhouse? Next week, the carpets go in. I plan to market it soon after."

"You've finished the work? Congratulations! I remember the dinner party where you told us you'd bought it. The same night Cole introduced you to Eric Lathrop. Um, I hear that's not working out."

"No, it's not. So Eric's your secret source on my social life, huh? I'll be interested to hear his version of events. Bye, Mom. Don't forget the key." She closed her phone and fell back against the seat. "Would you mind dropping me off at the Square?" She faced him and touched his arm.

Quinn leaned over to steal a quick kiss. "I don't mind at all. Shall we park and I'll walk you into the restaurant wearing in my tuxedo from last night?" He flipped the bow tie that hung loose around the open throat of his very wrinkled dress shirt.

"Hmm." She ran her fingers over his stubble. "Don't tempt me. But I'll pass. Neither of us needs *that* kind of rumor on top of the others that might be lurking in the wings. Mom obviously heard I'm on the outs with Eric, and that I went to your fund-raiser. She's on a fishing expedition. Otherwise she wouldn't have pressed Monique to set up a Sunday-morning spa treatment."

"I wondered about that."

"They're best friends who met at Smith College. Monique is really Myrna Goldman. She owns a chain of elite spas. She'll call in a couple of manicurists and masseuses, who'll give my mother and Myrna the works." April inspected her hands. "You have no idea how glad I am that I filed my nails so they wouldn't snag on the velvet dress I wore last night. Otherwise, Mother would nag me to join her for a manicure."

"If she'd seen you in that dress, she wouldn't nag." Quinn smiled secretively, kissed his fingertips and opened them to the air. "You were *magnifique*."

"And nuts. I'm glad you liked the dress, though. Robyn goaded me into trying it on and well, it shouted, *buy me!* I'll admit a little voice inside me said *wear that dress and Tori what's-her-name won't say you're a fashion victim.*"

Quinn laughed, handling the wheel easily with his left hand, his right hand on the back of April's neck. "It was my good fortune that you let Tori what's-her-name get your dander up. I'll drop you on the Square, go home and change, check on Hayley and Gram, and arrange for Ethel to stick close to the house today. How long do you need for breakfast with your mom? Shall I pick you up in an hour? We can spend some time figuring out how to approach the problem at the airport."

"Nine's good. But it'd help if you didn't think of Heinz as a problem but as an old friend of your grandmother's. A friend of Norma and Tony's. If you go all hostile on him, why would he want to clear up any mystery?"

"As usual, you're right." He slowed the car for another kiss. "That's why I need you with me, April. Guys tend to approach uncomfortable situations with a sledgehammer. Women pull out an olive branch."

"Not always. In this case, though, what you want is facts. Quinn…something else. Please don't be so hasty about pulling out of the Senate race. What's a few days? Maybe this thing with Paul Benson is much ado about nothing."

Quinn had pulled to the curb to let her out across from the restaurant.

He nodded slowly. "You have a point. I should know within minutes after meeting von Weisenbach whether he has plans to throw in his lot with Benson and Mattingly."

"Exactly." She glanced around; she was getting pretty good at checking for stray reporters. The street seemed clear, so she leaned over and delivered a kiss hot enough to burn his shoes. Drawing back, she opened the door and vaulted lightly out, then poked her head in and said, "One hour. I'll be waiting right here to hitch a ride."

He reached for her, but she shut the door and strutted confidently across the street. April was aware that Quinn's eyes were following the exaggerated sway of her hips. He didn't try to pull away from the curb until she'd arrived at the restaurant door and signaled him with a cheery wave.

Her most fervent hope as she entered the city's newest, trendiest eatery was that she'd beat Bonnie Trent and be seated before she showed up. No such luck. Quite the opposite; her mother had a ringside seat—right by the window.

Rising, Bonnie turned an unlined cheek for the requisite kiss.

"Mother. You're early. You must've been on your way to town when you phoned." April unbuttoned her jacket before she sat.

Bonnie signaled the waiter, all the while unnerving April with her scrutiny. "I'm annoyed that I am the *very last* in this family to learn that you're keeping company with the most talked-about sought-after junior Senatorial candidate." April's mother snapped open her menu and motioned impatiently for a hovering waiter to fill April's coffee cup. The moment he left, Bonnie leaned forward. "Roger's concerned. As is Miles. His friend at the *News Register* refused to give Santini's fund-raiser any press. However…" Reaching into her spa bag, Bonnie pulled out a folded newspaper—the *Register*'s rival. In the center of page one was a full-length photograph of Quinn with his arm draped possessively across April's almost backless dress.

She spewed coffee all over the picture.

Bonnie daintily stirred cream in her coffee. "I've always known there was a swan hidden beneath those ugly duckling clothes you insist on wearing." She raised her cup and clicked it gently against April's before she sipped. "I don't care who the man is," she said, lowering the cup. "I'm just glad he's special enough to put roses in your cheeks. I assume he's the one who dropped you off across the street. From the spring in your step, I trust he passes muster in bed."

"Mo…ther!" April gripped her cup in both hands. She could feel heat raging up her neck as she darted covert glances around to see if anyone nearby was listening to Bonnie's outrageous comments.

The waiter zipped over. In her usual high-handed manner, April's mother ordered healthy vegetarian meals for them both. With the waiter gone, Bonnie shook out her napkin. "April, what century are you living in? Mothers and daughters discuss sex freely and openly these days."

April couldn't imagine it. She scored the creamy linen tablecloth with her fork. "This isn't the lecture I expected. I thought you'd be defending Eric."

Bonnie added more cream to her cup. A gold wrist

bangle jingled. "Miles brought him to a dinner party to round out our numbers. For a few weeks, Miles, Paul and Eric were joined at the hip. The other day, though, I overheard Miles talking to your dad. I gather your brother's feeling uneasy about some deal of Paul's."

"No kidding. I hope my dear brother feels too guilty to sleep or eat. I asked you to bring the key to the farmhouse because I think he let Paul Benson have it to search my home for a packet of old letters I found in a wall I removed. Someone—Paul, I believe—accessed my private computer files. You know I have Miles's old computer." She didn't mention the hate e-mail she'd opened last night.

Bonnie drew the key out of her slacks pocket and pushed it toward April. "That could be why I heard Miles talking to your father about washing his hands of Paul. I assumed they'd had a falling-out, but I had no idea why. Well, other than that he mentioned some letters Paul apparently wanted that belonged to Quinn Santini's mother. Eric had seen them lying on someone's kitchen table."

"*My* table. Not Quinn's mother, his grandmother. Norma. Her husband built the house I'm renovating. You can tell Miles that Paul never found the letters because I'd already returned them to Mrs. Santini. Better yet, I'll tell Miles. I could have him prosecuted for handing a key to Paul and letting him rifle my house."

"Oh, but dear, Miles was furious that someone he thought was a friend broke a promise. It must have been Paul. I heard your father tell Miles the firm needed to back off from sounding too partisan. Coleman donated to Dan Mattingly's campaign fund, but that's the extent of what he's willing to do. So, April, if you're concerned that your father will snub your new boyfriend, I don't think you have to worry."

"Quinn's not my boyfriend. Besides, I hate that term for people our age. We're, well…sort of involved, I guess you could say."

Their breakfast came. April wasn't thrilled with her tofu, goat cheese and roasted tomato omelette. But she dug in so she wouldn't have to say any more about her fledgling relationship.

"You probably know that Coleman and Miles lost a big case to Quinn last year. Your father does hate to lose. Still, I'm sure he'll behave toward Quinn the way he does about your career. Complains to your face, but brags on your work to clients and friends."

"He does?" April dropped her fork. "He's always grumbling because his mom left me money to finance my business."

"Dear. Haven't you seen through his bluff? Coleman drew up Dixie's will. He loved that feisty woman, and… April, surely you know how much he loves you."

April thought she might cry. She tucked her head down and pretended interest in her plate. "I'm… For.me, Dad's always been hard to read. I wish we'd had this talk years ago."

"Well, you were hell-bent on riding your shooting star. You didn't want advice from anyone. Coleman got his feelings hurt."

April twisted her napkin. "Hurt feelings can fester and make a mess of people's lives. Dad might be interested to know that I'm going to buy a great historic home in Alexandria. They're asking top dollar, but once I gut the interior and turn it into three independent condos, it'll be worth a fortune. Maybe I'll drop over in the next few days to see if Dad has any tips on creative financing."

Bonnie patted April's hand and smiled. "Bring your young man."

"I don't think Quinn…well, I guess it depends. His campaign takes up a lot of his time." She paused. "Mom, if I asked, do you think Miles would tell me straight out if he knows whether Paul plans to try and smear the whole Santini family?"

"Smear them? Their name, you mean? I'm sure that won't happen. They're on all of Virginia's social registers! Why do you think I'm so pleased that my daughter is the mystery lady in the soon-to-be-senator's life?"

April downed a bite of spinach and asparagus hidden among the tofu. She'd learned her mother's priorities long ago. April gave up trying to dig for information that probably had flown right by her mother. She settled for making the most of their visit in other ways.

In the middle of filling April in on the infighting at her tennis club, Bonnie checked her watch and hopped up. "Mercy, I'm going to be late for the spa. Want to come along? Monique would call a masseuse for you." Bonnie nudged April as she handed the waiter a credit card to pay the bill. "I'm guessing you have all kinds of naughty aches after a night's romp with *that* gorgeous man." She wagged the folded newspaper before tucking it safely in her oversize purse.

This time April had a comeback. "Not one ache. That's the beauty of spending my day climbing ladders, toting wallboard and tiling floors. Keeps me agile."

"Mmm. If you say so, dear. Stay and have a second cup

of coffee. Wait, do you need a ride somewhere since Mr. Gorgeous dropped you off?"

"No, I'm…ah…meeting a friend in a little while." April didn't dare let on that Quinn was picking her up. She wouldn't put it past her mom to cancel her spa appointment in order to meet "Mr. Gorgeous."

She did linger over coffee, letting her mind wander in directions she usually had no time for. Where would she like this relationship to go? She had a thriving career that required long hours of physical work. Quinn was juggling a career and a half at the moment, as well as raising a daughter and looking after his grandmother.

A favorite saying of her dad's was "good things never came easy." Glancing out the window, April saw Quinn pull up across the street. Her heart beat faster in anticipation and that, she decided as she flew out of the restaurant, told her plainly enough where she'd like this relationship to go.

"Hi," she said, out of breath. She greeted him with a happy kiss through the driver's side window he'd rolled down.

"Hi, yourself. Whatever you had for breakfast, I want some, too."

She slung her bag over her shoulder jauntily and circled the car; Quinn leaned across the seat and opened the passenger door to let her in. She dived into the car, talking a mile a minute until Quinn interrupted her detailed account of breakfast with another kiss.

"I've missed you," he said after the kiss ended. He continued to hold her, their foreheads touching.

"Quinn, are we rushing into this?" April rubbed a finger over the slight cleft in his chin.

Drawing back, Quinn draped a wrist over the steering

wheel. "I've asked myself that, too. The answer I get is how happy I am to see you." He glanced away. "I take it your mother said something to cause you misgivings?"

"No, actually. The opposite. For probably the first time in…twenty years, I felt her wholehearted approval. There's a picture of us in the morning paper, by the way. She was pleased to see that my taste in men and evening dresses has improved."

Quinn brought one finger to his lips. "Ah, that photograph was under discussion at Gram's house, too," he said wryly. "Hayley said your dress was, and I quote, 'totally cool.' So your mom *wasn't* mad at you for dating her husband's political enemy?"

"She and I had an eye-opening chat on several issues. One you'll find interesting has to do with Miles, Paul and Eric. As we thought, Eric told Paul Benson I'd found the letters. I'm assuming Paul asked Miles to let him into my place to look at them. Mom tells me Miles didn't like whatever Paul did after that. He even went to Dad, who said the extent of the firm's political involvement should begin and end with their financial contribution."

"Really? So you think Paul and Eric took things a step farther than breaking and entering? That they contacted von Weisenbach on a hunch?"

"Probably not Eric." April tried to explain exactly what her mother had said.

Staring fixedly out of the Lexus, Quinn started the engine. "We've got quite a few hours to kill before the flight lands. Any ideas on how we should do that?"

"Well…we could track down Miles. And then, I'd value your opinion on the house I plan to buy in Alexandria."

"Perfect. Do you want to navigate or drive?" Quinn hesitated before pulling out.

"You'd let me drive your car?"

"Why not? You know how to get there. Alexandria's a maze."

"It's just that most men fuss about—" She saw his face and broke off. "Right, you aren't most men. Okay, trade places, Santini."

They made the switch. She eased away from the curb and took the next city block to get a feel for the luxury car. Quinn obviously expected some kind of comment. So she stepped on the gas.

"It drives okay," she finally muttered. "But you may as well know that I think a car is a car is a car. Beats me why designers include this great detail and then stick in a pansy-assed engine. If I spent this much money, I'd demand four barrel carbs and Hemi heads."

Quinn's eyes crinkled at the corners and he relaxed, leaning against the headrest as he laughed. "I had ten messages waiting at home from my media staff wanting quotes they can use about the woman I'm dating. I can't wait to hand them that one."

"Don't you dare." But her warning had no bite. She drove into an upscale, established area of Turner. They stopped in front of a large white house with an enormous yard. April and Quinn were surprised to see Miles Trent raking leaves that the storm had blown from a huge oak tree.

April left the engine running and prepared to get out.

"Need me for moral support or anything?" Quinn asked casually.

"I'll yell if I do."

Quinn felt a sense of pride watching her march straight up to her brother, who stood a foot taller. She gestured; Miles did, too. April moved closer and Miles backed up a few steps, then leaned on his rake, looking contrite.

It wasn't long before April bounded back, jumped in the car, popped the emergency brake and eased away from the curb.

"Well?" Quinn demanded. "Don't keep me in suspense."

"He gave Paul my key, the creep. He swears up and down that Paul promised all he'd do was look at the letters Eric saw on my kitchen table, although Eric knew I'd taken them into my bedroom. But I believe Miles. He said he met Paul in Smitty's bar to get the key back. And they had a huge argument when Paul admitted he and one of his employees tossed my bedroom and searched my computer. It fits with what Dennis Granger told us, about Miles storming out of the bar and Paul being inside. I told Miles I'd let him off the hook if he votes for you."

"Fat chance." Quinn's smile was droll.

"Yeah, well, the best part is he hates that we both know he did this. Miles is a lot like my mom. Image is everything. I doubt he'll do anything like this again."

They stopped talking about her brother as she entered the narrow streets of downtown Alexandria, which hadn't changed much since the colonial homes were constructed. She passed the distinctive octagonal tower of Christ Church, where Robert E. Lee was reportedly confirmed, and made a left turn at the intersection.

Quinn swiveled his head from side to side. "You're talking really high-rent district, April."

"Yeah. But don't you just love how long these homes

have withstood the years? Think of the historic people and monumental events they've witnessed. "

"Alexandria is one of our country's oldest ports."

"I walk along the river and I can almost hear the hammers from when they built ships here. I imagine listening for the shouts of tobacco auctioneers." She parked on a street shaded by tall brick homes, distinguished only by the color of their stoops or shutters. "That one," April said, grabbing Quinn's arm the minute he got out of the car. "There are three for sale on the street. This is the shabbiest. But it has the most potential. The wood interior has less dry rot, and the mortar can easily be repaired."

"I'll take your word for it."

"You don't like it?"

"I didn't say that." Quinn propped his hands on his hips and tilted his head back to try to see a glimpse of sky.

"Come and look inside." She dragged him down a narrow alley to a door with a combination lock, which she twirled until it opened.

"You memorized the combination? April, is this legal?"

"Yes, silly. The Realtor's a friend. That's why I have a prayer of stealing it from one of the big financiers." Taking his hand, she led Quinn up worn steps into big rooms where their footsteps echoed. As April talked and waved her arms animatedly, he began to see her vision. Soon, the various levels took on the warmth and life of a real home.

They clattered down from the highest floor, where the view had been magnificent. Just before April opened the door that led into the alley, Quinn braced the heel of his hand against the casing and blocked her exit. She glanced up in surprise—and instantly reveled in the emotion she read in his eyes. Respect for her occupation, pride in her talent and pure love of her as a woman lay bare for her to see.

Rising on tiptoe, she slid her arms around Quinn's neck and found his lips. The scent of his warm skin and citrusy aftershave filled her lungs. His long fingers tunneled beneath her jacket, which soon slid off her arms, and landed along with Quinn's in a soft heap.

Neither could probably have said which of them unsnapped and unzipped April's jeans. A moment after that, they were both on their knees, one step from lying on their jackets, when the shrill music of a cell phone drove them apart.

Quinn blinked. "It's your phone," April said, hauling in an unsteady breath.

He scrambled to locate his phone in the pocket of pants, which were puddled around his ankles. It continued to bleat as his head bumped April's when they both strained to see the readout.

"I don't recognize the number," he said, just as April said, "Quinn, answer it quick! Isn't that Heinz von Weisenbach's number in France?"

Taking her at her word, he flipped open the phone and shouted a breathless "Hello!"

April yanked up her jeans, tucked in her shirt and frowned at her watch. "I hope he's not going to say the plane landed early."

Quinn waved a hand in front of her face. In other circumstances she might have thought a man with his pants around his ankles had no business giving orders. But the serious set of his lips, and the worry in his eyes, drove everything else from her mind.

"Damn! The flight attendant thinks it was a heart attack?

Yes? Yes, I do happen to know a good heart doctor. They won't divert? No? So, Reagan National in forty minutes? I'll try to arrange for swift admission to the hospital. Right. Right. Thanks for the heads-up. We'll have your son call the minute we have any word."

Quinn closed his cell and struggled to pull up his jeans in the same motion. April didn't need to ask for a repeat of what the caller had said. Quinn blurted that out while grabbing their jackets and hustling them both toward the door. "Heinz Junior got a call via Airfone from his son. Senior collapsed on his way to the john. A doc on board says it's his heart. Well, you heard. Would you drive us to the airport while I try to get hold of Cecil Amhurst, a Maryland cardiologist? He helped a friend of mine."

"I'll drive." They ran to the car, all vestiges of their recent encounter erased. She merged with traffic at the intersection before voicing the concern uppermost in Quinn's mind as well. "Will he live? What if he doesn't? Oh, Quinn, shouldn't you notify your grandmother?"

"Why? She thinks he's already dead."

"But…we know he's not. And if she doesn't have an opportunity to speak with him, she'll never find out what did happen the day he defected."

"At the moment I'm more worried about handling this discreetly enough to keep the press from swarming all over us. April, I don't have time to sort out the moral or ethical issues. I need you to be quiet and drive so I can cut the red tape and have him admitted to a cardiac unit before the media turns the airport into a zoo."

"Okay," she said unhappily. "But maybe it's time you started thinking of *him* as your grandfather."

Chapter 11

As always the streets that led to the airport were crowded and traffic moved more slowly than an anxious April would've liked. She bit the inside of her mouth while listening to Quinn speak with Dr. Amhurst's assistant. That call resulted in a series of follow-up calls to secure an ambulance and hasten the ailing man through customs.

Quinn apparently calmed his nerves by dealing with the tangles of red tape. April, meanwhile, drummed her fingers on the steering wheel and worried enough for them both.

Quinn finally closed his phone with a satisfied exhalation seconds before she cut off a Beemer and stole the single parking place both drivers had eyed.

"Bravo." He pocketed his phone and flashed her the victory sign. "I'll let you chauffeur me to the airport any time," he said, making light of their situation.

April vaulted out of the car. "We've got less than seven minutes to make it from here to the international concourse." After he'd unfolded himself from the seat, she hit the lock mechanism on the remote and passed him back his keys.

He jogged to catch up. "Are you mad because I asked you to be quiet back in Alexandria? I didn't mean to be rude. I had to line up all the steps in my mind, then concentrate on those calls."

April rammed her hands in her jacket pockets and increased the tempo of her walk. "I'm not mad. Annoyed, maybe, because you're being so stubborn. The son told you his dad thought Norma died. Don't you find it really, really odd to think they had a mutual misunderstanding over something so…so cataclysmic? Forget it, I can see you still don't like the idea that your grandmother never got over Heinz. Yet the man's flown nearly four thousand miles on nothing but the word of a stranger he didn't even trust. And all because of a hint that Norma's alive."

Quinn avoided a loaded luggage cart. "So, shoot me for doing everything possible to help him and still look out for Gram's welfare. Would you be happier if I had Joseph drive Gram here when I have no idea how to begin explaining why *Heinz* happened to show up? Or how I knew he'd be here? Then they'd both end up on the cardiac care unit."

"Are you saying Norma has a bad heart?"

"At her age, you have to expect body parts to give out." Quinn remembered Norma's own words. "Dammit, April, slow down! On the phone, von Weisenbach stressed that his dad had no heart problems. I suspect he more or less blames us. At least he blames the circumstances that convinced his dad to make this long trip."

"Okay. It's your call, Quinn. If I were Norma, though, I'd want to see him, touch him, say a real goodbye if necessary. Something she was deprived of at the time she assumed he'd died. But I do understand your desire to protect her."

"Maybe I'll change my mind after I talk to the grandson. Unless he's as much in the dark about his grandpa's past as I've been about mine all these years."

April stepped on the moving sidewalk and began overtaking passengers. "Will we get close enough to customs to even see Marc?" she said. "No way will we be allowed in the concourse, since security's so tight."

"I requested a medevac air taxi to fly Heinz and his party to the hospital where Cecil Amhurst's chief of staff. A team will evaluate him en route, and if they feel he's had a coronary he'll go straight to ICU. Amhurst should be out of surgery by then, his assistant thinks. He'll take the case from there."

"How old is Marc? Your age? Or is he just a kid?"

"Beats me. He speaks English and had the wherewithal to phone his dad, who had a flight attendant talk to Heinz Senior's personal physician." Quinn took April's hand. "You're worried," he said, rubbing his thumb up and down her wrist. "Me, too. With this complication, the newshounds on the airport beat will consider any passenger who had a heart attack in-flight to be newsworthy. A reporter for the *News Register* might add two and two and end up with me. I'd rather that was later than sooner. I need your help, April."

"To do what?"

"Buy me time. I'm going to duck into this gift shop and

pick up an Orioles baseball cap, a sweatshirt and dark glasses. Will you see if you can track down information at the Air France counter without involving me by name?" Showing his nervousness, he aimed a pleading kiss at her lips, but missed and brushed her chin instead.

She avoided his mouth. "Oriole was your grandmother's code name. She told me that. Do you suppose Heinz knows?"

Quinn scowled. "I'd forgotten until you mentioned it. I hope she *didn't* tell him—or else what she said about not sharing state secrets with him wasn't true. Maybe I shouldn't—but the Oriole caps are right in front, and time matters."

"Buy the cap. He probably won't know an oriole from a blackbird. Where shall we meet? At the gate leading to customs? Forget the dark glasses, Quinn. It's been overcast for days. You don't want to be any more conspicuous."

He flashed a thumbs up and they separated.

April almost didn't recognize him later as she turned and bumped right into him. Quinn had his ball cap pulled low. "What did you learn?" His gaze darted over the crowd awaiting arrivals.

"No word on his condition. The rest of the passengers are being held up until they transfer a patient to a medevac plane. The Air France reservationist was reluctant to call anyone in the plane until I said I was here to pick them up and wasn't sure if I should wait for the grandson or go on to the hospital, instead. It turns out Marc got on the emergency flight, too. If we leave now and beat them to the hospital, maybe the staff there can hide us from prying eyes and nosy media before anyone's the wiser."

"Okay." Keeping his head lowered, Quinn threaded his way through the crowd, back in the direction they'd come.

They were waiting to pay the toll out of the parking garage when the medical chopper passed overhead. Quinn knew his way around D.C.'s one-way streets. They made good time crossing the border into Maryland.

"I know you're concentrating on driving," April said, drawing up one knee and turning her back to the side window. "But I've been thinking about something that just doesn't make sense to me."

"Join the crowd. A lot of this doesn't make sense to me. What in particular is bothering you?"

"Paul Benson's degree of involvement in this whole thing."

"He wants Dan Mattingly to win another term."

"That's too simplistic. Seems to me Paul risked his job as news editor when he tossed my place looking for the letters. And he, not Dan or his staff, phoned Heinz offering to pony up for an expensive plane ride. Just hoping for dirt so Mattingly could beat you? Quinn, Paul already has a bully pulpit to grind you down—his paper. There's *got* to be more. Otherwise, why fire Eric for allowing the letters to slip through his fingers? Eric's the one who gave Paul the tip. Why wouldn't he let Eric sniff out the story?"

"I get you. Like maybe Benson's in on some illegal business deal with Mattingly. A silent partner, say, who stands to lose his shirt if Dan loses the election. Hmm. Maybe you've hit on something. I'll phone a couple of aides at my campaign headquarters and start them digging." He opened his phone; in a matter of minutes his people were on the problem.

Quinn smiled at April, but found her still looking unhappy. "Now what?"

"I don't know. This feels more personal than business. I can't figure it out."

Shrugging, Quinn made a right turn from the busy street into the parking lot of a prestigious hospital. "Sweetheart, I've discovered that to a lot of men, business deals equal money, and money is very personal indeed."

She nodded. "I suppose. I have a hard time understanding it. I guess we'll have to wait and see if your aides stumble on an answer."

"Yeah. Right now, we need to find where they've taken our unwanted visitor."

"You really don't want to meet him and unravel the truth?"

Quinn parked and shed the Orioles sweatshirt. He resettled the ball cap, locked the Lexus, then took April's hand. "I wish the whole nightmare was over."

Moving closer, April latched on to his arm with her free hand. "Call me the eternal optimist. I'm hoping there's a good reason those letters surfaced after so many years."

"I can't think of a single one." Quinn urged her to step into the revolving glass door and scooted in behind her. Together they approached the information desk on the other side.

Removing his cap, Quinn gave a story he expected to have to repeat. But Dr. Amhurst's assistant had laid the groundwork. A hospital official was summoned to escort Quinn and April through the hospital with its maze of corridors.

The farther they walked and the more corners they turned, the quieter it got. "Even the gurney wheels are well-oiled," April murmured.

Their guide motioned them into a nicely decorated waiting area occupied by one man. As the door swished open, the lone person in the room, who'd had his head buried in his hands, glanced up.

April realized the guide had left and she'd advanced, but Quinn hadn't. She hurried back to where he stood outside. "What is it?"

"Gram's story is true," he said brokenly. "I've seen pictures of my dad as a young lawyer. That guy there looks just like my dad's photos."

April looked inside to judge for herself. She'd never met Brett Santini, but the man in the waiting room, studying her curiously, had the same startling blue eyes as Quinn's.

Neither man uttered a word. April managed a smile. "Marc? Marc von Weisenbach?"

The rigid shoulders squared even more if possible. "That's me. Have you news about my grandfather?"

"Oh, no." April shook her head, and aimed a kick at Quinn's shin to get his attention. "I'm April Trent. This is Quinn Santini. Your father phoned Quinn, who arranged to have your grandfather brought here."

"Ah, a relative of the government representative Grandpère worked for many years ago. Forgive my state of confusion," he said with a strong French accent. "Perhaps you will make clear the few muddy details Grandpère shared with me on the drive to Paris."

Still speaking for the stubbornly mute Quinn, April asked both men to sit down. She jerked a thumb toward the door. "I'll go see what I can find out about Mr. von Weisenbach's condition. You two get acquainted." Trusting Marc, at least, to break the ice, April rushed out and down the hall to the closest nursing station.

In the room, the guest extended his hand. "Marc von Weisenbach. You are a relative of Anthony, Grandpère's old friend? I learned from my father that he has died. May I extend our sorrow for your loss. Did he pass away some years ago?"

Sighing deeply, Quinn clasped the younger man's hand. "Yes. Almost forty years ago. Your grandfather has waited a long time to come and pay his respects to Anthony's widow."

"We did not know about the death. And I don't know why he felt the urgency now. Our family runs a busy landscape firm. On the drive to Paris, Grandpère said we owe it all to Anthony Santini, who made buying expensive land possible through contract jobs paid for by your government during the war and after. Papa said I should be careful who I talk with here about the war. But our benefactor was your grandfather, yes?"

"If you say so. What did your grandfather have to say about my grandmother? Norma Santini, formerly Norma Marsh. They were…friends during the war."

Marc got up and strode from one end of the small room to the other. "Grandpère started to speak of her on the plane. I gather he's most anxious to see her—if she is a woman he thought had died even more years ago than Anthony. According to Grandpère, Norma loved the color of a deep-salmon rose. We've developed a very similar one that has won our firm much recognition. It's called Mon Amour. My love, in English. When he spoke about the rose, Grandpère grew quite upset. He unbuckled his seat belt and walked to the back of the plane where he collapsed."

"My grandmother is very much alive. She's told me some interesting things about your grandfather. Where's his wife, by the way? What did she have to say about him charging off with you to find another woman?"

"I know little of her. She worked for the French underground, and died of a lung ailment she contracted in the Philippines when my father was five." Marc whirled toward the door when it breezed open.

April came into view, followed by a nurse who addressed the men. "Dr. Amhurst is in the process of conducting a thorough examination of Mr. von Weisenbach. He's ordered blood tests and an MRI. The patient's blood pressure is very low, and his pulse is fast and irregular. Notes from a minor work-up done on the aircraft indicate he isn't currently on blood pressure medication." She pulled a pen from her pocket and turned to a page clipped onto a board she carried. "Do you know if that's correct? It's unusual for a man of his age not to take any medications."

Marc detached a phone from his belt. "All the information that was relayed to a doctor who happened to be on our flight came straight from Grandpère's physician. It's past midnight in France, but I'd be happy to ring him again if anything needs clarification. I've never seen Grandpère take pills," he added

"Can't he speak for himself?" Quinn asked bluntly.

"The doctor on the flight administered a mild sedative to calm his heart and make him more comfortable," the nurse explained. "The notes say he suffered severe chest pains. He's awake, but a bit disoriented. I understand this is his first visit to the U.S. All the contact information is blank except for a phone number. Are all of you staying at a local hotel?"

"My grandfather and I are…were." Marc swallowed repeatedly. "But the airline can't release our bags until they clear customs. A flight attendant promised to have them held. Perhaps I can order a taxi to go and retrieve them. And I hate to leave the hospital until I have enough information to phone my father, who remained in France."

April nudged Quinn. "I could drive him to the airport to get the bags. Marc, do you have your passports? And your baggage claim tags?"

"Yes. However, I may wait to check into our hotel. Papa may prefer that I return home to look after the business and he'll replace me. It will depend on what the heart doctor determines."

Quinn seemed to rally. "In any event, you'll want to shave and change your clothes." He tossed his keys to April. "I'll hold down the fort here. What's your cell number, Marc? With luck, you'll be able to claim your bags and phone your dad with news before you get back from the airport."

"Thank you. You're very kind to a stranger in your country."

The nurse seemed slightly confused. "You aren't related? You could pass for cousins, if not brothers. Well, they say we all have a twin somewhere. I'll take this information to Dr. Amhurst and let him know someone will be here when he finishes his evaluation."

For the first time, Marc stopped to really look at the taller, broader-shouldered Quinn, who didn't flinch under the scrutiny. "It is happenstance, no?" he said at last, his statement lacking conviction. He released a breath as truth dawned. "Does Grandpère know? I think not," he muttered, still staring at Quinn.

April took it upon herself to hustle Marc out just then. "Well, let's go." She wiggled her fingers at Quinn.

He grabbed her arm and dragged her back for a harsh,

almost desperate goodbye kiss. "Drive carefully. If you run into any reporters, don't tell them *anything*."

She and the younger man exited the hospital in silence. As he saw the car, he gave a low whistle of appreciation. "I guess no one is going to appease my curiosity about why that man and I look so much alike," he said after they got underway.

"I'll only say that a few hours ago, Quinn sat in that same seat hoping your grandfather could resolve *his* unanswered questions."

"And if Grandpère dies?"

"I assume we're all praying he doesn't." She glanced over. His stubborn profile was enough like Quinn's to make her worry in case the press was hanging around the airport customs area.

"Marc, did you notice Quinn's ball cap? I'm going to stop at a gift shop in the airport and buy us each one as a disguise." Although she wasn't sure Quinn would approve, she talked about the need to remain unrecognized. "We think it's more than the usual mud-slinging by political hacks," she finished. "Unless you want to be relentlessly hounded by reporters who may track us to the hospital, I advise saying nothing to anyone."

He followed her lead. She bought them Washington Nationals caps, so no astute reporter would link them to the earlier man wearing an Orioles cap.

April watched people come and go in customs, leaving Marc to fill out forms and claim three bags. They were headed for the moving sidewalk, and she sighed in relief—when, of all people, she spotted Eric Lathrop on the opposite track. He saw her, too. She went into momentary panic as Eric vaulted the rail and started in her direction.

Then her brain kicked into gear. She snatched off her cap, shoved it and the Lexus keys into Marc's hand and hissed, "Trouble. Behind us. Don't look. Go right to the car and wait. I have to ditch a reporter I know. We parked on the top level, so if Quinn tries to reach you by phone, you should get a signal."

Spinning around, she watched as Eric made his way toward her, clutching his notebook, camera around his neck.

"Eric!" she said brightly, intercepting him, "What brings you to the airport?"

He dashed her a suspicious glance. "I might ask you the same thing. Who's the guy you were talking to?"

She pretended to look around "Who?"

"Don't bullshit me, April. I overheard a couple of staff guys from another paper at the café. The buzz is, some old geezer on an inbound Air France flight had a ticker problem. The other reporters are bummed because the airline personnel are being tight-lipped. But one of them overheard a name—von Weisenbach. Didn't mean a thing to him. It did to me. So I rush out here and who do I find? You. Where's Santini?" Eric craned his neck. "Give me *some* information, April. Or I'll take my suspicions to Benson."

"Why would you do that if Paul fired you?"

He clearly hadn't expected April to remember. "Yeah, well, he thought I blew it by not forcing you to hand over the letters. He went crazy and threw me out of his office. Said he'd handle this one himself."

She pulled Eric off the end of the moving sidewalk in the main terminal. A quick glance around told her Marc had just stepped on an elevator. "I'll buy you a coffee, Eric."

"Why are you being generous? Because you're hiding something?"

April joined the coffee line, thinking fast. "I'm trying to tie up loose ends to a puzzle. We can help each other, Eric."

"Yeah? I'll have a hazelnut latte. A big one. Shall I grab that table?"

"Okay, but I can't stay long." She hated to lie, but did, anyway. "I promised Mom I'd stop by the house and look at a new sweater she bought my sister-in-law for her birthday. She and Dad are meeting the Johnstones for bridge in two hours."

Acknowledging her need to rush, Eric commandeered the empty table. She quickly bought the drinks and sat down across from him.

"Shoot." He popped the lid off his drink to let it cool.

"Paul Benson has lots of reporters like you, all wanting to move up the ladder. He could snap his fingers and send you off in a dozen different directions, digging up clues here, there and everywhere. Yet he's obsessively followed a thin lead on Heinz von Weisenbach. By himself and in virtual secrecy. *Why?*"

"You tell me."

"Eric, come on. I have no idea. A man with Paul Benson's resources? I keep wondering why he's so pro-Mattingly that he'd cross lines, maybe even jeopardize his job, just to ruin Quinn. I know Paul talked Miles into giving him a key to my house. He told Miles he had to have those letters, then ransacked my house and found the name of the letter-writer on my laptop. Because of that, he and my brother argued and had a falling-out. But Benson didn't let it drop. He phoned France and offered to buy von Weisenbach a plane ticket here."

"So the old fool accepts, and now he's had a heart attack? That's rich. I can almost see Paul turning purple. He does that when things don't go his way."

"Listen, Eric. I'm trusting you, for old times' sake. Von Weisenbach had a bad feeling about Paul. He bought his own ticket, so Benson has no idea Heinz is here…yet. Quinn's got him under wraps," she added, not naming the hospital. "If you want a scoop, I'm trying to tell you how. Find out why Benson needs Dan Mattingly to win that seat at any cost. And don't share the information with anyone but Quinn, and I'll get you an exclusive with Norma Santini." She knew it was a reckless promise but felt she had no choice.

His eyes lit. Eric Lathrop was obviously weighing the advantages. "You're doing this because you're crazy about Santini, right?"

April thought it through for a minute, then stood and tossed her half-drunk coffee in the trash. "That's a good way of putting it, yes. I hope you aren't going to pretend, like you did that night at Cinalli's, that I mean more to you than a ticket to some of the right social events in town—like my mom's dinner parties."

He picked up his briefcase and camera. "Ya got me dead to rights, Trent. I have places to go before I tie myself down to a wife and mortgage. This offer better be for real, April, and not some smokescreen."

"Eric, I *never* deal under the table."

"Okay, I'll be in touch. Keep your cell phone on. Think I'll mosey on down to customs and see if any of Paul's pet reporters are hanging out there. If they are, or were, he's probably already got a tail on you and Quinn. Remember,

Benson didn't get to his position without knowing how to bird-dog a lead and grease a few palms. Says he has a nose for news because he came from a long line of reporters. His granddad and great uncle were foreign correspondents for some big-deal paper up north. His pop edited a small-town rag." He shook his head. "I've seen Paul destroy people with half truths. Just enough truth to get away with it—and a small retraction on page ten after the damage is done. That keeps him from getting sued. He has eyes and ears in more places than you can imagine. Tell Santini to watch his back."

April cast a nervous glance around. No one appeared to be lurking. "Unless Paul planned to have someone meet every incoming Air France plane landing here or at Dulles, he'd have to be clairvoyant to hit the right day."

"Don't bank on it. Paul's not a man to underestimate."

"I'll remember. Good luck, Eric."

April bounded into an almost full elevator headed to the top level of the parking garage. She crossed her fingers, hoping she hadn't put herself out on a limb. But her decision to trust Eric came from logic as well as instinct. She and Quinn agreed that Benson had to be the main person behind the probes into Quinn's background. And who better to ferret out evidence than Eric?

Marc was pacing back and forth in front of the Lexus. "I'm glad you finally got here! Quinn phoned. At first Dr. Amhurst thought my grandfather only suffered something called atrial fibrillation and atrial flutter." He spoke slowly and carefully. "But one test shows a partial vein blockage. He wants to do a procedure. Radio frequency ablation." He referred to a paper on which he'd scribbled the terms. "At the same time, they will install a pacemaker."

"I'm sorry to keep you waiting. Hop in. We'll go back to the hospital, okay?"

They climbed in and buckled up. Marc turned to April, saying worriedly, "Quinn asked why we weren't together. I said you'd stopped to talk to a reporter you knew. I hope that wasn't the wrong thing to say. Quinn…swore. He said that accounts for some article in the paper. I'm sorry if I caused you trouble after you were so kind as to drive me here."

"You have enough to worry about with your grandfather facing surgery. I haven't seen a paper in several days, so I don't know what article he means. But Quinn's used to negative press." As she drove, she explained a few things about Quinn's bid for the Senate. "I don't know how politics works in your country. Here it gets nasty. Quinn's tried hard to run a clean campaign. Not his opponent. That man's team is digging into Quinn's family background. Which is sort of how your grandfather's name came to light. That's the extent of what I'm comfortable telling you right now. For more, you'll have to sit down with Quinn."

"Thank you for giving me that much. Politics is not so different in France, and people's memories are long. Once when I was young, my school project was to write a detailed essay on one set of grandparents. I chose Grandpère von Weisenbach. Maman made me write about her father, instead, a very boring mathematics professor. All she'd say was that my father's parents lived with many secrets. My mother was never cross with me except on that matter. Much later, of course, I studied the war. I pieced a few things together and understood why Grandpère finds peace only working in the greenhouses."

"Yes," April murmured. "It was a harsh war." Her

thoughts centered on Norma Santini's confessions to Quinn. April found herself hoping that Quinn would let these two people, who'd suffered so much heartache for so many years, meet again.

Securing a parking place at the hospital, April kept looking over her shoulder as she and Marc hurried up the stairs. It was nerve-wracking and she wondered how anyone voluntarily became a spy.

Dr. Amhurst, a slight man with combed-back red hair, had just returned to the waiting room as they arrived. The doctor took Marc aside.

Quinn snatched up a folded newspaper and hustled April into the hall. He stabbed a finger at the *Register*'s front-page article. "This hints that you're warming my bed for the purpose of passing my campaign strategies to Eric Lathrop—who in turn shares them with Mattingly's team. Don't try to lie your way out, April. Marc described the guy you met at the airport for coffee. You did meet Eric, didn't you?"

A gasp exploded through April's lips. There was no mistaking how hurt she was by Quinn's tone, which implied that there was validity to the veiled accusations. "Do you believe this crap?" she managed to sputter.

He rolled up the paper and slammed it hard against the wall. "Well, I notice you aren't denying that you met Eric," he said bitterly.

"I waylaid Eric to give Marc time to escape! And it so happens I had an enlightening chat with Eric. Now, getting a look at this trashy article, I'm more convinced than ever that Paul Benson's using me and Eric to get to you, Quinn. I'm not your enemy. I've come to…care a lot for you. I'm sorry if you can't see that. Sorrier still if you choose to believe the worst. And when are you going to counter the garbage Benson prints? You have PR people. Have them send out a press release."

"And say what in our defense? Should I admit the intimate details of our relationship?"

April might have shot back something equally snide, but she was saved from an action she might later regret by the arrival of the doctor and Marc, who gripped his cell phone with purpose.

"Dr. Amhurst says it's crucial Grandpère agree to have a relatively new but simple operation. That stubborn old man refuses to authorize *any* surgery. He insists he made the trip to America to see Norma Marsh—or Santini, according to the fellow who first phoned him. Grandpère won't allow anyone to anesthetize him unless we either show him proof she's dead or he sees her in person."

All eyes swooped toward Quinn. "Uh, can't you sign the form authorizing life-saving surgery, Marc?"

"Not when a patient is awake and understands the procedure," the doctor put in.

"Surely your father has power of attorney in case his father is incapacitated."

"I talked to him. He has such a document, but it is no good in this case. Dr. Amhurst took my phone to Grandpère. He and Papa spoke. That document does not cover a man who is competent enough to speak his mind."

"Maybe he's not competent, just belligerent," Quinn suggested.

"Quinn!" April clutched his tense arm. "Listen to yourself! Please, put yourself in Heinz's shoes. Wait," she begged the others, then exerted considerable effort to pull Quinn farther down the hall. "Quinn Santini," she said earnestly, "if your grandmother has these…these holes in her past and in her heart, your stubbornness is keeping her from what may well be her last chance to fill in the blanks and maybe heal an old wound."

"You're right—about a lot of things." For a second, Quinn let his forehead touch April's. When he drew back, she could see the turbulence that carved gaunt hollows in his cheeks. "If you love her, Quinn, let her make the decision," she told him softly. "There's no question about her competence."

She watched as the struggle waged within him.

Dr. Amhurst bustled up before he could respond, Marc on his heels. "I'd like to give you more time, but I can't, Mr. Santini. I accepted this case in deference to your friendship with my neighbor, a Senator for whom I have immense respect. I have an opening on my surgery schedule tomorrow afternoon at three. Prepping of the patient will have to begin tonight."

"Will he die without the surgery?"

Quinn's question didn't faze Amhurst. "I'm not God," he said. "Although I do my best around this hospital to give that impression," he said, his smile fleeting. "In my professional opinion, this three-hour operation has a better chance of buying him another five to ten years than if he tries to control it with medication."

Quinn tugged hard on one ear. "Schedule his surgery."

The doctor immediately sped off down the hall. Appearing relieved, Marc turned away and opened his phone, no doubt planning to call his father.

April hugged Quinn impulsively. "I knew you'd do the right thing."

He unwound her arms. "Not so fast. What I did was buy some time. I never said I'd set Gram up for possible disappointment. What if I bring her to visit him, get her hopes up, and then his heart gives out during surgery? Wouldn't that be even crueler?"

"But you authorized Dr. Amhurst to prep him for surgery!"

"I need time to think. I'm going home to see how Gram is. I told you she has a cold. Maybe that's what I should've told the doc. He'd say not to expose his patient to any viruses."

"If you're going home, what about Marc?"

"What about him? I assume he booked a hotel."

"Yes, but…you seem to conveniently forget that he's technically your family." She kept her voice low, since Marc stood maybe ten feet away.

"I'm doing my best to forget," Quinn whispered back.

The subject of their conversation came up to them, looking more carefree than he had since they'd all met. "Dr. Amhurst told me about a motel called Country Inn within walking distance of the hospital. He spoke of three to four days of hospital time, followed by a week of home recovery before Grandpère should consider flying again. I can call a taxi because I have my luggage and Grandpère's. I'll walk out with you, since our bags are still in your car, Quinn."

"We can drop you at the motel," Quinn said, somewhat grudgingly. "You have my cell number if you need anything. Do the floor nurses know how to reach you?"

"Yes. It's kind of you to give me a lift. I considered renting a car. However, I don't see a need now."

April watched the two men, who bore a decided family resemblance, acting with the reserved politeness of strangers. "Marc, tell the nursing staff you're leaving. We don't mind waiting a few minutes, do we, Quinn? Perhaps they'll let him talk to his grandfather."

"Uh, no, I don't mind. Go ahead, Marc."

The young man smiled, and his whole demeanor changed. "Thank you." He loped a few steps toward the nursing station, then turned. "Grandpère will rest much easier once he knows you will be bringing the woman, Norma, to see him."

Quinn started down the corridor after Marc, clearly intending to stop him from saying anything to Heinz.

"Please, Quinn, will it hurt to give him a few hours of peace?" April urged Quinn to let Marc go. "I know Norma's your primary concern, but you have only to look at Marc—and then in a mirror—to see proof that the man lying in Intensive Care is the man she claims to have loved."

He sagged against the wall beside a potted fern. "You don't hold back, do you?"

"I've always believed that everything happens for a reason. I found the letters in the wall. They started a chain reaction that's not finished yet." She touched his arm, urging him to meet her eyes. "Dr. Amhurst says he can't play God. You shouldn't try, either, Quinn."

Rubbing his temples, he squinted at her through pain-clouded eyes. "You think I should just give in, don't you? Tell Gram about Heinz, take her to see him…"

"Yes, I do."

He shoved off from the wall. "You may be right," he said tiredly. "Will you come home with me and stick around while I figure out how to break the news to Gram?"

"With pleasure. Oh, Quinn, don't look like you've just lost your best friend! It's going to turn out fine, you'll see. Your grandmother's a strong woman."

Marc returned before April and Quinn had time to make firm plans. "They gave me three minutes with him," the younger man told them. "A nurse said he'd been sedated. I'm not sure he understood that his wish has been granted. I may visit him later. The nurse said when the sedation wears off, he won't receive any more until pre-op."

They left the hospital. Talk between the men would have been non-existent if April hadn't carried the conversation. She pointed out a strip mall with a convenience store to the visitor. "The Inn's across the street. I believe the rooms are more like suites, with small kitchens. There are a few restaurants, and a taco place at the far end of the mall. Or there's always the hospital cafeteria."

"Don't tell my mother, but I can actually prepare toast, eggs and a decent cup of coffee if the room does have cooking facilities."

That admission brought a smile from Quinn. "How old are you?"

"I'll be twenty-two in six weeks. I'm the youngest and the only boy. I have five sisters."

"I sympathize," April chimed in. "I'm the only girl, but I just have two brothers. I wouldn't have survived five. You poor man."

He smiled at her teasing as Quinn pulled into the motel drive. Marc got out to secure himself a unit.

"His old man must've done well growing roses if he could afford to feed that many mouths," Quinn remarked as he and April took the luggage from the trunk. "I should've asked how many kids Heinz Senior produced, besides his dad—and mine," Quinn said dryly. "If Heinz Junior has six kids, all working in the landscaping business, maybe they won't be looking to cash in on—"

He broke off, but April finished for him. "—on Norma's estate, you mean? I don't think that's what they're after, Quinn."

He slanted her a sheepish glance, but was happy to see Marc dashing back brandishing a key. He slung one carry-on over his shoulder and lifted the other two bags, declining their offer of help. "Again, my profound thanks. I'm in room 112. I hesitate to make additional requests, as you've done far more than my father expected. But I wouldn't object if one of these days, you or someone else sat down and explained how our family trees came to be grafted together. I'm making the assumption that it's through our grandparents."

Not waiting for an answer, he took off and soon disappeared into his ground-floor motel unit. Quinn watched the lights go on inside. "He's obviously guessed that it happened because of a wartime affair," Quinn muttered, twisting the key to start the engine. "Or is he too polite to say so?"

April was silent. The day had been difficult for everyone. She didn't feel like talking. Quinn hadn't properly apologized for harboring even a passing thought that she might have done what that article in the *Register* suggested.

Outbound traffic was a snarled mess. Quinn appeared content to listen to the soothing sounds of a classical CD already in his player.

Closing her eyes, April enjoyed the piece but didn't recognize it. This was a quiet, romantic song and she sensed that Quinn was softening. Or she did until they turned down his street and approached the automatic gate. Vans bearing the *Register* logo and TV vehicles were parked haphazardly on both sides of the road. Men holding big cameras milled about, blocking the entrance to Quinn's estate.

"Don't turn in," April said, grabbing his arm. "Drive past and phone home first. What on earth do you suppose has happened?" Her heart beat faster as she struggled to avoid reporters and cameramen swarming toward the car.

"Probably you should ask your pal Eric," Quinn snapped as he pulled off the road and into a driveway over the next hill. "Joseph," he yelled, after punching a number on his cell. "What the hell is that ruckus at our gate? Are Gram and Hayley okay? You and Ethel, too?"

Straining to hear, Quinn rubbed a thumb and finger over the lines thatching his forehead. "The afternoon edition of the *Register?* No, I saw the earlier edition. You mean there's an even worse article than that garbage this morning?"

His tight expression told April the afternoon news *was* worse, but the fact that he'd called it "garbage" was heartening.

"Okay… Listen, Joseph, sneak out and down to the gatehouse. When I get close, slide the gate open just enough to let my car in, then shut it manually. They might recognize my car, but I'm wearing a ball cap and dark glasses. April's with me. Oh, and tell Gram we're coming directly to her house."

April didn't wait for him to ask her to duck. She crawled into the back seat, handed Quinn the props he'd mentioned, then curled up on the floor. After they'd streaked down the hill, she heard a commotion. Shouts. Fists pounding on the driver's window. But she didn't raise her head.

Quinn swore succinctly.

April felt a slight breeze and figured he must have opened his window a crack, because he shouted, "The first person setting foot inside my gates gets arrested for trespassing."

The ride was jerky for several seconds, then she heard the gate roll closed. A puffing Joseph jumped into the passenger seat April had vacated. Her heart sank when he said, "The front page of the afternoon *Register* is devoted to sly innuendo about some old letters April found in a wall. Where is she? I thought you said she came with you?"

"I'm here." April sat up. "So help me, if Eric's name is on that article, I'll *kill* him. Quinn, I swear to you Eric figured out on his own that Heinz is the one who had the heart attack on the flight. As for the rest," she fumed, "what you said at the hospital, you owe me an apology." She didn't care that Joseph was present; she had to say this. "I didn't betray you or Norma. I never would."

"I know. I knew the minute the comment left my mouth. I hope you'll forgive me, April." He reached back to touch her and relaxed when she kissed his fingers.

At Norma's, the trio jumped out and ran into the house before long-range telephoto lenses could catch them.

Quinn snatched up the paper lying on the love seat. April hung over his arm to read. "Not Eric," she breathed. "I don't recognize the byline. I'll bet dollars to doughnuts Paul Benson's behind these slimy remarks that cleverly fall just short of libel."

A dazed-looking Norma Santini entered the room.

"Ethel's taken Hayley out the back door to your place on the pretext of bringing her new building blocks down here. It'll take them a while to gather up the blocks. That ought to give us time to discuss how to disperse that mob. I'm so sorry, Quinn. You wanted me to destroy the letters. I can't imagine how anyone guessed they were from Heinz. Or worse, come to the conclusion that he served in the German army." Suddenly, her gaze lit on April and her eyes turned accusing.

"Mrs. Santini, uh, Norma, I never told anyone. I wouldn't. You have to believe me. I care too much for Quinn—for all of you."

Norma nodded and left the room. She was back a moment later, thrusting the bundle of yellowed envelopes into Quinn's hand. "There—throw them in the fire. Be done with it once and for all. Tell whoever's guessing that they've guessed wrong. I don't have any idea how they learned his rank, but they're dead wrong about the kind of man Heinz was. He's no war criminal." She pulled Quinn toward a fire crackling behind a glass enclosure. Untying the ribbon, Norma crumpled the top letter, her face streaked with tears. She retrieved the fragile pressed rose and stroked its petals as she dropped heavily down on the love seat.

April didn't realize she'd stifled a cry until Quinn and his grandmother spun around. She kept her fingers flattened against her lips, but her eyes implored Quinn to do the right thing and confess the day's events to his grandmother. *Now.*

"No, Gram." Quinn gently removed the letter from her hands. He attempted to straighten the crumpled edges as he led her to the love seat. "I don't care what those jackals do to me. Paul Benson went on a fishing expedition, that's all. I've got no idea why he's aimed so much venom at us. At me. I swear, Gram, I'd quit the race before I let him or anyone cause you more grief." Sinking to his knees, Quinn set the letters in his grandmother's lap.

Sighing, April shrugged off her jacket and sat on a chair. Glancing from one serious face to another, Joseph mumbled, "I'll go help Ethel and Hayley locate all those blocks."

"Gram, I don't know where to start." Picking up the top letter, Quinn reiterated how April had found them. He went on to her innocent Internet search, followed by the not-so-innocent break-in. He finished by describing that day's events. As the story unfolded, Norma sat straighter and straighter. Her eyes glittered with unshed tears.

She accepted the tissues April shoved into her fidgeting hands. "But…I saw Heinz fall. Blood spurted everywhere. His blood, and so much of it." She released the letters and they spilled out onto the tapestry of the love seat. "He's *alive?*" she asked in a dumbfounded voice. "And he's here? Oh, but his heart! Quinn, you said he's in the hospital awaiting surgery. I have to go to him at once. I can't believe any of this," she said fretfully. "Please, oh, please, let's not waste another precious minute. And my goodness, he has a grandson? So he got married." The last word fell almost sadly from her quivering lips. "What if the doctor won't allow him to have visitors? What if…he refuses to see me? I can't bear to upset him. I'd never want that. I loved him so very, very much. More than life itself."

April turned away from the tears trickling down the softly lined cheeks. A huge lump formed in her own throat. This was Quinn's opportunity to set everything right.

"Get your coat, Gram. He'll see you. In fact, he refused to have surgery without talking to you first. We'll take the Lincoln. Ask Ethel to bring Hayley over here—we'll all go to the hospital. Joseph can drive us. I'll phone Marc and have him meet us there. Marc is his grandson. You'll be shocked to see how much he looks like the old pictures you have of my dad." Rising, Quinn went to the mantel and collected a few family photographs.

Before their eyes, Norma became girlish, giddy, insisting on taking a few minutes to change clothes and repair her makeup.

April noticed, even if Quinn didn't. It was as if the news had put a spring in Norma's step and taken years from her age.

It was as if the news had brought her hope.

Chapter 12

Quinn drew April aside as Joseph went to the garage for the Lincoln. "I don't like taking Hayley, Joseph and Ethel, but I worry more about leaving them alone with a bunch of aggressive reporters surrounding the house."

"I don't blame you. If you pull off a meeting between Norma and Heinz, and if you can keep the press at bay a little longer, maybe you'll get answers that'll defuse the crap in those articles. Benson may not have written them, but you've got to know they have his stamp of approval."

He gazed into April's concerned face and looped a wind-blown strand of hair over her left ear. "A lot of women would've written me off before now. Do you know how much it means to me that you didn't? And that you stuck around to nag my conscience? And you were right. Gram didn't fall apart. Far from it, in fact."

"Quinn, has your staff dug up any reason for Benson's vendetta yet? That's what his onslaught feels like, doesn't it?"

"Neither Mike nor Jim has called back. I'll track them down while we wait for Gram at the hospital."

"Or phone Eric. I dropped a hint about Paul at the airport. Eric may have sources closer to Paul than your people do."

"You really believe Benson's attacks are more than a political zealot wanting his candidate to win at any price?"

"I went back and read his editorials on the Internet. His comments had a personal tone from the get-go."

Quinn moved his thumbs back and forth across April's cheekbones. "I'm resigned to the fact that I may still have to drop out of the running to keep Benson or his cronies from smearing Gram's good name."

"So, she had a love affair more than half a century ago. Women are no longer tarred and feathered for getting pregnant before marriage, Quinn. As for Heinz, we don't know his story, but his son said on the phone that he received a Distinguished Service Medal given by *our* president. I saw it on a Web site, too."

"So what? Is that enough of a reason for Gram to flip over an old guy she hasn't seen for sixty years?" He aimed an almost angry glance in the direction of Norma's bedroom. "She looked just fine in what she had on. But she left us to cool our heels so she can doll herself up for Heinz."

"Love makes women act crazy." April smiled tenderly at Quinn.

"I wouldn't know about that. Or…well, I know my outlook improves when you're with me, April."

"The feeling's mutual, Quinn. And no one's more surprised by that than me."

"I'm in no position to request any kind of commitment from you."

"I don't recall asking for one, Quinn. I'm fine with waiting until your life calms down. Aren't you?"

His answer was a sudden flare of desire in his eyes, and his kiss seared the air between them.

April's fingers dug into his arms. She wanted more, and he would've complied, except that Ethel and Hayley appeared on the path and Joseph backed the car out of the garage just then. Norma emerged from the house, hurrying toward them.

"We'll return to this when we're alone," Quinn said roughly in April's ear. He turned away to open the car door.

They all fit nicely inside the big car, with room to spare. Joseph, Norma and Quinn sat in front, with Ethel, Hayley and April in back. Hayley cuddled up next to April. She'd brought along a plastic case of Barbie dolls, plus a coloring book and crayons.

As the automatic gate opened to let them out, reporters leaped at the car and banged on the windows and the trunk lid. Some ran for their vehicles.

"Who are all those mean people?" Hayley asked worriedly.

In an undertone, Quinn told Joseph to try to shake anyone who decided to follow them, which left April to allay Hayley's fears.

"Honey, you know your dad's running for an important government job. The race between him and another man is over soon, so now everything they do is big news. In less than two months, the voters will decide which man wins, and those reporters at the gate will be on to the next story."

"After Halloween, Daddy finds out if he won." Hayley

jiggled her feet. "Can I still be a princess for Halloween, Daddy?" She gazed up at April. "April, can you come trick-or-treating with us? You can wear that queen cape you wore to Daddy's party. He can be king, you can be queen, and I'll be a princess. Won't that make us a perfect family?"

"Where did you see my cape?" April tightened her hold on Hayley as Joseph made a series of sharp turns and sped down a side street.

"Ethel and Gram had a newspaper picture. More than one. I bet your dress with the sparkly straps is way prettier than in that picture."

Her comment got Quinn's attention. "Way prettier is right, honey. Uh, Hayley, at our grocery store or other places, people may talk about stuff they read in the paper. Sometimes the stories are wrong. I just want you to know."

"Huh? Okay, Daddy. Why are we going to a hospital? Is somebody gonna be born? Gram showed me a c'tificate in my baby book that says I was born in a hospital."

Norma hadn't spoken a word until then. "I'm visiting a dear friend. Someone you've never met, Hayley. He lives far away and got sick on the plane coming here to visit. The doctors will try to make him well again. You'll wait in a special room while I visit him. Now, I'm counting on you to play quietly and be good."

The child appeared to understand for the first time how tense they all were. She curled her hand in April's and whispered, "I'll color a picture for Gram's friend. He'll like that, won't he?"

April smiled. "He will. I'll help you color."

Marc beat them to the hospital. Not surprising, as Joseph took a circuitous route in order to ditch one very stubborn reporter. After Marc nervously shook hands all around, Ethel gave Hayley's toys to April, and said, "I'm starved."

"Me, too," Hayley murmured.

"I thought so. Joseph and I will take Hayley and scout out the cafeteria. That'll give Norma time to visit. Would anyone care to have us bring back a sandwich or coffee?"

Grateful, April hugged the housekeeper. "I'd love some coffee. Marc, do you take anything in yours?" Deciding for Quinn, who'd gone to give their names at the nursing desk, April told Ethel, "Make it coffee for everyone. I take cream only."

"Everything in mine," Marc said, obviously embarrassed by Norma's scrutiny and glad of the distraction. He pulled out his billfold, but Quinn returned and handed Joseph two bills, saying, "Gram, the nurse will check to see if the patient's awake, and if so, she'll give us a wave."

The chatty threesome left in search of food, leaving silence in the otherwise empty waiting room.

"Marc, I apologize for staring," Norma finally said. "It's uncanny how much you resemble my son, Brett, Quinn's father. He died in a plane crash. I see a similarity between you and Quinn, as well. No doubt you were quite confused to discover—" Norma's voice broke and she gestured futilely. "If I'd had any idea Heinz had survived being shot…" Her eyes misted, and she shook her head.

Marc and Quinn shifted uncomfortably. Neither knew how to help Norma.

April slipped a bracing arm around the older woman's shoulders. "The nurse just gave the okay for your visit. What happened to him back then is a good place to begin your conversation with him. Only he can tell you how he survived."

Norma licked dry lips. "Now that I'm here, I'm afraid the shock of seeing me will be too hard on him."

"It'll be fine," Quinn said. "The nurse told me that Marc phoned Dr. Amhurst after I called to say we were bringing you. The doctor left orders to allow you to visit at any time."

"I'll walk you to the room," April said. "Or Quinn can."

Norma squared her shoulders and let April guide her the short distance to ICU, since Quinn made no move to do the honors. Once there, April gently urged her toward the door, but Norma hung back. She waited long enough to see the long-limbed, sun-tanned man, hooked up to needles and monitors, open his eyes. Brilliant blue eyes the color of Quinn's and Marc's. They shone with pure joy the moment he saw Norma. And his mouth formed her name.

Not caring to intrude on what was surely going to be a private moment, April backed away and quickly returned to the waiting area.

"Well?" Quinn asked abruptly.

April smudged unexpected tears from her eyes. "He's very glad to see her."

"Then why are you crying?"

"I can't explain. Don't ask. Probably for the same reason people cry at births and weddings."

The men shared a puzzled glance. Marc sat facing the hall that led to his grandfather's room. He propped his elbows on bony knees and after linking his hands, rested his chin on his thumbs.

Quinn buried his fingers in his back pockets and strolled restlessly around the room. He, too, kept one eye on the door. "How long do you think this'll take?" He stopped in front of April, who sat leafing through Hayley's coloring book.

"Well, I don't hear any shouting," Marc put in. He rose and made a counter-clockwise turn of the room, pausing to stare down the empty hall.

"Guys, relax. They're trying to catch up on sixty-some years."

The men continued their nervous pacing until April's nerves were ready to snap. The tension grew each time either of them passed her or each other.

Finally, Marc threw himself back into a chair near the door. "Do you know when Grandpère was supposedly shot? I wasn't even aware he'd been injured during the war."

"I know Gram's side of the story. It's safe to say there are some major discrepancies between what she thought occurred and what did happen. She served as an American agent in France and supposedly facilitated your grandfather's defection. Or so she assumed. Maybe he didn't defect." Quinn frowned at the younger man.

Marc leapt out of his chair. "He did! He has a medal, for distinguished service from *your* government. That proves he risked his life many times over for Allied troops."

"Big deal," Quinn shot back. "I know he got a medal. But he could've been a spy for both sides."

"Impossible! My grandparents didn't only join the French Resistance but worked underground in other theaters as the war changed. After the war ended, Papa said an American official visited often. He remembers that from when he was a boy. In the fifties, Grandpère helped train American agents for work behind the Iron Curtain, and again before war broke out in Korea. Grandmère contracted lung disease in the Philippines. That was when Grandpère said *no more!* He went to university, became a landscape architect and built the nursery on land he said was bought with money Anthony Santini paid him. Money from your government. You will take back your insult." Marc advanced, hands balled into fists.

Norma materialized in the doorway. "What's all the fussing? Heinz and I could hear you shouting."

Quinn, who hadn't moved, whirled around. He attempted to control his voice. "Marc took exception to my suggestion that his grandfather may have duped you the day you thought he was defecting. I said maybe Heinz was a double agent."

"I was duped all right, Quinn. Not by Heinz, but by Anthony." She passed an unsteady hand across her eyes. "It seems Anthony hatched a…complicated plan. We think he did it because he was determined to marry me from the time I was recruited for the job. The day he contacted Heinz and set up his transfer, Tony told him my superior had it in for me. He asked Heinz to pretend to die or else he said my boss would spread the word that I was spying for both sides. Tony was in charge of the defection. He even sent Heinz pockets of fake blood to make it look like he'd been killed. Tony promised Heinz he'd see to it that we were reunited in Paris, and that we'd work together under a new team leader."

Quinn gaped at her. "Heinz didn't question what happened when you didn't show up?"

"He did. I figured out that Tony slipped off to see Heinz and concocted more lies while he had me stashed with his underground friends. Later, Tony informed Heinz that I'd suffered a mental breakdown. He convinced Heinz I'd been sent home and died in an institution. Anthony did it all."

Norma wrung her hands. "He went to great lengths to make each of us think the other was dead."

"The joke was on him, I guess, when you turned up pregnant with von Weisenbach's kid," Quinn said. April could hear the scorn in his voice.

"Yes." Norma only sounded sad. "I believe Anthony paid for his sin. He probably lived in fear that one or the other of us would accidentally learn the truth. I assume that's why he jumped at the opportunity to join the new CIA and spent so much time abroad. To keep track of Heinz. Tony's the one who arranged for Heinz and Simone to serve in Paris, pretending to be husband and wife. After five years, Heinz said they simply decided to make their sham marriage legal. But, like my marriage to Tony, something was always missing," he said. "Oh, Tony tried to make amends by lavishing me with material things. And who knows what he went through to keep Heinz and Simone employed? All the years, all the lies—took a great toll on Tony. I have no doubt it's what made his drinking spiral out of control."

Quinn dropped heavily into a chair. Sweat beaded his forehead. "Here I've been worrying that Paul Benson stumbled on your romance with a possible traitor. But it turns out that Grandpa Santini was a liar and manipulator. He may have been a son of a bitch, but Mom, Dad, you, me, Hayley—we all have his name."

"Not for long. Me, I mean," Norma said, blushing wildly. "One thing Heinz and I agreed on in the short time we talked was that our feelings for each other haven't diminished. Every second we have left on this earth we want to spend together. In fact, that's what I came to tell you. I'm staying here through his surgery and recovery. You can all go home if you wish. Marc, he'd like a word with you. I think he'd like you to phone your father to break the news."

"What?" Quinn yelped. "How can you possibly know you haven't both changed in sixty years? This is a rash decision, Gram. Where will you live? Are you leaving me and Hayley to live in France? Or does he intend to give up his business to move here?"

"We haven't settled all the details, of course." Norma's jaw jutted out stubbornly. "Quinn, we were robbed of spending our lives together. We're in our eighties now, and I think you should give us credit for knowing our own minds."

Marc didn't look happy, either, and bobbed his head when Quinn roared, "The two of you talked for twenty minutes, now you're both ready to throw out the lives you've lived for the past sixty-plus years?"

April, who sat taking everything in, uncoiled from her chair. "Quinn," she said quietly, "they've earned the right. Maybe it seems hasty to you, but you haven't lived with heartache and loss for as long as they have."

He dragged a hand through his hair, and his eyes lost some of their dark shadows. "Not for sixty years, but I've lost Mom, Dad and Amy. Okay, so I selfishly want things to remain as they are. I should've realized when those letters surfaced and Gram told me her story that all our lives would change. I should've gotten out of the senate race then."

"Why?" April looked from one to the other. "The only people who know the real story are in this room and in the ICU. Except for me, they're also the only people affected by Anthony Santini's elaborate deceit."

"True. But what are you getting at?"

"Well, correct me if I'm wrong, but it seems to me that with a few minor omissions you're sitting on a great human interest story. Tony's record with the military, the OSS and CIA was exemplary as far as anyone knows. Right? And the whole world believes he and Norma had a good marriage. Anyone digging around in France will find the same in Heinz's background. He's a decorated hero who lost his wife to the cause. *No one* committed treason, Quinn. Norma, a former OSS agent, met Heinz through Tony when they all worked in France." April paused, then said poignantly, "Isn't it wonderful that two old friends have found each other after they both gave so much to their countries and each lost a spouse? Things like that *do* happen."

The light dawned for Quinn and Marc simultaneously. "So," Quinn said slowly, "We leak this story to the media. And…Paul Benson has egg on his face."

April's cell phone rang. She left them plotting, pulled it out of her purse and started to shut it off, having forgotten to do that when she entered the hospital. But she signaled Quinn. "It's Eric," she said, frantically pointing to the readout.

"Call him back," Quinn said. "There's a payphone in the corner."

They moved to the phone and she returned the call. "Eric? Wait…talk slower. You've found out why Paul Benson's making trouble for Quinn? But you won't tell me." She lifted a brow at Quinn. "Yes, we know reporters have been camped out at Santini's gate. Everyone figured that's thanks to Benson, too."

April lowered the receiver, whispering to Quinn, "Eric wants to trade what he's got for a scoop on your grandmother's association with ex-Colonel von Weisenbach. You can control what you tell him," she said, covering the receiver. "It's a fair trade, Quinn."

"No. No dice," Quinn snapped. But then his eyes followed April's nod. "I do want to deal?" he asked, trying to understand what she was signaling. "All right, April. You haven't steered me wrong yet. Wait, I'm beginning to see. This way, the story about Gram doesn't come from my staff but from Paul's former reporter." Quinn's slowly dawning smile made an impact on everyone in the room.

"Eric, if you take precautions to ensure that no one's on your tail, you can sit down with Quinn and Norma."

Quinn watched her smile.

"Okay, we have a deal then," she said next. "Come to the lobby of Mason Lee Hospital in half an hour." Eric apparently gave an affirmative answer because she hung up. She dropped into a nearby chair. "Lord, I hope this is the right thing to do." Her concerned gaze flashed from Quinn to Norma and back. "Eric saw Heinz's signature on one of the letters. Oh, no! How do we explain the letters?" She hopped up frantically, again prevailing on the others, this time including Marc.

Norma came to her rescue. "Does he need to know they're love letters?"

"*I* knew they were love letters. I can't recall if I mentioned that to Eric," April said, rubbing her temples as she thought back to the day she'd discovered the letters. "I'm quite sure he didn't see the postmarks."

"If this reporter didn't actually read them, he can't very well prove they were anything more than letters from Heinz to *Anthony* and me. Heinz did come over to our side, and Anthony did facilitate it. Who's to say we didn't keep in touch for a while after we left the OSS? Simply say the letters were lost during the building of the farmhouse. Then we moved, and Tony reconnected with Heinz for work-related reasons, but I was busy raising Brett, and then Anthony himself died. We can say it was a huge surprise to me when you found Heinz's old letters, April—which it was. We concluded they must've been accidentally knocked into the space during construction. But you made the effort to track me down and the result was…this." She indicated the room down the hall.

"That's all true—or true enough. And the rest, as they say, is history," April tossed out excitedly. "It's not uncommon for old friends who've lost their spouses to marry for companionship or the sake of friendship. Although Eric probably doesn't need that much information to have a good story."

"Written right, it can be one helluva drama." Quinn eyed his grandmother to see if, knowing that, she was still prepared to talk with Eric. It was plain that she was, and wanted to put this behind her and get on with her life.

He muttered thoughtfully, "Can we trust Eric?"

"I think so," April said. "You're handing him a golden opportunity to sell a major article to a competitor of the man who fired him. Now, if you two have your stories straight, you'd better go. Eric will be downstairs in a few minutes."

"You're not coming, April?" Quinn asked. "Aren't you wondering what he has to say about Paul?"

"You can tell me later. I'll stay here and keep Marc company. Joseph, Ethel and Hayley should be back soon. I promised Hayley I'd help her color a get-well picture for Mr. von Weisenbach."

"It's best if I don't show my face to your reporter friend," Marc said. "He seems too intelligent to miss the family likeness."

Quinn frowned. "I hadn't thought that through."

Norma again took charge. "Stories come and stories go. By the time Heinz recovers from surgery, Marc will have gone home and our family will be old news."

Marc nodded, looking a little dazed, "If April's staying here, maybe I'll go see Grandpère. He's probably upset about all the shouting he heard. His mind may be made up, but he'll rest easier, I'm sure, if I go and tell him I approve of Norma."

She smiled gratefully and spontaneously hugged the younger man. "That means the world to me. I want you and your father to understand that I've never stopped loving Heinz. If God grants us a chance to live our remaining years together, we'll be splitting our time between our two families."

Her words excited everyone. There was a moment of back-slapping and hugging. Then Quinn sobered. "Gram, there'll be time for this later. As April said, we need to go and give Eric Lathrop his big scoop."

April had barely ten minutes to reflect on everything that had gone on as a result of her finding the old letters. She was considering how—or if—she'd fit into the family, when Hayley Santini skipped into the waiting room, followed by Joseph and Ethel. They carried trays with wrapped sandwiches and several cups of coffee.

"Where's Daddy and Gram?" Hayley asked. "Miz Ethel bought cheese and ham sandwiches, and Mr. Joseph has loads of coffee." The girl pulled sugar packets and plastic containers of creamer out of her pockets and passed them to April.

"Everyone but me is off doing important stuff. I'd love

a sandwich and coffee. And, Miss Hayley Santini, I've been waiting here to help you color a beautiful get-well picture for your great-grandmother's friend."

"Goody. Can I pick? My coloring book has animals and flowers."

April accepted a steaming cup of coffee and stirred in cream. "Heinz likes roses, I've heard. He grows them to sell, in fact. I saw a picture in your book of a vase of roses. Shall we color that for him?"

"Okay. April, you and Daddy are bringing me roses at my first school open house, right? 'Cause roses are special and so's open house." She flipped through the book to the page April had mentioned. "Let's color these 'xactly like the roses Daddy gave you, April. What color were they?"

April gazed confusedly at Hayley over the rim of her cup. "Your dad's given me beautiful gerbera daisies, and another time, Dutch irises. No roses," she said.

The little girl shot her a wide-eyed look that quickly turned to guilt.

"It's all right, Hayley," April assured the girl. "I loved both bouquets."

"No, ev'rybody says you get roses when you're special. It's my fault. I acted bad, April. I said I didn't want Daddy buying you roses." The girl dashed over and flung her arms around April, which meant she had to juggle the cup to keep Hayley from splashing hot coffee on both of them. "At open house, I'll tell Daddy he's gotta bring roses for you *and* me."

"Honey, don't worry. I liked the other flowers a lot. Honestly."

"I love you, April. Daddy said me and him weren't always gonna be alone, but one piece of his heart will always be for me. I want you to have a piece, too," the girl said as she stepped back and dumped the box of crayons in April's lap. "You wanna have a piece of his heart, don't you, April?"

April didn't hesitate. "Yes, Hayley, I do. And thank you for sharing your father with me. That's an incredibly nice thing to do. Very unselfish." April set her coffee down and hugged the child. She had no idea Quinn and Norma had returned and stood in the doorway observing and listening to the entire exchange.

Norma jabbed Quinn's ribs, causing him to wince and crack his elbow on the door casing.

The noise caught April and Hayley's attention. The little girl squealed with delight and launched herself at her dad. Catching her on the run, Quinn swung her aloft, but his gaze roamed April's crimson face.

"Oh, you're back so s-soon," she stuttered, unable to rise because of her lapful of crayons. "Didn't Eric show up? Or…"

"He was waiting when we got there," Norma said. "He took notes on everything I said and seemed pleased with what he had."

"And did he keep his part of the bargain? Did he give you the goods on Paul Benson?"

Quinn set Hayley down and watched her run back and settle in to color again. He came and sat opposite the spot where April was outlining salmon-pink roses as Hayley colored the vase a soft blue.

"Benson has apparently been nursing a long-time family grudge against my grandfather. Well, against Anthony Santini," he said, acknowledging for the first time that Heinz was his rightful grandfather. "Eric tracked down a source who said Paul's grandpa and a brother, Paul's great-uncle, were foreign correspondents for the *Baltimore Sun* during the Cold War and the first throes of Korea. The men were on the trail of a story and somehow ended up in North Korea. The version of the tale Eric got from a shirttail relative of Benson's said Tony and two agents were also in North Korea gathering intelligence when the area got overrun with North Korean soldiers. Tony radioed for a military chopper. The Benson brothers asked, begged, to go along. According to the relative and a *Sun* article run posthumously, Anthony Santini flatly refused them passage. The article was based on notes found on the men's bodies later, when our troops stumbled upon them at a tea plantation. It looks like Anthony left the Bensons to fend for themselves. Left them to die is what's implied in the *Sun* article."

"No wonder Paul's out to derail your career! But, Quinn, maybe your grandfather, uh, Anthony, was under classified orders those reporters knew nothing about."

"Eric said he wasn't able to get any further information. He came up blank when he tried digging into the archived files stored by the Pentagon. I hope you're right, April. I'd hate to think one of our agents would consign any Americans to death."

"I'm sure there's much that's still cloaked in secrecy." Norma sat on the arm of Quinn's chair. "Even before I left France in 1944, reporters had begun flocking abroad in search of Pulitzer-winning war stories. Their number had increased after Pearl Harbor, of course, and more went to Korea and later, Viet Nam. I know that reporters have difficulty with the concept of undercover agents, and the military and intelligence officers have to operate covertly to keep an enemy guessing."

"Do you think Eric's freelance article will make Paul back off?" April curled a hand over Quinn's and squeezed lightly.

"Time will tell. Paul may still try to sully Tony's reputation, and by association, mine, by reprinting that old *Sun* article Eric uncovered."

"Your PR team can counter with what Norma just said, can't they? Surely you're not going to leave the race now, are you?"

"I'll have to give it more thought. What Paul's done has left me with a bad taste. Maybe I don't have the stomach for politics."

"If a man of your integrity," April said softly, "won't stand up against lies and corruption, who will? It's not right to hold you accountable for something that happened—that *may* have happened—back in the 1950's, any more than its right to hold the atrocities of Hitler against Heinz, who defected and spent many years working for our side."

A smile flickered on Quinn's lips. "Gram, this is the woman who used to swear she was apolitical."

"If you recall, I was against your entering politics, Quinn. But I agree with April. I wish I could offer more support, but my place is at Heinz's side. Do you mind if get back to him? Every minute we're apart now feels like an eternity. We've missed so much because of lies I'd never have thought Anthony capable of."

Quinn stood. "I should go meet this guy. Before he goes under the knife, he has a right to see his other grandson. This is one time, no matter what, when I need to put family first."

Norma seemed deeply touched by Quinn's offer. April saw the luster of tears in her eyes. April felt a bit weepy herself. She'd recognised Quinn as solid and honorable once she got to know him. But too many people believed everything printed in newspapers.

On her knees, Hayley ripped out the page with the vase of roses. "Don't cry, Gram. Take this picture to Mr. Heinz. I wrote, *love, Hayley.* April, you want to sign it, too?"

Norma blotted her tears and smiled when April printed her name under Hayley's. "This says it all," Norma murmured. "Family first."

"Family first," April repeated. Almost without thinking, she included Joseph, Ethel and herself when she added, "I can't see any of us going too far away until Heinz is out of the woods, Norma."

Clutching the get-well picture, Norma left to go see Heinz, accompanied by Quinn. They met Marc in the hall, and Quinn said, "I know you were just in to see your grandfather, but come back with us, why don't you? I brought some of our family photos to show him." When Norma looked shocked and yet pleased, Quinn mumbled, "These are some of Dad and me I slipped out of the frames you had on the mantel."

Stretching up, Norma kissed him on the cheek and linked arms with both of the younger men as they entered her old love's room.

Chapter 13

The next afternoon, Norma Santini sat alone in an empty ICU cubicle, awaiting word on Heinz's surgery. His son in France had sent a large refrigerated box of roses; they were the deep-salmon shade she'd once cherished. Today their heavy scent overwhelmed her. She hadn't slept a wink all night. Rather, she'd spent the long dark hours holding his hand. Norma hadn't shared with him, or with her family, the constant fear pounding in her head and chest. No one else would understand the terror she'd felt the day she thought this man she loved had been killed. *Fake blood*. His death was staged by Anthony, a man, it was now clear, she never really knew.

She told herself Heinz could die today. For real this time… What if this *was* the end? What if she'd found him, only to lose him again?

Each time Norma dozed, she woke, suffocated by a nightmare. It was silly, but she wondered if Anthony somehow still controlled their lives from beyond the grave. Or that she didn't really deserve the happiness her heart felt at the possibility of being reunited with Heinz?

"Norma." She gave a start and leapt up. Dr. Amhurst, still wearing blue scrubs, blocked the light from the hall. Her chest felt tight and her throat burned as she tried to gauge his expression.

"I went to the waiting room first and got waylaid by your family, who'd just arrived. They said you'd chosen to stay here. Heinz came through the surgery like a champ. There were two blocked arteries. The veins I took from his leg to replace the bad ones showed no sign of disease. The pacemaker smoothed out his fibrillations. I expect that by this evening we'll move him out of ICU, into his room. We'll keep him here for a few days, but I understand from Quinn that my patient's home recovery will be supervised by you."

"Yes, oh, yes! He's really out of danger? He's going to live?" She clutched a locket in which she'd placed a small picture Marc had given her. A wrinkled one he'd carried in his wallet. Heinz aping for the camera with his infant grandson...

The doctor chuckled. "I wish all my patients were as robust as that man. Perhaps I should take offense that you had so little confidence in my ability."

Norma blushed automatically, and yet all she could think was that her fears had been groundless. "How long before I can see him?"

"Soon." Amhurst glanced at the clock on the wall. "In fact, right now. The nurses will be bringing him in." He smiled. "I've already answered the families' questions. Yours and his. Which, if I understand correctly, will in the not-too-distant future be one and the same."

She blushed harder and covered her cheeks with icy hands just beginning to thaw. "I suppose a young man like you considers us doddering old fools for discussing a wedding when his future was so uncertain."

"On the contrary. I'm delighted for you both and I hope Heinz exceeds the life expectancy of this pacemaker, which the company claims is fifteen to twenty years. I've always believed that happiness keeps us alive a lot longer."

Norma clasped her hands over her heart, and her first genuine smile in days burst through the lingering fear.

"Here's our patient now. He'll be groggy, Norma. I'll check on him this evening."

White-gowned nurses in rubber-soled shoes fussed over Heinz, hooking him up to monitors after orderlies had transferred him to a bed. Norma gave the professionals room to work, but when the nurses left she remained vigilant in spite of the doctor's encouragement.

Heinz's eyelids barely fluttered, and he seemed pale beneath his tan. Crossing to his side, Norma gingerly enclosed one of his big, scarred and callused hands between hers.

The patient's eyes slowly opened. As he focused on her face, his brilliant blue eyes cleared, and crinkled at the corners in delight. "There you are, *mon amour,*" he whispered hoarsely. "You're even more beautiful than the roses on that stand."

"I thank you, but my hair's grown pure white, and my skin certainly shows the passage of time. By the way, your son sent the roses."

"I asked him to send them for you, my darling. These

roses are descended from the roses I once grew in pots and cut for you. With each new crop that thrives and blooms, I remember you, my love, the way you were. In my eyes, you haven't changed." He'd spoken in French but now switched to English. "You're the same girl I held close to my heart."

She knelt in the chair and rested her head on his unbandaged shoulder. "You made me feel beautiful then, and now. I promise that I'll do my best to be the girl you fell in love with. A girl filled with hopes, dreams and a passion for life."

"Will you marry me soon, my love? This week? I have no idea what our future holds. I don't want another day to pass without knowing we're bound together legally and in the eyes of God."

"Yes, oh, I will. Except…I'm not sure how to arrange it."

Their private moment was interrupted by sighs and hand-clapping from the door. Lifting her head, Norma saw Marc, Quinn and April huddled there.

"You heard?"

"We did," they chorused.

"Dr. Amhurst plans to move Heinz into a private room later," April said. "Having a quiet family ceremony here is quite manageable, I should think, if the doctor approves. Marc can get on the phone and call area clergy. Quinn and I will go to your place, Norma, and pick up a dress. Do you have a favorite? Oh, and Ethel and Joseph can witness, unless you'd rather Quinn and Marc did the honors." She paused. "How about Thursday late afternoon, after Hayley gets out of school?"

The men let the women make plans and list the chores that needed to be done. As they prepared to leave, Quinn snapped his fingers. "I almost forgot why we came in." He pulled a folded newspaper from his back pocket and opened it to Eric Lathrop's article. The headline in bold print read: Old Letters Found in a Wall Lead To Internet Search That Reunites World War II Friends.

"Friends," Norma murmured, smiling at the man she loved. "Oh, yes, Eric bought the story we gave him."

Quinn passed her the article, which she scanned. "It's been picked up by a wire service and has probably run in most state papers," he said.

"Eric wrote with more human emotion than I knew he possessed," April put in. "I'd be surprised if this leaves a single voter in the district dry-eyed. Well, with the exception of Dan Mattingly and Paul Benson," she added smugly.

"Don't you think they're crying, too?" Marc grinned. "Considering Lathrop's listing of Grandpère and Anthony Santini's medals, Benson would look petty and prejudiced if he ran his story accusing Anthony of cowardice for leaving his relatives stranded."

"What's this?" Heinz peered over Norma's arm. "Who did Anthony ever leave stranded?"

Quinn offered a short version of the story Eric had given them about the fate of Paul Benson's grandfather and great-uncle.

"Non, non!" Heinz sliced the air with a hand taped with needles and lines dripping saline and antibiotics. "I know that incident. Those reporters were repeatedly warned not to stray from safe territory. We've learned that, in matters having to do with Norma, Anthony crossed moral boundaries. Not so in his work. He was, how do you say, straight-arrow. I was among the operatives waiting to disseminate

the information he'd gathered in North Korea. They limped in, their helicopter badly damaged by anti-aircraft fire. The pilot said if Anthony had agreed to bring out two more, they would've been overloaded and forced to fly lower. As it was, the copilot died. With the information Anthony delivered to us, an entire company of men changed course and was saved, because two days later war officially broke out in Korea. Anthony, though, hated leaving those reporters. He spent weeks trying to get them out. Good men died in those rescue expeditions. Tell Cyril Benson's grandson *that*."

Quinn, who stood with a shoulder propped on the door, lifted his head sharply. "Cyril was one of the *Baltimore Sun* reporters. The other was Hal or Harold. I really appreciate your clearing this up, Colonel. If I ever go head to head with Paul, those are facts I can use. Although I doubt I will. Rumor has it he may be looking for another job. The *Register's* owner reportedly isn't too happy with the way his editor has slanted recent articles. The owner wants an unbiased paper, which he hasn't had with Paul at the helm of his news desk."

"I am glad I could help. But please, I have not been a colonel for many decades. I would prefer to forget those years I served with the German army."

"As you wish," Quinn said, his respect for the man rising.

A nurse briskly entered the room. "There are entirely too many guests here. Our patient is only a few hours out of surgery."

The guilty parties scattered, after assuring Norma and Heinz their wedding would take place Thursday afternoon if Dr. Amhurst gave his okay.

★ ★ ★

More than once on her wedding day, Norma declared them all miracle-workers. She looked beautiful in an ivory silk suit, and thanks to Robyn, April had come up with a small hat that had a short, sparkling veil.

Heinz insisted on standing to say his vows. He had Marc bring him a dark suit jacket from his luggage, which he slid over one arm. They pinned his empty sleeve across the other arm. He seemed refreshed and much stronger.

Quinn, Marc and Joseph showed up in suits that ranged from pale gray to black. Ethel's dress was Valentine-red. Bustling around, she fussed over Norma. "Nothing like a wedding to bring out the romantic in all of us."

Quinn's eyes were drawn to April, pretty in pale blue. She saw him and said, "It's fall, not spring, but love is in the air."

Having divided his day between keeping tabs on his campaign, getting Hayley to and from school and doing whatever was requested of him by the women planning the festivities, Quinn hadn't had much opportunity to think of this as a *real* wedding. Until now.

Yes, he'd helped Hayley dress up in her favorite long pink taffeta gown. Now he watched April tuck a pink tiara among the little girl's curls. She also gave Hayley a basket filled with rose petals to scatter over the floor between the happy couple and the priest Marc had engaged. He'd explained that the von Weisenbachs were staunchly Catholic, and he wanted this wedding by the book.

Norma glowed. Heinz's color was markedly improved. Marc took at least a hundred photographs with disposable cameras he'd bought while out doing errands.

Nurses were grouped in the open door, their faces

wreathed in smiles. The charge nurse kept an eye on her patient, but the floor staff had clearly gone out of their way to make the occasion as wedding-like as possible, despite the sterile atmosphere. Vases of roses were everywhere, in every color under the sun.

April tugged Quinn's head down so she could whisper in his ear. "I love the way Heinz managed to surprise Norma from his sick bed. He not only had Marc buy every rose from all the florists in town, but when Norma slipped out to have her hair done, they convinced a jeweler to bring Heinz a tray of rings. It's so romantic, don't you think? And don't they look so happy they could burst?"

It so happened that Norma and Heinz had bought rings that were very similar. Each had chosen a wide gold band entwined with tiny diamonds that could pass as roses. "Roses, roses and more roses," Quinn murmured.

"Don't you like roses?" April asked. She recalled Hayley's saying she wanted her dad to buy roses for her school's open house. "If not, Hayley's going to be disappointed. She's hoping, more than hoping, that you'll buy me and her each a dozen roses for her first open house."

"I know. She told me." He paused, then whispered, "I planned to bring you a dozen red roses the evening of my fund-raiser. I got cold feet, I guess, when Hayley went on about how roses were meant for special people and how she was supposed to be the one who was special to me. She is, of course, and so are you, and…" He sighed. "I ended up buying you irises. Are roses your favorite flower, April?"

"I like all flowers. It's *who* gives a woman flowers that matters." She gestured around the room. "This is overkill, but Norma said they're planning to have the nurses donate all the bouquets to the cancer ward, except for the one Heinz's son sent. Those salmon-colored blooms are apparently just like the roses he gave her during the war. Every luxury was hard to come by then. It's easy to see how she was bowled over by his thoughtfulness."

"The room looks like a mortuary," Quinn grumbled. April nudged him as the priest began to speak. Norma's dearest friends, Ethel and Joseph, stepped up to serve as witnesses.

After the vows had been said, the priest and nurses departed, and soon only family was left. Quinn raised a cup of the punch April had made. "Gram, Heinz, I've decided to buy the farmhouse April remodeled as my wedding gift to you both."

Quinn expected his grandmother to be pleased, as she'd professed to loving the farm. Plus, this grand day would never have come about had April not bought the house and ripped out a wall....

The "oldyweds," as Norma and Heinz had taken to jokingly calling themselves, traded a wary glance. Norma was the first to react to Quinn's news. "That's very thoughtful, dear, but H and I have made other plans."

"H?" Quinn blinked and his cup of punch wobbled.

His grandmother leaned over the bed where her new husband again lay, and slipped her arm through his. Their fingers twined naturally. "Two men in the family have the name Heinz, so calling him H simplifies things."

"Fine. Getting back to the farmhouse... You've never really liked the home where you live now, I believe *ostentatious* and *mausoleum* are words you've used to describe it."

"True. But...April was telling me about a marvelous row

house in Alexandria she's set to remodel into three condominiums. H and I talked it over. Since we plan to divide our time between his cottage in France and here, a condo with minimal upkeep appeals to us both. Would you be terribly hurt if I refused your gift, Quinn?"

"But…you said you loved the farm."

"I did, but the life I led there—and in my current house— was one big deceit. I want to begin over somewhere without sad memories. I can do that now, since I know the truth. Poor Tony—he must have suffered so much guilt…. I did love him and I hope that he's at peace. But Heinz and I need a fresh start. April said that with luck, the condos should be livable by the time we return from our European honeymoon. I'm sorry to spring this on you so abruptly, Quinn. I know you rely on me to watch Hayley, but—" Norma cast an almost sly glance from her grandson to April, who was helping Hayley box up the sheet cake they'd cut and shared with everyone in the ward. "—I rather imagined you might be planning on rearranging your life, too," Norma finished.

"If I win the election, you mean? That's looking more possible by the day. My campaign manager phoned to tell me that they ran a poll after Eric's story hit. It shows my numbers are up by double digits."

"Quinn, that's fantastic." Norma beamed at him, and Marc gave him a friendly slap on the shoulder.

"Uh, did April mention that I'd expressed an interest in maybe buying one of her condos myself?"

Heinz spoke up then. "The way we understand it, she's planning three units. Sounds ideal—the place could house the whole family. We've spoken of putting Joseph and Ethel in one, Norma and me in another, which leaves one."

If April heard any of the byplay, she didn't let on. She bagged the leftover paper plates, cups and plastic forks, and stacked the bags on the cake box before she and Hayley headed for the door. "I still have your car keys, Quinn. Hayley and I are going to store this stuff in the trunk. Then…we should probably wind down. The afternoon's been quite hectic for a man only a few days removed from heart surgery. Remember, he had bypass as well as mitral valve repair, which means his hospital time will be longer than we first expected."

"I'm resting," Heinz protested. But it was evident the fuss and flutter was wearing him down.

Sliding off his bed, Norma dispensed hugs all around. "How can we ever thank you enough for making this day one of the most perfect days of my life?"

"*Our* lives," Heinz corrected.

"Most of the credit goes to April," Quinn said proudly.

"Yeah," Marc agreed from where he'd gone to shake his grandfather's hand. "April's *fantastique*." The younger man kissed his fingertips. "I asked her to marry me and add her many talents to our landscaping firm. Alas, she refused. She said I was too young for her."

It didn't escape Norma's notice that Quinn scowled at his young relative, but Marc went right on.

"Grandpère, since I'm leaving you in good hands, I believe I'll try and get a flight home tomorrow. Papa and Maman are hounding me for photos of the wedding."

"Be sure you tell them I've never been happier," H insisted. "Dr. Amhurst said if it weren't for having to take veins from my leg, I'd be able to travel much sooner. But I'll be recuperating at Norma's for about three weeks, which will give her and Quinn an opportunity to list her home for sale. And let Quinn make arrangements for Hayley's care."

"If Quinn had a drop of French blood in his veins instead of American and German, he'd cease dallying and ask April to be his wife. I know he's the reason she turned me down," Marc announced baldly, which gained him more than a scowl from Quinn.

"Hey, Mr. Romantic, I planned to offer you a lift to the Inn, but if you're going to make statements like that, you can walk."

"Boys," Norma said, grabbing each by an arm. "April is not a toy to fight over."

The two men immediately stopped needling each other, out of respect for the grandmother they now shared. Although Marc declined to accept a ride to the Inn, saying he knew Quinn needed to get home.

"Did Marc decide to stay at the hospital?" It was April's first question to Quinn after she'd buckled Hayley into the Lexus.

"If you're so worried about him, I'll let you out and you can go back and see for yourself," Quinn muttered.

"What brought *that* on? I just assumed you'd give him a lift."

"I like Marc," Hayley said. "He showed me really neat string games. How far away is France? He said he hasta go home to France, 'cause that's where his mama and daddy live."

"He works in the family business, Hayley," April said. "And he's taking classes to become a landscape architect like his father and grandfather."

"I know. I heard him say you could come remodel houses in France, April. And then he'd plant trees and roses and stuff in the yard. I don't want you to go, April."

"Oh, honey. Marc was teasing." Laughing, April glanced back at the girl.

Quinn shifted in his seat. Pulling up to a red light, he braked so hard they were jerked forward and then back again. "Sorry. Are you quite sure he was teasing, April?"

"Don't be silly! Of course he was. Well, even if he was partly serious, do I strike you as a woman impulsive enough to throw away everything I've worked for to go globe-trotting on a whim? And for heaven's sake, the man is eight years younger than me."

"Isn't that what my grandmother's doing? The globe-trotting part."

"No, Quinn, it's not. Her heart has never been a hundred percent invested here."

The light changed and Quinn crossed the intersection without further comment. But he wore a bleak expression, prompting April to lay a hand on his knee. "Her getting married and leaving must seem sudden and impetuous to you. I know she's been a rock for you since you lost Amy," April added in a voice too low to carry into the back seat. "I never stopped to think that their getting married repre-sents another major loss in your life."

Quinn hiked a shoulder. "If I win in November, I'll be moving on anyhow. For the last year, I've turned more and more cases over to a couple of junior partners I took into the firm a few months after the plane wreck. I could go back there and pick up where I left off if Mattingly's re-elected. But I'm thinking, win or lose, I should consider making a change. My life's been sort of a lie, too."

"I don't imagine you'll want to live in the carriage house, or whatever you call it, after Norma sells her home."

"Yeah. It's zoned as one property. Did you hear any of our conversation after Gram and Heinz refused my wedding gift? I won't be buying the farmhouse, after all."

"Should I apologize for telling Norma about the place in Alexandria?"

"You won the bid for sure?"

"Yes, my dad, bless his heart, made some calls. I heard from the lender while I was across the hall helping Norma and Hayley dress for the wedding. I would've told you, but things got pretty hectic right afterward. Quinn, I hope you aren't feeling guilty because you mentioned buying the farmhouse and now you have to renege. I have at least three possible buyers who've made inquiries. It's not like I'll be out any money. But if you're hurt because they refused your generous gift, that's something else altogether."

"Any mixed emotions have to do with all the changes you've brought to my family, April."

She snatched back her hand. His words pricked feelings that had grown deeper these past weeks and continued to expand with love for him. She'd foolishly thought he felt the same way.

Quinn felt the loss of warmth when she removed her hand. He glanced over and saw the mask of pain settle over April's face. "That didn't come out sounding right," he rushed to say, reaching to take her hand. "I meant, *I'd* like to be the one sharing a home with you, April. That's why I didn't want you living with my family without me. Without us. Hayley and me."

Her chin shot up. "That's, uh, probably all the wedding atmosphere getting to you, Quinn. It's understandable, after all, you and Hayley are heading into a new life, so you'd want to stick close to your family."

Quinn's hand tightened. "This is a helluva place to say *I love you*, April." They were at a busy intersection, and thank heaven the car in front of Quinn's skated through on the yellow light. He stopped the car so he was able to focus his full attention on the woman beside him.

"I heard you take a breath," he said. "Does that mean *forget it*? Does it mean *stop, you're rushing things*? Or—please—does it mean you're interested?"

"The latter comes the closest," she admitted, leaning across the console to collect the kiss he was dying to deliver.

"Uh, Daddy and April, you did kissy-face like Gram and Mr. H. Oh, goody! Does that make you husband and wife like the priest guy said to them?"

Unlocking their lips, the couple turned sheepishly and laughed. "Hon, the priest has to come and say words about loving each other through sickness and health and stuff like that," Quinn informed his daughter.

Hayley's face fell, prompting April to add, "Hayley, when people kiss, especially if they kiss often, it means they're probably thinking of getting married." She deliberately caught Quinn's chin and kissed him again.

The light changed and the driver in the car behind them laid on his horn.

Quinn was too affected by the kiss to continue driving. He pulled over to the curb. "April, are you serious about saying yes to a guy who might become Virginia's next junior senator? When we met, you said you hated attending parties at your parents' house. Entertaining would be part of the job, I'm afraid."

"Didn't I do okay at your fund-raiser?"

"You did. You were the envy of every man there." He

let the car idle and picked up both her hands. "But I twisted your arm to get you to go with me."

She smiled, unhooked her seat belt and looped both arms around his neck. "I'll let you in on a secret. I liked having my arm twisted. Other men who've tried to drag me into the social scene lacked the methods you employed."

"Flowers? You said no one ever brought you flowers."

"Hmm. Well, the flowers put you in a different league. I was actually alluding to the kiss that knocked my socks off. That's what changed me from an isolationist to someone who wanted to know everything there is to know about your politics…and, well, other skills you seemed to have."

The light burning deep within her eyes told Quinn that April's mind had traveled back to the fantastic night they'd spent in her bed. And after that, it was tough for a man who wanted a repeat performance—but who'd proposed marriage in front of his six-year-old daughter—to retain control.

"Ahem. I believe the question about our future is settled. All we've got to decide is when," he said, kissing his way along April's arms as he unhooked them from around his neck and turned to release the car's brake.

"My mother would never forgive me if I told her I wanted a wedding pulled together as quickly as Norma's was. How do you feel about a holiday wedding, Quinn? If I subcontract more jobs than I usually do, there should be enough done on the Alexandria house by Christmas to give us all places to live."

"Like old H, I'd be happier tying the knot tomorrow, or at least by Thanksgiving. But for the sake of not antagonizing my future mother-in-law, tell Bonnie she has until

Christmas to pull off the miracle. Norma, with your help, managed in under a day."

Time didn't stand still. Quinn was kept busy with fundraisers and other events. He crisscrossed the state holding town-hall meetings, arranged by Eric Lathrop, now Quinn's press officer. As a result, he won the election the first week in November by a landslide.

In the midst of deciding things like wedding colors, what they'd serve at a buffet at the Trents' country club, and the style of type to go on three hundred invitations, Quinn remembered to order two dozen roses to present to his two favorite women on the night of Hayley's first-grade open house.

"Quinn, these roses are spectacular! They're almost purple. Hayley's pink ones are beautiful, too. I've never seen a color as rich as this."

"I know a grower," Quinn said, tucking April's arm under his as they entered the school, looking for all the world like the happy family they'd soon become. "I phoned H and tried to explain the color of that dress you wore to my fund-raiser."

"Eggplant. That's right, this is a similar color."

"H called it *aubergine,* which is French for eggplant. What really sold me was the name of this rose. *Avril Amour.*"

Her raised eyebrow prompted him to bend and say huskily near her ear, "April Love."

The air between them was so steamy, they almost didn't make it through the open house. When they'd met Hayley's teacher, they took the little girl back to Ethel and Joseph's, where she showed off her roses and regaled them with a blow-by-blow description of the evening.

Quinn took the old couple aside and said he'd be back in a while to collect his daughter. Ethel and Joseph lived in the middle condo, the one most recently renovated. The top apartment was where Norma and H intended to live for half the year. They were due to arrive at the end of the month to take part in Quinn and April's wedding.

The bottom-level condo, earmarked for Quinn and family, was the place April currently called home. That night they walked into an echoing, sparsely furnished apartment with peeling paint, bare unfinished floors and a hissing old-style radiator.

Quinn stripped off his tie. "Is this a case of the cobbler's children having no shoes?"

Dumping nails out of an empty coffee can, April filled it with water and arranged the roses. She made room for the can on the old Formica counter. Crossing over to Quinn, she took his tie, wadded it up in his pocket and with a huge smile on her face, slowly divested him of his jacket. She let it fall to the scarred floor. "Aren't you being a little picky, Senator Santini?"

She rose on tiptoe and unbuttoned the first two of his shirt buttons, then deliberately pressed her lips to the spot where his pulse beat wildly.

"On second thought, this soon-to-be condo already has everything it needs."

"You and me?" she murmured as she shoved down the suspenders he'd taken to wearing.

"Well, yes, but I was thinking of the bed."

April took his hand and led the way to the big room where the bed sat, looking lonely.

Quinn stopped. "Whoa, you tore out a wall since I was in here last."

"It was disappointing. No cache of Confederate coins and no love letters."

He sat on the bed and pulled her between his legs. "Give me an hour and you'll hit the jackpot anyway."

"An hour? I'm giving you a lifetime, Quinn. And you, sir, need to keep sending me those sizzling e-mails. Maybe I shouldn't tell you, but I printed off the last dozen or so, tied them with a red ribbon and plastered them into the center island I just finished building in the kitchen."

Quinn helped her out of the soft gray dress he'd found so touchable the first night he took her to Cinalli's. "The minute you walked out wearing this dress," he murmured, "I knew I'd never be able to keep my hands off you."

Later, as they lay luxuriously in each other's arms after reaching heights they'd never reached before, he asked the last question of the evening. "Exactly which X-rated e-mails did you put in that wall for some unsuspecting future April to haul out?"

"I chose the juiciest ones, of course. And unless, my esteemed senator, the U.S. is taken over by invaders from outer space, the good parts won't need translation."

Epilogue

Christmas was in the air. Heinz and Norma had stopped decorating their tree to stand at their big picture window overlooking the Potomac River. They were admiring the lights dancing on the water and testing out a cinnamon Wassail recipe Norma had received from Heinz's daughter-in-law before they flew to the States for Quinn and April's wedding.

They clinked cups, hooked little fingers and each made a wish to the other. It was a habit from their brief time together during the war years. A habit they'd naturally slipped into again.

"You always wish for the same thing," Norma chided gently. "Twenty more years together is asking a bit much, don't you think, for people in their mideighties?"

Heinz leaned down and kissed her. "Twenty more years

with you isn't nearly enough. Besides, your wishes take care of all the other things I want. That Quinn and April have as fantastic a time on their honeymoon in Paris as we did on ours. That Marc will marry that sweet botanist he met in Holland when he went to buy tulip bulbs and we'll be a truly international family. And that our first Christmas in our new home will bring our whole family together for laughter and good cheer."

She took her eyes off her beloved and stared into her aromatic cup. "Am I a foolish old woman who wants our family's lives to be as wonderful as ours?"

"Not foolish at all, *mon amour*. What was foolish was me dragging that seven-foot spruce up eight flights of stairs because you and Hayley said no other tree would do."

She smiled and squeezed one of his arms. "Ah, but Heinz, you looked very manly. So manly we sent Hayley downstairs to stay with Ethel and Joseph for a couple of hours. Remember?"

His blue eyes brightened. "How can I forget something that beautiful? How could I not wish for another twenty years in your bed?"

"And you shall be in my bed—just as soon as you finish stringing the lights on that tree. Oh, and after you assemble the beautiful dollhouse we bought Hayley in Bavaria."

Dismay crossed his features. "If you'll put a shot of something stronger than apple cider in this Wassail."

She did, because she loved granting his every wish. And because she wanted Christmas to be perfect. She looked forward to the day Quinn and April returned from their honeymoon. Their wedding had been the gala kick-off to a Virginia holiday season. Secretly, though, as wonderful as every detail was, Norma was partial to her own wedding in Heinz's hospital room.

The week flew by in a frenzy of last-minute gift-buying and secret package-wrapping. Quinn and April's plane came in just ahead of a storm that dusted everything with snow the evening they all attended Hayley's dance recital.

Norma shed a tear. "She is the most talented and cutest sugar plum fairy there ever was."

"Gram, you're prejudiced," Quinn teased. "She lost her star and tripped over the shoe ribbons of the fairy standing next to her."

"Quinn," April and Norma scolded together. April dug an elbow in his ribs and said, "You march right up to that stage and bring her these roses. Tell her what a marvelous job she did in the show."

"Yes, ma'am," he said, leaning over to kiss his wife.

And he left with the roses.

The next day was Christmas Eve. Heinz, Quinn and Joseph disappeared for what seemed like hours. April, Norma, Hayley and Ethel spent the time in Ethel's kitchen trying out a host of recipes Norma had brought home from her newly acquired relatives. The women all laughed continually and had a lovely afternoon as they trudged upstairs with the gourmet dishes and stored them to bring out when the family gathered at Heinz and Norma's later, in anticipation of Santa's arrival.

The men, however, arrived first. They stomped in, shaking off snow, followed by Marc and a pretty red-haired young woman. Then his father and mother, his five sisters, their spouses and children. Amid shouted introductions and a lot of hugging, kissing and chatter, Norma felt that her happiness had never been this complete.

It took an hour before everything settled down. The rest of the family went to inspect the other apartments, Heinz held Norma back on the pretext of readying their place for the onslaught and making room for the bags full of presents that had come with their guests. First, however, he led her to their bedroom door. Holding mistletoe over her head, he kissed her. "Before we're inundated again, I have a very special gift for you."

"Oh, Heinz. It's enough of a gift that you granted my wish to have our whole family meet and share this, the best Christmas I've had in sixty years."

"I know, but this is a present between us, *mon amour.*" With that, he left her side and came back with a fifteen-inch square foil-wrapped box.

She sat on their bed and removed gold ribbon and brocade foil to reveal a photograph album. There were two oval picture frames on the front of the white leather book. The picture on the left was the one taken in 1943, when they first fell in love. And on the right, a photo Marc had snapped of the two of them kissing at their wedding. Inside, carefully preserved in plastic sleeves, was each letter from the packet April had found in the wall. The letters and their envelopes, the pressed rose and the faded red ribbon, all preserved for posterity. "It's a pity I had to destroy your letters to me," he said. "I had to keep them from falling into the wrong hands. But at least we have these."

Norma cried openly and happily as she kissed Heinz and tried not to let go of the wonderful album filled with poignant memories. "I shall hold these dear for however many years we have left. But, with your permission, Heinz, I'd like to add a note in our trust passing this testament of timeless love on to April. If she'd dismissed the letters, or hadn't been the romantic she is, you and I wouldn't be here now. Together."

"There are twenty letters, did you know that?" he murmured, enfolding her in his strong arms. "I intend to read one to you every year on our wedding anniversary."

"Heinz, my love, I have a secret to tell you. I intend to write you a letter every year for the next twenty. And I've already written the first one." Norma set the heavy album aside and slid her arms around his neck. An hour later, they almost weren't ready to greet their family who tramped, singing and laughing, up the many stairs to share Wassail and the tree.

* * * * *

Welcome to cowboy country...

Turn the page for a sneak preview of
TEXAS BABY
by
Kathleen O'Brien
An exciting new title from Harlequin Superromance
for everyone who loves stories about the West.

Harlequin Superromance—
Where life and love weave together in emotional
and unforgettable ways.

new, it needed either a wash or a new paint job or both.

"Damn it, what's wrong with you?"

CHAPTER ONE

CHASE TRANSFERRED his gaze to the road and identified a foreign spot on the horizon. A car. Almost half a mile away, where the straight, tree-lined drive met the public road. He could tell it was coming too fast, but judging the speed of a vehicle moving straight toward you was tricky.

It wasn't until it was about two hundred yards away that he realized the driver must be drunk…or crazy. Or both.

The guy was going maybe sixty. On a private drive, out here in ranch country, where kids or horses or tractors or stupid chickens might come darting out any minute, that was criminal. Chase straightened from his comfortable slouch and waved his hands.

"Slow down, you fool," he called out. He took the porch steps quickly and began walking fast down the driveway.

The car veered oddly, from one lane to another, then up onto the slight rise of the thick green spring grass. It just barely missed the fence.

"Slow down, damn it!"

He couldn't see the driver, and he didn't recognize this automobile. It was small and old, and couldn't have cost much even when it was new. It was probably white, but now it needed either a wash or a new paint job or both.

"Damn it, what's wrong with you?"

At the last minute, he had to jump away, because the idiot behind the wheel clearly wasn't going to turn to avoid a collision. He couldn't believe it. The car kept coming, finally slowing a little, but it was too late.

Still going about thirty miles an hour, it slammed into the large, white-brick pillar that marked the front boundaries of the house. The pillar wasn't going to give an inch, so the car had to. The front end folded up like a paper fan.

It seemed to take forever for the car to settle, as if the trauma happened in slow motion, reverberating from the front to the back of the car in ripples of destruction. The front windshield suddenly seemed to ice over with lethal bits of glassy frost. Then the side windows exploded.

The front driver's door wrenched open, as if the car wanted to expel its contents. Metal buckled hideously. Small pieces, like hubcaps and mirrors, skipped and ricocheted insanely across the oyster-shell driveway.

Finally, everything was still. Into the silence, a plume of steam shot up like a geyser, smelling of rust and heat. Its snake-like hiss almost smothered the low, agonized moan of the driver.

Chase's anger had disappeared. He didn't feel anything but a dull sense of disbelief. Things like this didn't happen in real life. Not in his life. Maybe the sun had actually put him to sleep....

But he was already kneeling beside the car. The driver was a woman. The frosty glass-ice of the windshield was dotted with small flecks of blood. She must have hit it with her head, because just below her hairline a red liquid was seeping out. He touched it. He tried to wipe it away before it reached her eyebrow, though, of course that made no sense at all. Her eyes were shut.

Was she conscious? Did he dare move her? Her dress was covered in glass, and the metal of the car was sticking out lethally in all the wrong places.

Then he remembered, with an intense relief, that every good medical man in the county was here, just behind the house, drinking his champagne. He found his phone and paged Trent.

The woman moaned again.

Alive, then. Thank God for that.

He saw Trent coming toward him, starting out at a lope, but quickly switching to a full run.

"Get Dr. Marchant," Chase called. "Don't bother with 911."

Trent didn't take long to assess the situation. A fraction of a second, and he began pulling out his cell phone and running toward the house.

The yelling seemed to have roused the woman. She opened her eyes. They were blue and clouded with pain and confusion.

"Chase," she said.

His breath stalled. His head pulled back. "What?"

Her only answer was another moan, and he wondered if he had imagined the word. He reached around her and put his arm behind her shoulders. She was tiny. Probably petite by nature, but surely way too thin. He could feel her shoulder blades pushing against her skin, as fragile as the wishbone in a turkey.

She seemed to have passed out, so he put his other arm under her knees and lifted her out. He tried to avoid the jagged metal, but her skirt caught on a piece and the tearing sound seemed to wake her again.

"No," she said. "Please."

"I'm just trying to help," he said. "It's going to be all right."

She seemed profoundly distressed. She wriggled in his arms, and she was so weak, like a broken bird. It made him feel too big and brutish. And intrusive. As if touching her this way, his bare hands against the warm skin behind her knees, were somehow a transgression.

He wished he could be more delicate. But he smelled gasoline, and he knew it wasn't safe to leave her here.

Finally he heard the sound of voices, as guests began to run around the side of the house, alerted by Trent. Dr. Marchant was at the front, racing toward them as if he were forty instead of seventy. Susannah was right behind him, her green dress floating around her trim legs.

"Please," the woman in his arms murmured again. She looked at him, the expression in her blue eyes lost and bewildered. He wondered if she might be on drugs. Hitting her head on the windshield might account for this unfocused, glazed look, but it couldn't explain the crazy driving.

"Please, put me down. Susannah… The wedding…"

Chase's arms tightened instinctively, and he froze in his tracks. She whimpered, and he realized he might be hurting her. "Say that again?"

"The wedding. I have to stop it."

* * * * *

*Be sure to look for TEXAS BABY,
available September 11, 2007,
as well as other fantastic Superromance titles
available in September.*

Welcome to Cowboy Country...

TEXAS BABY

by Kathleen O'Brien

#1441

Chase Clayton doesn't know what to think.
A beautiful stranger has just crashed his
engagement party, demanding that he not
marry because she's pregnant with his baby.
But the kicker is—he's never seen her before.

Look for TEXAS BABY and other fantastic
Superromance titles on sale September 2007.

Available wherever books are sold.

HARLEQUIN
Super Romance

**Where life and love weave together
in emotional and unforgettable ways.**

www.eHarlequin.com   HSR71441

ATHENA FORCE

Heart-pounding romance and thrilling adventure.

Professional negotiator Lindsey Novak is faced with her biggest challenge—to buy back Teal Arnett, a young woman with unique powers. In the process Lindsey uncovers a devastating plot that involves scientists from around the globe, and all of them lead to one woman who is bent on destroying Athena Academy...at any cost.

LOOK FOR

THE GOOD THIEF

by Judith Leon

Available September wherever you buy books.

REQUEST YOUR
FREE BOOKS!

2 FREE NOVELS PLUS 2 FREE GIFTS!

 HARLEQUIN®

EVERLASTING LOVE™

Every great love has a story to tell™

YES! Please send me 2 FREE Harlequin® Everlasting Love™ novels and my 2 FREE gifts. After receiving them, if I don't wish to receive any more books, I can return the shipping statement marked "cancel." If I don't cancel, I will receive 4 brand-new novels every other month and be billed just $4.47 per book in the U.S. or $4.99 per book in Canada, plus 25¢ shipping and handling per book and applicable taxes, if any*. That's a savings of about 15% off the cover price! I understand that accepting the 2 free books and gifts places me under no obligation to buy anything. I can always return a shipment and cancel at any time. Even if I never buy another book from Harlequin, the two free books and gifts are mine to keep forever.

153 HDN ELX4   353 HDN ELYG

Name _____ (PLEASE PRINT) _____

Address _____ Apt. _____

City _____ State/Prov. _____ Zip/Postal Code _____

Signature (if under 18, a parent or guardian must sign)

Mail to the **Harlequin Reader Service®:**
IN U.S.A.: P.O. Box 1867, Buffalo, NY 14240-1867
IN CANADA: P.O. Box 609, Fort Erie, Ontario L2A 5X3

Not valid to current Harlequin Everlasting Love subscribers.

Want to try two free books from another line?
Call 1-800-873-8635 or visit www.morefreebooks.com.

* Terms and prices subject to change without notice. NY residents add applicable sales tax. Canadian residents will be charged applicable provincial taxes and GST. This offer is limited to one order per household. All orders subject to approval. Credit or debit balances in a customer's account(s) may be offset by any other outstanding balance owed by or to the customer. Please allow 4 to 6 weeks for delivery.

Your Privacy: Harlequin is committed to protecting your privacy. Our Privacy Policy is available online at www.eHarlequin.com or upon request from the Reader Service. From time to time we make our lists of customers available to reputable firms who may have a product or service of interest to you. If you would prefer we not share your name and address, please check here. ☐

HEL07

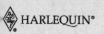

HARLEQUIN®

E V E R L A S T I N G L O V E ™

Every great love has a story to tell ™

Desperate times call for desperate measures.

The late 1930s and early 1940s were years
when many Americans were still struggling
with the Dust Bowl and the Depression…
struggling to survive. In their almost fifty
years together, Evvie and Edgar Clyburn have
known this better than any other two people.
And yet their love has survived it all….

Look for

Upstairs at Miss Hattie's

by

Ken Casper

**Available September
wherever books are sold.**

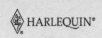

HARLEQUIN®

EVERLASTING LOVE™

Every great love has a story to tell™

COMING NEXT MONTH

#15 UPSTAIRS AT MISS HATTIE'S by Ken Casper

In the late 1930s and early 1940s many Americans were
still struggling with the Dust Bowl and the Depression…
struggling to survive. These were desperate times that
sometimes called for desperate measures. In their almost fifty
years together, no two people have known this more than
Evvie and Edgar Clyburn. And yet their love has survived it
all….

Ken Casper is a popular author with Harlequin
Superromance. His first title for Everlasting Love is a story
that has the direct emotional appeal of books by writers like
Nicholas Sparks.

#16 SUMMER AFTER SUMMER by Ann DeFee

Texas summers. Charlie Morrison. Jasmine Boudreaux has
always connected the two. Her relationship with Charlie
begins in high school, and then it ends. Twenty years later
it begins again—and ends again. But their romance finally
reaches its rightful conclusion as the love it was meant to be.
Charlie and Jaz together—forever!

Ann DeFee's first Harlequin American Romance novel,
A Texas State of Mind, was a double RITA® Award nominee.
Now *Summer After Summer* features her trademark warmth
and humor, plus the kind of engaging characters for which
she's received consistent acclaim.

www.eHarlequin.com

HECNM0807